TRUSTING THE BODYGUARD

MAURA TROY

Autumn Spring Enterprises LLC

CHAPTER ONE

THE EYES of the dead were unforgiving.

Especially the eyes of a beautiful sixteen-year-old girl, her lifeless body tossed into a garbage-filled dumpster. Thrown away as if she were nothing more than worthless refuse instead of someone's beloved child.

A screech of brakes pierced his thoughts, and he looked toward the street. The passenger door of a silver Mercedes-Benz opened, and a middle-aged blonde woman flew down the alley.

"No, no, no, no, no!" She skidded to a halt and grabbed his arm. "Where is she? Where's my daughter?"

He couldn't answer. His eyes were locked on the dumpster containing Tabitha Spencer's corpse, a mute testimony to his failure. Memories of his sister rose up, and he pushed them back. It wasn't his family in that dumpster, and he needed to remember that.

"Noooooooo!" the woman keened as she whirled and lunged toward the dumpster.

A police officer blocked her way, holding her around the waist. "It's a crime scene, ma'am!" he shouted, barely heard over her agonized wails.

"No, my baby, my baby! Peter!" she cried as her husband caught up to her and took her into his arms. "She needs us. We have to get her."

Peter Spencer kissed his wife's head and hugged her as she sobbed and struggled to get to the dumpster. "She's gone, Barbara." Tears streamed down his face. "Tabby's gone."

The woman's cries intensified, burning a hole in his gut as if he'd swallowed lye. A wicked voice whispered wretched things in his head, like how if he'd left the scene as soon as he'd given his statement to the police, he wouldn't be trapped in the alley, witness to the Spencers' pain. And even worse, the voice whispered, if he'd gotten there a few minutes sooner, Tabitha would still be alive. Mere minutes.

Timing was a merciless bitch.

"Close that file. Now."

Reeve Buchanan tore his mind from the nightmarish memory as October "Tobie" Armstrong, his boss and the owner of October Armstrong Security and Investigation Services, aka OASIS, arrived for their upcoming client meeting. She strode into her office and took a seat at her large oak desk. Through the window behind her, the sprawling Manhattan skyline stood at attention. "The Spencers will be here any minute. They don't need to see that again."

He snapped the folder shut, avoiding one last look at the crime scene photo of Tabitha's body lying in the dumpster. Not that it mattered. He saw it in his head every time he closed his eyes. The hole in his stomach burned a little wider. Not even the deaths of some of his Navy SEAL team-mates in Afghanistan had eaten at him like this. Then again, the deaths of his fellow SEALs hadn't been his fault. "I suppose the Spencers want to chew me out to my face," he said as he sat in one of the four chairs in front of Tobie's desk. "Hell, they probably want to see me drawn and quartered."

"I don't think so."

"I killed their daughter! They hired us to save her, and I killed her."

"You made a mistake—"

"No, don't even bother with that. I should have known better."

Tobie's assistant came to the door. "Excuse me, Ms. Armstrong. They're here."

Reeve braced himself for the moments ahead. He deserved whatever the Spencers dished out and more. Tabitha was dead because of him, and at the very least he owed her parents the dubious satisfaction of lambasting him to his face.

The Spencers walked in, their slumped shoulders and pain-ravaged eyes a heartbreaking distortion of the strong, hopeful parents who'd hired OASIS a week ago. Reeve couldn't speak past the lump rising in his throat, unable to even offer his condolences. He was scum.

Mr. Spencer cleared his throat as they all took their seats. "I'll get right to the point, Ms. Armstrong. My wife and I want your agency to find our daughter's killer."

Stunned silence filled the room. Tobie leaned forward. "The police—"

"The police will do everything they can, but it won't be enough. Their resources are limited. Your team came so close to finding her. That's why she was murdered."

Reeve flinched at the words, but he couldn't deny them.

Mrs. Spencer reached for his hand. "We know how hard you tried," she whispered.

He raised his eyes to meet her red-rimmed ones. "I'm so sorry," he choked out. "I'm sorry I didn't get her back

3

for you. I'll turn over all my files to the agent Ms. Armstrong assigns to the case. To the police too. Anything I can do."

"No!"

Reeve flinched again at her sharp tone, but he couldn't blame her. She didn't want him anywhere near her daughter's case, not after he'd screwed up so badly. "Don't worry, Mrs. Spencer, I won't get in the way."

She snatched her hand back and turned to her husband. "Peter—"

"You misunderstood, Mr. Buchanan. My wife and I want you to head the investigation."

Tobie cleared her throat. "I don't think—"

"Ms. Armstrong, please, he was so close." Mrs. Spencer turned back to Reeve. "Mr. Buchanan, I buried my sixteen-year-old daughter this morning. No parent should ever have to do that. Whoever did this can't get away with it. Please, don't let Tabitha down now. Not after all you've already done to try to help her."

The tears rolling down her face poured more acid into that hole in his gut.

"Find him," she wept. "Find whoever did this to our little girl."

Tobie shook her head. "Mrs. Spencer—"

"I'll do it," Reeve said quietly, his eyes locked on Mrs. Spencer's. And he would. The mission had gone horribly wrong, but he could do this for her. He would move heaven and earth to give her that small piece of closure.

"Thank you," she whispered.

"Money is no object. Do whatever it takes to catch Tabitha's killer." Mr. Spencer shook Reeve's hand and escorted his wife from the office.

Tobie waited until the elevator doors closed behind

them. "I'm going to call them tomorrow and tell them you won't be working the case."

"You'll be lying."

"No, I won't. You need to let someone else take this on. Someone who can maintain the proper detachment."

"None of us are detached from this."

Tobie nodded. "You're right. We all feel awful about what happened. But I still don't want you on this case. You came back to work too quickly after Ann Marie's death, and now you're too raw from what happened to Tabitha. I'm placing you on leave. Take some time and get some rest."

"Fine," he growled and headed for the door.

"Wait a minute." Tobie glared at him as he turned to face her. "If I force you to take vacation, you'll just go after him alone, won't you?"

"I owe them this much, Tobie. So, yeah, I'm working this case. And I'll do it with or without the agency's support." Reeve returned her glare yet hoped his boss didn't fire him on the spot. No one could ever call her a pushover, and OASIS was her baby. He meant what he said about working the case on his own, but he'd rather not have to resort to that. Their one possible lead from the crime scene was iffy at best. The agency's state-of-the-art resources would help considerably.

Tobie tapped her finger on the edge of her desk. "All right. I'll get the team together and we'll figure out a game plan."

"Thanks, boss."

"Don't thank me. I'm only saying yes because the last thing the Spencers need is you going all rogue on their daughter's case. But you had better stick with the plan this time, and remember your training. If I think for one second you're letting your emotions overrule your common sense,

I'm yanking you from the investigation, even if it means I have to fire you." She snatched up her phone and jabbed at the keypad.

He swallowed the retort that came to his lips. No need to press his luck any further.

Tobie finished dialing and threw him another glare. "I'm trusting you on this, Reeve. Don't make me regret it."

"Ah, this is the life."

Jessie Haynes smiled but didn't open her eyes. "You got that right," she replied groggily. The soothing ministrations of her masseuse along with the warm salty breeze floating over her skin were a combination built for napping. She and her best friend, Candy, had been in Key West for a week, and this was their third outdoor massage. Jessie's individual philosophy dictated there could never be too much of this sort of decadence in a person's life.

Candy spoke again. "What do you say we extend our stay for a few more days?"

"No can do."

"Oh, come on. We could go to that party those two guys we met last night told us about."

"I told you. I have no interest in getting to know those guys any better."

"Why not? They were perfectly nice. You need to loosen up. Get out there in the dating world. Those booty calls you indulge in are going to get old pretty soon."

"So you keep telling me. But no strings attached is just the way I like it. You know that."

"Yeah, I do." Candy sighed. "And I know why. But that doesn't mean I agree with you. It was fine for a while, but you just turned twenty-nine. It's time to let go of the past and embrace the future."

"Sweetie, you are my best friend on this earth and I love you more than anything, but if you insist on spoiling this massage by waxing all philosophical about my love life, I may never forgive you."

"Oh, fine. Be that way. But let's stay a few more days anyway. This is our first vacation since we started the company. What's the point of running our own business if we can't take extra time off when we want to? We don't have any clients lined up for another week. I, for one, am not looking forward to turning my cell phone back on."

"I know, but I promised my neighbors I'd dog-sit for them. They leave for their daughter's wedding the day after tomorrow. Much as I'd rather stay here, I can't back out on them at this late date."

Candy heaved a dramatic sigh. "Bummer. I hate it when you get all responsible."

"I'll make it up to you. I'll buy us a pitcher of margaritas after we're done here."

"Deal."

An hour later, reclining in lounge chairs on the hotel beach, they sipped their drinks as they took in all sorts of scenery—the waves, the sunset, the...

"There's a hot one." Candy nodded toward a rather buff-looking specimen of man coming out of the water.

"Not bad. A little too blond for me, though. I prefer that one over there." Jessie jutted her chin toward a dark-haired man slowly pacing the beach near the water. His tall, broad form had caught her attention earlier, and she'd been sneaking peeks at him from beneath the wide brim of her straw beach hat. His pacing had brought him close enough once or twice that she could see his strong, even features, although mirrored aviator sunglasses hid his eyes. She guessed him to be about six feet tall, every inch of those six feet dedicated to tasty-looking muscle. No doubt about it, this one would definitely be added to her mental collection of fantasy men, the ones she pulled out on quiet evenings and dreamed over when none of her aforementioned booty call pals were available.

He turned his head just in time to catch her nodding in his direction. A smug little smirk danced on his lips as he gave her the slightest of nods in return. She looked away. Discreetly watching hot guys on the beach was one thing, but she had no interest in flirting with them.

Candy gave a low wolf whistle. "Damn, he *is* a babe. Pecs of a gladiator. He keeps looking over here too. Are you sure you don't want to stay a few more days? You could get to know him."

Jessie stole another peek. Sure enough, he was still looking her way. Only now she detected a hint of a frown on his features.

"Excuse me."

Jessie jumped at the voice so close to her ear. She whipped her head around and found her face mere inches from that of a strange man down on one knee next to her chair. His thick hair was completely white, but his fair skin showed very few wrinkles. She guessed him to be around forty-five years old. But it was his eyes that struck her most. Black and lifeless, they held her captive. A ripple of revulsion fluttered in her stomach.

"Can I help you?" she asked, barely keeping a shake out of her voice.

"Have you seen a little boy come by here? He's wearing bright blue trunks."

"N-no. I haven't seen any children around here at all."

"You're sure of this?" He placed a hand on her thigh, sliding it up and down.

"Yes," Jessie whispered. The touch of his hand on her leg was cold and reptilian, but she found herself unable to voice an objection or tear her gaze from his dead eyes.

"Look, here comes one of the waiters," Candy said. "We'll ask him to get hotel security to help you find your boy."

His lips tightened, and he rose to his feet. "No, thank you, that won't be necessary. I'm sure he's returned to our room by now." He gave a soft brush of his fingers to Jessie's cheek before he walked away and disappeared into the hotel.

Candy twisted around and watched him go. "Jeez, that guy gave me the creeps. And I can't believe you let him touch you, control freak that you are. He was practically climbing into your lap. Are you okay?"

"Yeah, I'm all right. I'm just glad he's gone."

"Me too. But it sucks that he frightened off your boyfriend."

Jessie took a deep breath, and her stomach relaxed a bit as Candy's words sank in. "Boyfriend? What are you talking about?"

"I'm talking about that magnificent mountain of muscle you were checking out. He's gone too."

Jessie looked back across the sand. Her tall, dark, and handsome beach boy had indeed disappeared. "Fine by me. I've had enough encounters with strange men for one day."

Candy picked up the pitcher and topped off their margaritas. "To our last night in paradise."

They clinked glasses, and Jessie eagerly embraced some false courage from the tequila. The eerie stranger had shaken her more than she cared to admit. *Those eyes!* She sipped her drink, vowing to put the encounter behind her. Like hell she'd let some weirdo ruin her last evening on vacation.

Enjoying the tangy scent of the warm sea breeze caressing her skin, Jessie leaned back and closed her eyes. From the privacy of her imagination, she shamelessly entertained some racy thoughts regarding her sexy-looking, dark-haired beachcomber.

Bingo! A tingle of excitement rushed through Reeve as he spotted the shock of white hair emerging from the hotel bar.

He and his team had scant information about the man they sought, just a bare-bones physical description from a career drug dealer named Artie Pugliesi. According to Pugliesi, their quarry was a thin man with snow-white hair. Everyone called him the Iceman, and he was always looking to get his hands on teenage girls. What exactly he did with them, Pugliesi swore he didn't know. He did know, however, that Tabitha Spencer had last been seen alive with the Iceman shortly before her body had been found in the dumpster.

Because you handed her over to him, you little prick. Traded her for the cash the Iceman paid for girls. If the fates ever provided an opportunity for him to get ten minutes alone with that slimeball Pugliesi again, Reeve wouldn't waste them talking.

A small piece of paper found stuck to Tabitha's shoe had the name of this hotel scribbled on it, providing OASIS with a tenuous lead on her murderer's whereabouts. Looked like they'd just caught a break.

The Iceman scanned the patio area for a moment before

his gaze settled on the redhead and the blonde. No surprise there. From the moment they'd arrived at the beach and settled into their lounge chairs, the women caught the eye of every straight guy in the vicinity. And why not? The blonde was tall and stacked while the redhead was a little shorter but equally curvaceous. With their barely there bikinis and sheer sarong wraps, they'd been hard to ignore, even for Reeve —especially the redhead. If he hadn't been on assignment, he would have found a way to introduce himself. He'd always had a thing for redheads.

His impression of the woman took a nosedive as the Iceman swooped down beside her. The wide brim of her hat hid their faces, but their proximity and the sensual caress to her thigh left little doubt of the intimate nature of their conversation.

Reeve hurried into the hotel and took a seat at the bar, making brief eye contact with his fellow OASIS operatives, Ian Westlake and Maddie Barnes, and nodding toward the trio outside. This could be the next break they were looking for. So far, they'd had no luck in identifying the Iceman's real name. The women, however, might be traceable.

The Iceman stood up and left the women. He passed through the bar and headed straight for the hotel elevator. Ian followed him in. A minute later, Ian sent a text to Reeve's phone. *He's staying in suite 801. I'm monitoring from the stairwell.*

Reeve nursed a beer for an hour as the women giggled their way through their pitcher of drinks. They gathered up their beach totes and towels and proceeded to the elevators. Maddie, dressed as a hotel employee, slipped in behind them. A few moments later, she returned and stepped behind the bar. Grabbing a cloth, she wiped the marble top and made her way to Reeve.

"They got off on the sixth floor. It looks like they're sharing room 614."

"Okay. I'll find out who they are. Ian's watching our target from the eighth floor, but I want you to stay sharp in the lobby. Call me immediately if any of them come back down. Otherwise I'll relieve you in a few hours."

"You got it."

He headed for his own room and placed a call to Jake Hooper, their research and computer expert at headquarters. Within minutes, Jake had information on all three.

"The Iceman's suite is registered to a Dean King from Phoenix. His record is clean, but Tobie is sending Fitz out there to check out the address on the driver's license and see if he can find any evidence to nail the sleaze-bag."

"Good. What about the women?"

"The blonde is Candace Bartlett and the redhead is Jessica Haynes. They both live in Candlewood, Connecticut, and there's no criminal record for either of them. All three are booked to fly into LaGuardia tomorrow, but his flight is earlier than theirs."

"Book Maddie on the same flight as Haynes and Bartlett. Book me and Ian on the Iceman's flight. We'll need cars ready and waiting at LaGuardia."

"I'll take care of everything, buddy," Jake said. "I'll be there too. We won't let him out of our sight."

"Thanks. See you tomorrow."

Reeve hung up, confident Jake would forward the appropriate information to the rest of the team. He tried to get some rest. But sleep wouldn't come because all he really wanted to do was go up to the eighth floor and nab the Iceman this minute. However, Pugliesi had disappeared, and without his testimony, they couldn't connect the Iceman to

Tabitha. They had no evidence the police could use to arrest him. All they could do right now was follow.

Muttering the old saying about patience being a virtue, Reeve rolled over and punched his pillow. His thoughts turned to the redhead, Jessica Haynes. Too bad such a pretty package hid an ugly character. Why a woman who could have her pick of men would choose someone like the Iceman, Reeve would never understand. He knew all about how some women were attracted to so-called bad boys, but this was another league entirely.

None of that mattered to him anyway. If Jessica Haynes had assisted the Iceman in Tabitha's murder, Reeve would make damn sure she felt the consequences.

CHAPTER TWO

JESSIE WAVED goodbye to Candy as the taxi pulled away, and with a bone-weary sigh, she unlocked her front door. Some mechanical glitch with the plane had delayed their flight, landing them in New York just in time to hit evening rush hour traffic. The commute from LaGuardia to Candlewood had taken twice as long as it should have.

Jessie glanced up and down the block, letting the comfort of being home soothe her mood. She loved the tranquil glow the setting sun cast on her quiet little street. She'd lived here for three years now and never tired of the view of lush lawns and carefully tended gardens. While not a ritzy or particularly affluent area, her charming little neighborhood was filled with hardworking people who took pride in their homes. Several years of her own hard work had allowed her to purchase her small bungalow. The day she'd signed the closing papers and received the keys had been one of the proudest and happiest of her life.

She inhaled deeply, the scent of her neighbor's roses a delightful welcome home, and stepped inside. Leaving her roller suitcase at the foot of the stairs, she walked into the living room to open some windows.

"Hello, Miss Haynes."

Jessie let out a small squeak as she jumped about a foot in the air before whirling around. *What on earth?* The white-haired man with the dead black eyes sat on her couch. The picture of relaxation, he had one leg bent with the ankle resting on the other knee, and he sipped an amber liquid from one of her Waterford crystal glasses. Even the fingers of his free hand idly tapping the butt of a handgun lying on the end table conveyed no hint of tension or nervousness.

Run! her mind screamed, but stunned fear rooted her feet to the floor. "What are you doing here?" she croaked out, barely able to form the words.

"I came to see you."

His mischievous tone sent her heart pounding into overdrive. "I don't understand."

"We never got to finish our chat in Key West."

"I told you, I never saw your son."

"Oh, don't be obtuse. We both know there was no little boy."

"Then what—"

"As I said, I wanted to see you again." His eyes raked her up and down, and she fought the urge to cross her arms in front of her chest. "Normally, I don't pay attention to redheads, but you are quite exceptional."

Words lodged in her dry throat as her white-knuckled fingers clung to the strap of her tote bag, still draped across her chest. Finally able to send a signal to her feet, she backed away slowly.

"Oh, no, no, no, Miss Haynes. Don't leave yet. We're just beginning to get to know each other."

His calm, playful demeanor only increased her terror.

Those soulless black eyes stared right through her, and his fingers closed on the butt of the gun. Whatever his intentions were, there would be no mercy from this man. "How do you know my name?"

He put down the glass and pulled one of her business cards from his shirt pocket. "I slipped this from your bag last evening while we spoke. Then it only took a few clicks on the computer to find your address."

Her mind raced. She hadn't locked the front door yet. Maybe she could make it out before he was off the couch and on her.

He stood and swiftly approached her, dashing her plan. Jessie shuddered as he took her arm and led her to the little side table she used as a bar. He picked up a glass. "Fix yourself a drink. You'll feel better."

"No... I-I don't want a drink."

He squeezed her arm. "I *said* you'll feel better."

She reached for the stopper of the nearest crystal wine decanter, and he released his hold. Her hand shook violently as she poured, and the cabernet splashed over the rim of the glass he held, splattering to the carpet. She stared at the spreading stains, slowly processing this horrifying turn of events.

This man was going to rape her, and most likely kill her. Most likely? Ha. She'd seen his face, knew he'd been at the hotel in Key West. Plenty of information to give to the police. But that wasn't the only reason she knew she would die today. Even if he'd worn a ski mask, his eyes told her everything she needed to know.

Tears welled up, and the blood-red wine stains wavered in her vision as if they were living things performing a danse macabre, courting her death.

He rubbed his finger very lightly up and down her bare

arm before wrapping his hand around her elbow. That final touch acted as a detonator, and she exploded in a wild burst of fury. Swinging her hand up, she caught him cleanly across the jaw with the heavy crystal stopper still clutched in her fingers. Wrenching her elbow free, she ran for the door. She might not make it, but she ran anyway, and if he caught her she would fight him with everything she had. Rage at his audacious attempt to destroy the life she'd worked so hard for had supplanted her fear. No way would she be a meek little lamb for the slaughter.

She flew to the hallway, his footsteps booming after her. He emitted a surprised grunt, and his fingers grazed her butt just before a loud thud sounded. She risked a quick look back as she yanked open the front door. He'd tripped on the hallway area carpet, falling to his knees. He bounded back up, and Jessie raced outside, screaming at the top of her lungs. "Help! Fire!"

"You bitch! Get back here!"

He gained on her as she bolted across the lawn toward the street. A dark SUV screeched to a stop in front of her, and she slammed her hands on it to stop herself from going over the hood. The angry crack of a gunshot sounded by her ear, and the passenger side-view mirror shattered and was nearly ripped off the door. Jessie's jaw dropped and her mind moved in slow motion as she tried to grasp the reality of being shot at.

The driver's door opened. A man got out, stepped on floorboard, and fired a gun over the roof of the vehicle, the sharp report echoing up and down the street. "Get in the car!" he shouted.

What the hell? The man from the SUV was the dark-haired man from the beach she'd been looking at last night. Two other people ran toward them from the other side of the street, guns drawn and firing at her white-haired attacker. One of them, a woman with long, dark hair, was suddenly thrown back to the ground. She gripped at her shoulder, and Jessie's stomach turned to lead as blood poured through the woman's fingers.

"I'm with the FBI! Get in!" the man from the beach roared.

Jessie still struggled to make sense of the gunfire mutilating her sweet, placid neighborhood as well as the appearance of the two men from Key West at her house. Two more gunshots rang out. The back passenger window of the SUV exploded, snapping Jessie's brain out of its fugue state.

Screw it, figure it all out later! She jerked the door open and scrambled onto the seat, staying low and keeping her head down. The dark-haired man fired another round toward her house before he jumped behind the wheel and raced down the street with a squeal of tires.

She twisted around and peered over the back of the seat to see her assailant running back into her house and slamming the door. A tall man with reddish, wavy hair and a scruffy beard came out from behind the cover of a parked car and ran over to the woman on the ground. Jessie could hear the howl of sirens in the distance, and just before the SUV whipped around a corner, a police car raced up toward her house.

"Stop! Go back!" she cried. "The police are here."

"We can't go back. How many other ways out of your house are there besides the front door?"

"What?" Her dazed mind kept seeing that poor woman lying in the street with blood running through her fingers. Jessie didn't think she'd ever seen so much blood before.

"How many?" the dark-haired man all but shouted,

jolting her attention back to him. "If he goes out the back, can he escape?"

"Y-yes. There's a gate that opens to the alleyway."

"Shit!" He grabbed a cell phone from the center console. "Jake, you there?"

"Yeah," came the disembodied response.

"The bastard's in the wind. There's an alley behind the house. Get over there pronto."

"On my way."

"Ian?"

Another voice crackled through the phone. "Yeah, boss, I'm here."

"How is she?"

"The paramedics just got here. They're working on her now. But it looked to me like it went clean through, so I think she'll be all right. I'll know more soon."

"Stay with her. And make sure she goes to the hospital. Don't let her say no."

"Yeah, sure. Like she'll listen to me."

"Just do it, Ian. Make sure she sees a doctor."

"Yeah. Out."

He winced as he lowered his arm to drop the phone back onto the console. A splotch of blood seeped through a rip in the shoulder of his black tee shirt.

"Oh my god! You've been shot!"

"It's nothing, just a graze. It barely broke the skin." He grimaced again as he gripped the steering wheel.

"You can let the paramedics look at it when you take me back to my house."

"We're not going back."

"Why not? Please, just take me home!" The shrill pitch of her voice raked against her own ears, but she didn't care. This man claimed to be with the FBI, but until she had proof of that, she wanted the comfort of police cars and lots of men in uniform.

He kept driving, making no attempt to turn around.

"Who are you? What do you want with me?"

"My name is Reeve Buchanan." He looked directly at her for the first time, and Jessie was struck by the intensity of his eyes. They were a deep azure blue, and she might have found them attractive if it weren't for the naked fury they blazed at her. She shrank back in her seat.

"Who are you?" he snapped. "What's your relationship to the Iceman?"

The *Iceman?* Actually, she couldn't think of a better name for the man in her house. She'd felt chilled to the bone when she'd looked into those obsidian eyes.

"He was going to kill me." Just saying the words brought the horror of those moments in the living room roaring back.

"Why?"

"I don't know."

If anything, her response seemed to antagonize the stranger beside her even further. He took another turn at warp speed. Jessie fumbled for the seat belt, anger erasing her confusion and fear. "Slow down before you kill us both!"

"Yeah, you'd know all about that sort of thing, wouldn't you?" he sneered.

"Look, uh, Reeve, is it?" At his brief nod, she continued. "I don't know who you are, and I certainly don't know that lunatic back there."

"Oh, sure. I suppose it was your identical twin I saw cozying up with him in Key West last night."

"I wasn't cozying up with him! That's the first time I ever saw him."

"Yeah, right."

They came to the highway entrance and Reeve took it, thwarting her hope he might slow down enough that she could jump out. Like it or not, she was stuck in this vehicle until he decided to stop it. She could only pray he had been telling her the truth, and they were heading to the nearest FBI office. *Was* there an FBI office in Candlewood? She had no idea. "Where are you taking me?"

"The hospital. You're bleeding."

"What?" she screeched. She looked down at herself, terrified she would see blood gushing out of some as yet unfelt wound. Nothing.

"It's your head," Reeve said calmly, as if he were reporting the weather.

One hand flew to her head as the other flipped down the sun visor. A few bits of mirrored glass glittered in her hair, and two thin lines of blood were dripping down the left side of her face. She probed around her scalp and found two small lacerations. They didn't feel that deep, and she was about to tell him they didn't need anything more than a little disinfectant but thought better of it. The hospital sounded like a good idea. There would be lots of people around, and she would have a doctor or nurse call the police.

"Forget it," he said, startling her from her thoughts.

"Forget what?"

"Whatever it is you're thinking about the hospital. You have to keep your mouth shut about what happened back there. We're going to tell them you tripped on your way to the car and bumped your head into the mirror."

"You're not with the FBI, are you?" Jessie said, willing her voice not to shake.

He didn't answer as he whipped the SUV through the busy traffic, giving her nothing more she could use to determine if he was a good guy or a bad guy. On the plus side, he'd saved her from being attacked and gunned down on the street. But on the down side, he thought she was a criminal. She looked at his profile, noting the grim set of his mouth as he gave his full attention to the crowded highway.

Gone was the laid-back-looking beach dude. The tight scowl on his face, the short, jagged scar along the side of his chin, and the near-black hair falling to the tip of his collar in thick waves all shouted danger. Her eyes traveled lower, taking full note of the impressive biceps bulging from the sleeve of his tight black shirt and the powerful hands gripping the steering wheel as he expertly wove through the rush hour traffic. He'd been an attractive package last night, but right now all his attributes did nothing but intimidate.

"Who are you?" he asked again.

"Jessie Haynes."

"I know that! I meant who are you to him?"

"I told you. I don't know him."

"Stop lying."

"That's it. I've had enough of this crap. Who are *you*?" she demanded as she poked him in the arm. "How do *you* know this guy? Why were *you* at my house? It seems to me that you know a hell of a lot more about what's going on than I do."

Reeve shifted a bit in his seat, ignoring the nip of pain as she poked a little too close to his wound. He had to admit the whole situation back at the house was strange. If she and the Iceman worked together, why had the creep been shooting at her?

She must have double-crossed him somehow. Reeve didn't buy her "I don't know him" act. Not with all that touchy-feely going on at the hotel patio.

"Well?" she asked. "Who are you?"

"I'm the guy who's going to make sure your boyfriend gets what's coming to him."

"He's not my—"

"Spare me. I'm in no mood for bullshit."

He took the exit for the hospital and pulled into the emergency room parking lot. She reached for the door handle, but he seized her arm. "I mean it. Don't try anything stupid. You're going to tell me everything you know, and if it helps me to catch him, then maybe I'll forget about you altogether. But if you cross me on this, I promise you I will make your life a living hell."

"Let go of me. I'm not going anywhere but to the first doctor who can stitch up my head."

He squeezed her arm a little tighter as he pulled his gun from his pocket. "This may be out of sight, but it will be pointed at you at all times."

Her eyes widened and she gave him the barest of nods, her arm trembling in his grasp. She looked so vulnerable he almost felt sorry for her until a replay of her cuddling with the Iceman on the beach ran through his mind. She didn't deserve sympathy. He dropped her arm in disgust.

"Don't move," he warned. Slipping his gun back in his pocket, he got out, walked to the passenger side, and snatched open her door.

"Let's go."

———

WALTER FOX PARKED his '68 cherry-red Mustang on a side street around the corner from the emergency room. As he hurried toward the corner, he quickly inspected his uniform, making sure his badge and nameplate were straight. He'd dressed in such a rush he wouldn't have been surprised if one or both of them were upside down. Satisfied he looked his part, he turned the corner and made a beeline toward the emergency room entrance, determined to get there before the Haynes woman and her escort.

He had no idea who the man was. Nor the woman either, really, other than her name. All he knew was that his past was coming back to haunt him. That psycho, the Iceman, called him a little over an hour ago, told him to put on his uniform and then go sit tight down the street from the her house. Fox hadn't wanted to get involved, but he'd learned long ago that saying no to the Iceman led to very unpleasant consequences.

When the shooting had started, Fox nearly bolted. He had no qualms about conning people out of their cash and valuables, but he avoided any kind of violent criminal activity. Only his fear of incurring the Iceman's wrath made him stay put.

Just as the SUV had roared past his Mustang, the Iceman had called Fox again, ordering him to follow and to intercept the woman if he could.

Some of Fox's tension slipped away as it became clear the couple were on their way to the hospital. He quickly devised a plan and knew he could sell it. But it wouldn't work if he didn't get inside before they did. He doubled his pace.

The sooner he delivered the woman, the sooner he'd be done with the Iceman.

REEVE LED the Haynes woman through the emergency room doors into the waiting area. Two police officers spoke to a nurse at the admitting desk, their backs to the entrance. A third officer stood in the waiting area itself, scanning the faces of the several people waiting to be seen. The pair by the desk moved toward one of the exam rooms, and the third officer followed, casting a final glance at the entrance. He turned away and then did a double take before veering away from his buddies and heading straight for them.

"Miss Haynes?" he asked. "Jessica Haynes?"

Reeve tightened his grip on her arm, sending her a silent warning to deny it, but she ignored him.

"Yes, I'm Jessie Haynes."

"I'm Officer Fox. We need you to answer some questions about the incident at your house. You'll need to come with me." He reached to take her other arm.

"Miss Haynes needs medical attention. I'm taking her to see a doctor now." Reeve inwardly cursed the efficiency of the police to have gotten here so fast.

"I'll make sure she gets checked out," the officer persisted.

"I don't need a doctor." Jessie smiled at the officer before glancing up at Reeve. "You were sweet to insist on coming here, but all I really need is a Band-Aid."

"I think you're making a mistake. Let's get you taken care of and then I'll drive you to the police station," he lied, having absolutely no intention of letting his only solid connection to the Iceman slip through his fingers. He couldn't afford to wait for the police to find out what she knew.

He bumped the pocket with the gun in it, hoping to frighten her into submission, but she pulled her arm from his grasp and stepped back toward the doors. "Really, you're a dear, but I'm fine, and I don't need to take up any more of your time. Let's go, Officer. I'd like to do whatever I can to help."

"This is Fox," the officer said into the microphone on the front of his shoulder. "I'm bringing Miss Haynes in for questioning."

"Copy that," a voice replied. The policeman stepped around Reeve and escorted her out the door.

Dammit! Reeve didn't waste time by following them out. It wouldn't accomplish anything other than rousing the officer's suspicion, a headache he really didn't need right now. Law enforcement had a frustrating habit of slowing things down with policies and procedures.

He fumed at his stupidity for bringing her here rather than taking her to the OASIS offices. One of the team members with some medical training could have looked at her head. But with agonizing results, he'd learned the painful lesson that head wounds were often far more serious than they looked. As bad as he wanted to nail the Iceman, he wasn't willing to put anyone's life on the line for it. No matter what the hell kind of relationship she had with that bastard, Reeve didn't want to see her dead.

Seeing her and her boyfriend serve a long sentence in a maximum-security hellhole of a prison would be far more satisfying.

CHAPTER THREE

JESSIE ALMOST DISSOLVED with relief as she walked outside, Officer Fox right on her heels. Reeve had shown no qualms about using a gun on her quiet street—even if that did look like self-defense—so she'd taken a pretty giant leap of faith he wouldn't want to pull his gun in front of a cop.

Now that she'd gotten away from him, her nerves calmed a little and the questions really started swirling in her mind. Why were the two men from Key West suddenly here in her town? And one of them *in her house?* Why was the Iceman after her? And just who the hell was Reeve Buchanan, really?

Too many questions, not enough answers. "What's going on, Officer? And I should tell you that man we just left has a gu—"

"We'll talk about everything at the station, Miss Haynes." Placing a hand firmly on her back, Officer Fox steered her away from the main parking lot and out to the quiet side street bordering the hospital.

Jessie stopped walking. "Look, I don't mean to be rude, but I'm on my very last nerve here. I've just been attacked, shot at, and kidnapped. I intend to cooperate, but I want some answers first, and I want them right now." She planted her hands on her hips as she stared him in the eye. "So I repeat, what is going on?"

"I'm not authorized to tell you anything."

"Are you kidding me? What the hell does that mean?"

He ignored her questions, taking her by the arm and tugging her toward an old red sports car. The hair lifted on the back of her neck. That certainly didn't look like any police car she'd ever seen.

"Wait a minute. I want to contact my attorney," she said, stalling for time as she groped at the opening of her tote bag.

"You can call him from the station." His grip on her arm tightened, and Jessie's sense of unease inched up another notch.

"Please let go of me." She pulled away, but he pulled her back with a fierce yank, cranking her panic level to high alert. "You're not a policeman, are you?"

"Never mind that now. We have to get going." He fished a set of car keys from his pocket and opened the driver door. "Get in and slide over."

Like hell I will. She jerked her arm in earnest and aimed a slap at his face. He dodged it easily and kept a tight hold on her.

"Oh, no you don't, Miss Haynes. There's a friend of mine who wants to see you."

AFTER A FINAL GLARE at Jessie's departing back, Reeve strode to the admitting desk. Anxious to discover Maddie's condition, he hoped the paramedics had gotten her here already, and he needed to talk to Ian. Both Ian and Maddie grew up in this area, and they were going to have to utilize any connections they might have with the Candlewood Police Department to have any prospect of picking up the Haynes woman again.

Once they did, Reeve vowed she wouldn't get away so easily a second time.

Three other people waited at the desk. He groped in his pocket for his ID, hoping to speed the process along.

"Reeve." Ian emerged from the hall leading to the exam areas, a grim look on his face.

Reeve's stomach dropped. "Is Maddie...?"

"She's fine." Ian's beleaguered tone explained it all. Maddie was no doubt fine enough to rip her partner a new one for insisting she get checked out at the hospital. She wouldn't have come willingly if her injury was anything less than a limb amputation. Maddie had a lot of grit and guts, but sometimes Reeve wondered about her common sense.

"What did you tell the police?"

"The usual cover story. We're private investigators working a divorce case, and Jessie Haynes is the suspected mistress of the husband of our client. I claimed ignorance about the Iceman and the shooting. Ditto on the Haynes woman's whereabouts."

"Good work. Although we've lost the Haynes woman."

Ian's eyebrows sprang up. "What? I thought you had her."

"I did, but not anymore. She had a slight head injury, so I brought her here. A cop headed us off in the waiting room. Haynes jumped ship as quick as she could and went with him." Reeve's pride still burned at how neatly she'd maneuvered herself away from him. "She knew I wanted answers about her boyfriend."

"Did you get anything useful before she bailed?"

"No. She denied knowing the Iceman, which has got to be a load of crap. She was practically making out with him on the beach last night."

"Yeah," Ian agreed. "Although if she's involved with someone like him, it's a dicey move on her part, putting herself right into police hands."

"It is, but I was pretty clear about how I wanted to take down the Iceman. I guess she saw me as a bigger threat than the police. And my gut tells me she can help us."

"You'd think she'd want to tell us whatever she could. I mean, he just tried to kill her."

Reeve shrugged. "Yeah, I don't get it either. He shoots at her, and she *still* wants to protect him? I'll never understand a woman like that."

"She's probably got secrets of her own to hide."

"Agreed. And who knows what her plan is now. Maybe she figures she can sweet talk her way out of police custody."

"You want to pick up her trail from the police station?"

"Definitely."

"Okay. Let's go talk to the officers who just took my statement. I sort of know one of them. Name's Reilly. He was a kid the last time I saw him, but I graduated high school with his sister. Seems like a decent guy. He might help us out."

Ian led the way down the hall and around a corner. The two police officers he'd seen earlier now stood at the foot of a bed. One of them had a pad and pen in hand.

A striped curtain concealed the bed's occupant, but her voice carried loud and clear. "I want to file a complaint. The nurses stole my clothes."

Reeve rounded the curtain and met Maddie Barnes's

mutinous glare head on. Her ferocity intensified when she spotted Ian. "And you helped them, you traitor!"

"Doc says she's gotta stay overnight for observation," Ian muttered.

"I'm not staying. I'm fine!" She sat up and flung her blanket off. The hospital gown slid off her shoulder, revealing the large bandage wrapped around her wound. She grimaced as she tried to get to her feet.

"Knock it off, Maddie," Reeve said. "Get back into bed." She sent another searing glare in his direction, but he didn't care. He wasn't about to let her aggravate her injury. He had enough to worry about. "I mean it. You're white as a sheet and in no condition to go anywhere."

"We've got work to do," she snarled.

"And I'll need you at your best. Get some rest tonight. We'll see where you're at in the morning. That's an order."

Maddie grumbled her way back under the blanket. "Don't let being team leader keep going to your head. It was fat enough to begin with."

"Yeah, okay, thanks for the tip," Reeve said.

He turned to the officers. One of them bit his bottom lip, not even trying to hide his amusement. The other looked down at his utility belt as he slowly and carefully replaced his pad. Reeve couldn't blame them. Maddie's personality evoked a wide variety of reactions from people.

"You haven't changed a bit, have you, Maddie?" the first officer said.

"Bite me, Reilly. Just because you've got a badge now doesn't mean you've gotten any smarter. You don't know anything about me, so you can take a flying—"

Ian cut her off. "Reilly, this is my boss, Reeve Buchanan. We were wondering if there's any way we can find out how long Miss Haynes will be kept at the station for questioning?"

The officers exchanged a curious look between them. "Miss Haynes is at the station? When did that happen?"

"Just now," Reeve said. "I brought her here to attend to some minor injuries. Officer Fox met us in the lobby and took her in. He called it in on his radio. Didn't you hear it?"

"No, nothing came through the radio." Reilly looked at his partner, a frown wrinkling his brow as he asked, "Do you know Fox?"

"Uh-uh. Never heard of him."

A knot of lead tightened in Reeve's stomach. "Is it possible he's new? Someone you haven't met yet?"

The second officer—Parker, according to his nameplate —shook his head. "I've been on the force here for twelve years. It's not that big and word travels fast. I'd know if somebody new came in. There's no one named Fox."

The knot in Reeve's stomach became a vise. He spun and raced back the way he'd come. Ian and the officers were right behind him, and he was vaguely aware of Maddie's voice stridently demanding someone bring her some clothes. He dodged several people as he tore through the waiting room and then burst out into the parking area. Frantically scanning the lot, he saw no sign of Jessie Haynes or the police imposter.

"What do they look like?" Reilly asked as he skidded to a halt.

"She's a redhead, about five foot six. He's about five ten with light brown hair, and he's wearing a uniform just like yours."

"Okay, let's split up and see if we can spot them. Parker, you go with Buchanan. Ian, you come with me." Ian and Reilly ran to the right and disappeared around the side of the hospital. Reeve and Parker sprinted in the other direction and out of the parking lot. A cry for help came from his left, and Reeve spotted the Haynes woman struggling with Fox near the end of the block.

"This way!" They raced down the street as Parker shouted a command for Fox to get away from her. The imposter looked at them in surprise, and the woman wasted no time yanking free and sprinting away, disappearing around the next corner. Fox dove into a red Mustang and screeched out of the parking space. With gun drawn, Parker dashed into the street to head him off, but Fox swerved around him and sped away.

As Parker alerted his partner, Reeve flew down the street and around the corner after the Haynes woman. This street was a main thoroughfare, and he anxiously scanned the pedestrians, failing to spot her gleaming red hair. He looked to the other side of the street as well, but he didn't see her. *Shit!*

Parker caught up with him as Ian and Reilly came around the opposite corner of the hospital and hurried toward them. "Where'd she go?"

"I don't know," Reeve answered, still scanning the street. "You didn't see her?" he asked Ian as he approached.

"No."

A group of smokers dressed in hospital scrubs or white lab coats huddled around an ashtray several feet away from the entrance. Reilly and Parker walked over, asking if they'd seen anything. Reeve pulled out his phone and called OASIS headquarters.

"Jake, we've lost the Haynes woman. She was last seen outside of the hospital. See what you can find." Jake could tap into just about any computer system in existence. If she started leaving any kind of an electronic trail, Jake would find her. With any luck, one of the many cameras Reeve could see on the hospital building would show where she went. Jake could access those too. "Time is important, Jake. She's in deep shit and needs our help."

"I'm on it," Jake said.

"You don't think she's his partner anymore, do you?" Ian asked as Reeve ended the call.

"No. Not a willing one, anyway. But I'd bet a year's salary this Fox guy definitely works with the Iceman. The question is, what does she have to do with all of it?"

"I don't know. According to what Pugliesi told us, she doesn't fit the profile of his usual victims."

Reeve agreed. That was why it had never occurred to him that she might *be* a victim. She was voluptuous and beautiful, true, but also about a decade older than the teenage girls the Iceman supposedly preferred.

The image of Tabitha Spencer's body in the dumpster crept into his mind's eye, and he pushed it away, forcing his focus to the here and now. It didn't matter that Jessie Haynes wasn't a teenager. Whatever the reason for the Iceman's fixation on her, it certainly wasn't going to be in her best interest.

"Stay with these guys," he told Ian as he nodded toward the policemen. "See if they come up with anything we can use. I'm going back to her house in case she heads there. We have to find her before the Iceman does."

As he ran back to his SUV, the sharp fingers of guilt gripped his chest. She'd asked to go to the police right from the get-go, and he hadn't paid that any attention, desperate to believe she would have evidence against the Iceman. Now she was alone facing a treacherous threat. He'd screwed up, big time. Again.

He slammed his palm against the steering wheel before

starting the ignition. *No, dammit!* He would fix this mistake. He had to.

No way would he let the Iceman claim another victim.

———

JESSIE DARTED around the corner and spotted a young man getting out of a cab. He wore a besotted grin on his face as he wrestled a huge bouquet of flowers and an enormous stuffed teddy bear out of the vehicle. She dashed over, nearly knocking the flowers out of his hands.

"Sorry!" she said as she flung herself into the back seat.

"Can't get me down today. I just became a dad!" He bumped the door shut with his hip.

"Drive!" she shouted to the cabby. "Please, just go!"

He gave her a startled look but then, to her immense relief, pulled into traffic. Jessie slouched down in the seat. As the cab pulled through the intersection, she stole a quick glance out the back window just in time to see Reeve Buchanan charge around the corner. She ducked down again, taking deep breaths as she tried to quiet her hammering heart.

After a few blocks, she sat upright. The cabby caught her eye in the rearview mirror as she dug a tissue from her tote bag and wiped the blood off her face.

"Hey, lady, you okay?"

"It's just a scratch. I'm fine," she lied. She was anything but fine. Oh, her head was all right, but a slew of strange men—*armed* men—were after her, and she hadn't the faintest clue why.

"You want to give me an idea where we're going?"

Good question. "Can you just drive for a little while? And stay away from the hospital?"

"You got it."

Jessie mulled her options. Her first instinct was to go back to her house and the swarm of police officers bound to be there by now. But how would she know which of them were real and which ones might be phonies? Meaning she couldn't go to the police station, either. Not yet. They couldn't all be imposters, but she hadn't any idea how to tell the difference. She'd been so easily fooled by that sleazy Fox person, and the fact that he had been at the hospital waiting for her suggested there was a definite plan in play. All these strange men wanted to get their hands on her and were going to great lengths to achieve that goal.

She needed time to herself, time to get out of sight and think until she figured out what to do. She'd go to a hotel. No one would know where she went, and she could think in peace. She checked her wallet, so glad now she hadn't had time to put down her tote before this insanity started, and instructed the cabby to take her to the bank so she could get some more cash to add to what little she had left from her vacation money. Call her paranoid, but she didn't want to use her credit card for the hotel.

Jessie leaned back, closed her eyes, and tried to relax. Going to pieces would only compound the problem. Checking into a hotel was a good idea. She'd get a little rest and decide who to call for help. If the police couldn't be trusted, maybe she'd try the FBI. Although Reeve Buchanan had claimed to be with the FBI. Another lie from another imposter?

Crap, isn't there anyone I can trust?

If push came to shove, she supposed she could contact her father. Her stomach clenched. That would have to be her very last resort.

She already had enough trouble.

"WHAT DO you mean you lost her?"

"I couldn't help it," Fox whined on the other end of the phone. "She figured out I wasn't a cop and put up a fight. Then a real cop showed up. I had to get out of there."

Iceman slapped the lid of his laptop shut. "So she's with the police now?"

"No, I don't think so. As soon as she got loose, she hauled ass in the other direction. I got the feeling she didn't want to see them any more than I did. Not even the guy who brought her to the hospital. She couldn't wait to ditch him."

Interesting. Why would she run away from someone trying to help her? There must be more to the situation than he'd been told. "Did you dump your car?"

"No! I love that car. It's the only thing I got that's worth anything."

"Do it! It's too conspicuous, and they probably got the plate number."

Iceman hadn't anticipated needing any help in snatching the Haynes woman. But he believed in being prepared, so he'd contacted Fox and had him standing by with his phony police uniform, telling him to park a few doors down from her house. But Fox managed to screw up a perfectly good opportunity. *Asshole.* This was why he liked to work alone. Unfortunately he'd had little choice this time.

He'd suspected there were people following him as soon as he'd arrived in Key West, making him hesitant to snatch the Haynes woman right away. But now he wondered if they'd really been after him at all. Maybe they were there to look after the redhead. Had Cochran gotten cold feet about the whole thing? Changed his mind and decided to protect her by calling in some sort of bodyguard service? He'd check it out. In his line of work, one could never be too careful. Something he needed to make clear to the idiot on the other end of the phone.

"Get rid of that damn car. I won't tell you again."

"Fine," Fox grumbled. "Anything else you want me to do?"

"Just hang tight. I'll call you with the next move." He broke the connection and leaned back in his chair. *Could* Cochran have double-crossed him? It didn't seem likely. The snake had too much riding on making the woman disappear. Nor had he shown the faintest trace of remorse when he'd approached Iceman with his scheme. Cochran had been more than eager to see her gone, especially since he would be getting the finder's fee Iceman paid to anyone who supplied him with a usable woman.

So if Cochran didn't send them, who were those people? How were they connected to the woman? She'd been just as surprised by their arrival as he had, so it wasn't as if she'd been expecting their assistance. And judging by her choice to get away from them, she clearly didn't *want* their help. Curious.

Whoever they were, he needed to get rid of them. Thanks to the death of the Spencer girl, things were getting hot and he needed to leave the country, sooner rather than later. He never should have agreed to take care of the woman for Cochran. If he'd never gone to Key West, he'd be free and clear by now. But the job had seemed simple enough.

Rookie mistake. Now this nasty situation threatened his future financial security as well as his ability to stay out of prison. If he wanted to continue living free and rich, he had no choice but to finish what he'd started.

And he wasn't about to forget the tasty bonus in store at

the end of this job. The redhead's lovely curves had not been lost on him, and he looked forward to spending at least a few days with her. Images of her naked body tied spread eagle to a bed had happily occupied his thoughts ever since he'd laid eyes on her at the beach. Oh yes, he definitely wanted some quality time alone with this one.

He sat up in his chair, laced his fingers together, and cracked his knuckles. If he wanted to spend some time with her, he had to find her before anyone else did. Perhaps a little hacking would give him some more information on the whereabouts of the luscious Miss Haynes and her mysterious bodyguards. At the very least, he could hack into her bank and freeze her accounts. Cutting her off from cash would force her to use her credit cards. And once she did, he'd find her in seconds.

He flipped open his laptop and got to work.

CHAPTER FOUR

FROM A DISCREET DISTANCE, Reeve kept a vigilant eye on Jessie Haynes's house. Tobie was keeping a similar vigil at Candace Bartlett's house. He doubted Jessie would show up at either place now, but at the moment they had no other place to start looking. The police still milled around the Haynes property, and several neighbors clustered together on lawns here and there as they watched the proceedings. Night had fallen in full, and the flashing lights from the police cars cast a sickly red and blue throb through the darkness.

His cell phone buzzed and flashed Jake's name on the readout. About time. "What have you found?"

"Somebody's been messing with her accounts. She tried to get cash from an ATM on Jackson Road, but she couldn't get anything. They didn't close off her credit cards, though, so if she's short on dough she'll have to use plastic pretty soon. And then we'll have her."

Jake sounded optimistic, but Reeve couldn't shake his own unease. "Any idea who froze her accounts?"

"I can probably trace it to the source, but it won't be quick. Whoever did it is one sharp SOB. I'll bet it's our guy."

"Which means if she shows up on the radar, he'll know about it too."

"Most likely," Jake agreed, and Reeve's anxiety jumped up another notch.

"Did you get anything from the hospital cameras?"

"Yeah. She grabbed a cab. I got the number. The bad news is the driver never called it in to his dispatcher, so we don't know where he dropped her off. He's off duty now. We've tried calling, but he's not answering his home phone or his cell. Ian is on his way over to the cab company to see if he can get any more information. You can meet him over there."

"Good idea." Reeve punched the address into his GPS as Jake reeled it off. "Got it. I'm on my way. Anything else?"

"Not really. So far, I haven't found anything to suggest she's a criminal. No arrests, no warrants, nothing. She and her friend started their own job coaching business a couple of years ago. It all looks legit. But I've only just started. I'll dig deeper into her past and see what I can find."

"Okay. Keep in mind it's a whole new ballgame now. The connection could be anything."

"Don't worry. No matter how big the haystack, I'll find the needle." Jake disconnected.

Reeve pocketed his phone. With a last wishful scan of her house and the surrounding properties, he started the SUV and drove off. He pulled up in front of the cab company just as Ian walked out of the building, a grin of success on his face.

"Meet Tim Miller," Ian said, showing Reeve a grainy copy of a hack license. "The dispatcher said Miller has the hots for a waitress at one of the local bars. We might find him there."

"You know where this place is?"

"Yeah. The Wagon Wheel Tavern. It's not far. Follow me." Ian climbed into an SUV identical to Reeve's own—minus the shattered windows—and led the way to a street several blocks over.

The Wagon Wheel Tavern looked more or less like any other neighborhood bar that stood the test of time thanks to its clientele's thirst for booze and laughs over any real interest in updated decor. Lots of heavy wood fixtures, old neon beer signs and placards, and a jukebox blasting out an old Bon Jovi tune. A few kids of questionable drinking age clustered around an antique-looking pinball machine near the back. A long bar, full to near capacity, took up most of one side of the room. Reeve scanned the faces but didn't spot anyone who looked like the picture. Ian nudged his arm and nodded to one of the high tables scattered about the room.

The man in the photo had a full beard, but the guy at the table had only the stubble of two or three day's growth. He wore a baseball cap low on his forehead, further hampering positive identification.

A blonde waitress in a tight pink tee shirt and even tighter blue jeans emerged from the kitchen. She deposited a plate loaded with a burger and fries in front of the man while his eyes greedily roved up and down her shapely figure. She paid no attention to his obvious lust and quickly stepped back to the bar after delivering his food. Ignoring his plate, the guy stared at her curvy ass as she put one foot up on the foot rail and leaned over the bar to grab some napkins, fairly threatening to split her jeans.

"The man said he had the hots for the waitress," Ian said. "Let's talk to him before he starts drooling."

They approached the table, and Reeve waved his hand in front of the guy's eyes. "Excuse me, are you Tim Miller?"

The guy jumped, his face flushing as he quickly tore his gaze away from the bar. Reeve swallowed back a snort. *Did he really think he'd been subtle?* Even now his eyes kept darting over to the waitress's backside. Ian stepped between him and the girl, his bulk effectively blocking Tim's view.

"Who's asking?" Tim whined, like a child whose mom just took away his toy.

"We're looking for a woman who took a ride in your cab earlier," Reeve said. "Red hair, about five foot six. You picked her up at the hospital and drove her to the bank on Jackson Road. Ring any bells?"

"Yeah, so what?"

"Did you leave her at the bank or did you take her anywhere else?"

"Who are you guys? You cops?"

"No, we're private investigators. It's very important we find this woman. She's in trouble."

Tim's eyes narrowed as he looked back and forth between Ian and Reeve. "How do I know you're not the ones she's running from?" He folded his arms across his chest. "What if you were the ones who gave her that cut on her head? I tell you guys anything and maybe she winds up dead or something. That ain't right."

Part of Reeve admired the fact that Tim appeared to have a chivalrous conscience. A much bigger part of him wanted to grab this guy and shake him until his teeth rattled out of his head. They didn't have time to waste on his knight-in-shining-armor routine.

Ian took out his wallet and showed the cabbie his private

investigator's license. He made no attempt to conceal the large wad of cash also in his wallet, and Miller's eyes were drawn to it like a magnet. He didn't even look at the OASIS business card Ian handed him.

"I might know where she is," he muttered, stuffing the card into his shirt pocket.

"And?" Reeve snapped.

Tim scowled, folding his arms across his chest. "And maybe I don't."

Reeve opened his mouth to reply, but Ian headed him off. "Dude, wouldn't you like to leave a nice tip for the waitress?" He slid a hundred-dollar bill across the tabletop.

Tim's expression softened as he snatched up the cash. He looked around to make sure he wouldn't be overheard. Reeve wondered if the jerk thought he might be conducting espionage.

"I took her to a motel."

"Which one?" Ian asked.

Tim eyed them both speculatively before focusing his attention solely on Ian. "Well," he said slowly, "it would be nice if I could invite Karen out to a really nice dinner. Maybe bring her some flowers too." He dropped his eyes to Ian's wallet, and once again Reeve had the overwhelming urge to do this putz harm.

Ian slipped another hundred across the table and held up a third. "Which motel?" he asked, keeping the last bill out of reach.

"The Oak Motor Inn, over by the highway," Tim said quickly. Ian tossed the bill on the table as Reeve turned and ran out of the bar. Ian caught up with him outside.

"Reeve, slow down."

"No way. We've got to get to her before that piece of slime does." He jumped into his SUV and leaned out to close the door, but Ian braced a hand on the frame. "What are you doing? We've got to go!"

"You need to take it easy. You're not going to do her any favors going off half-cocked."

"I'm not—"

"Yes, you are." Ian looked him squarely in the eye. "We all know how you feel about Tabitha Spencer's death. Hell, we all feel terrible about that. And maybe it's worse for you because she kind of looked like Ann Marie—"

"Leave my sister out of this."

"I can't because I think you're letting her death, and Tabitha's too, cloud your judgment. You nearly lost us getting any information out of that guy because your impatience is getting in the way."

"That guy would have sold us his mother for another couple of hundred."

"Maybe. Maybe not. The point is you were making him hostile. Hostility always slows down an interview."

"I really don't think now is the time for a lecture," Reeve bit off. His body hummed with the need to take action, and he couldn't shake the feeling they were going to be too late. "We need to get moving."

"Yeah, we do," Ian continued. "But we're going to do it smart, like the highly trained former SEALs that we are. *Not* like reckless amateurs." He ignored the glare Reeve leveled at him. "I know where the Oak is. Follow me and we'll be there inside of ten minutes. We'll go in quietly and calmly."

Reeve nodded as his gut twisted into a braid of guilt. Ian was right. Panic and guilt were pushing him into haste. If he wanted to help Jessie, he needed to screw his head on straight.

True to his word, Ian got them to the cheap dive in a few

minutes. They went inside, and a few more hundred-dollar bills slipped to the desk clerk got them her room number.

"Let me go up," Ian said.

"No, man, I'll do it."

Ian looked at him doubtfully, apparently not convinced Reeve had calmed down enough to handle talking to the Haynes woman with any sort of finesse.

"She knows me," Reeve said. "She may not like me, but she knows I'm not working with the Iceman. It will take you longer to convince her to let you in. I'll bring her down the back stairs. Meet us at the door there." He didn't wait for an answer as he headed across the lobby and got in the elevator. Knowing he'd found her made him feel a bit better. But he wouldn't fully be able to relax until he saw for himself that she was all right.

And then he would do whatever it took to keep her safe.

———

JESSIE'S KNEE bounced up and down as she tapped her pen on the cheap motel room desk and looked at the notepad before her. She loved lists. Loved making them up and crossing tasks off as they were done. Nothing gave her a better feeling of zen and self-control as a completed list.

Tonight, however, the habit failed to bring her any comfort. Mainly because she hadn't written down more than two items and, worse, only crossed one of them off—she'd called her neighbors to let them know she couldn't look after their dog after all. Thank goodness she'd gotten their machine because she didn't need the million questions they were sure to ask about the shooting on her lawn. Especially since she hadn't a clue as to what the hell was going on.

As for the second item, she hadn't been able to reach Candy. No surprise there. Candy had given up her landline years ago and, true to her word, hadn't bothered to turn her cell phone back on. Jessie sent a text to Candy's number anyway. Ever since they'd met at college, Candy had been her best friend and her rock, and Jessie would feel better when she could actually speak to her.

She glanced at the door to the room, confirming for the umpteenth time since she'd gotten here that the chair she'd jammed up against the door was still in place before returning her attention to the notepad. The nearly blank page silently screamed at her. She didn't know what else to put on the list. Well, actually, she could put a lot of things on it. What she really couldn't figure out was what to do about them, which meant she couldn't cross them off. She despised adding an item if she couldn't be sure of crossing it off. And she had a sick feeling this might be the one list she couldn't conquer.

Oh, if only my clients could see me now. The majority of them were women looking to land a job after being out of the workforce for years while raising their children or staying too long in a bad marriage or getting over a lengthy illness. So many of them were broken in spirit and didn't believe they could get back on their feet. She never let them get away with it for long. She made each one of them dig deep to find their inner strength and prove to the world and themselves they could stand on their own. She'd been there, done that, and it was the creed by which she lived her own life. Now was no time to stray from it, no matter how frightened she was.

Sucking in an angsty breath, she tapped the pen against the desk a little bit harder, flipped to a clean page and started writing.

1 – A crazy man broke into my house and tried to kill me.

2 – A second crazy man thinks I'm a criminal working with above crazy man.

3 – A third crazy man (a corrupt police officer? an imposter?) tried to kidnap me.

4 – ATM card won't work. Coincidence? Or deliberately tampered with?

She dropped the pen and ran both hands through her hair, her heart tap dancing once again as the words stared back at her.

The first item chilled her the most. He'd been *waiting* for her. Sitting calmly on the couch and staring at her with those eyes of black ice. Her mouth went dry, and she couldn't stop shaking.

She looked at the second item. She didn't really think Reeve was crazy. Dangerous, scary, and judgmental, yes, but not crazy. If forced to pick which of the three new men in her life she'd prefer to see, he'd be the one she'd choose.

A pang of longing assailed her as she pictured his handsome face. Why did he have to be a domineering idiot who accused her of consorting with a criminal? Why couldn't he have been an actual good guy? Someone who explained rather than demanded and bossed.

Yeah, right, as if she'd ever actually known a good guy. Even so, she knew what she'd want in one. Like any other young girl, she'd often thought about her fantasy future husband. But reality had soon set her straight. She'd learned the disappointing lesson a long time ago that Prince Charmings and white knights lived only in fairy tales.

Her body jittered with nerves, and she rubbed her eyes, which were so gritty from lack of sleep, she knew how the Sandman got his name. She would rest for now, and maybe the items on her list wouldn't seem so insurmountable in the morning. She eyed the double bed with distaste and a churning stomach, longing for the amenities of the four-star resort she'd enjoyed in Key West. This dump had only two redeeming qualities—cheap rates, and staff who accepted cash without asking for any identification.

A telltale squeaking sound followed by a woman's lubricious wail came screeching through the paper-thin walls. "Oh yeah, baby, give it to me! You don't need that frigid cow you married when you've got me!"

Could this night get any better?

"Well, at least someone's having a good time," she muttered as she reached for the plastic bag containing the sparse toiletries she'd picked up before she'd had the cab driver drop her off. Frugal as she'd been, her small supply of leftover vacation cash wouldn't last long. Hopefully, she could reach Candy in the morning and borrow some money. Until she got this situation under control, she didn't feel safe going to the bank to straighten out the ATM card problem.

The bed-squeaks and moans from the next room reached their predictable crescendo before blessed silence descended once more. Jessie peeled off her shirt and tossed it over her tote bag on top of the dresser. She padded to the bathroom and splashed water on her face. The pockmarked mirror returned a reflection she barely recognized, fear and exhaustion taking its toll. She could only hope she'd be able to get some sleep. Between the surrealism of her predicament and the scuzziness of the bed, she somehow doubted Morpheus would come calling.

She filled a water glass and carried it to the bedroom. A quick glance at the door verified the chair remained jammed in place, and she switched off the light. Clutching her glass of water, she took a step toward the bed.

A sharp knock on the door broke the silence, and Jessie

let out a small shriek. Water drenched her cotton camisole as her glass tumbled to the floor, and she clapped her hands across her mouth. *Jesus! How had that psychopath found her?* She looked around the room for a weapon. Nothing, not a lamp or even a lousy clock radio to bash him on the head. With nowhere to run, she quivered like a cornered rabbit.

"Jessie, open the door."

Relief surged through her, and she almost collapsed to her knees as she recognized Reeve Buchanan's voice.

Now what? While definitely the least of three evils, Reeve was still potentially an evil. She plucked up her cell phone, but with a flash of Officer Fox in her head, she couldn't bring herself to finish dialing 911.

Reeve pounded the door this time. "Jessie! Are you all right? Answer me."

"Yeah, Jessie!" a groggy male voice shouted through the wall. "Open the damn door. Some of us are trying to sleep!"

"I want to help you," Reeve called through the door. "I know you don't know the man in your house today." His tone softened. "I believe you, Jessie. I'm sorry for what I said earlier. Please let me in."

The woman from next door joined the party. "Let him in, Jessie. He sounds sorry. Time to kiss and make up."

Jessie's mind raced as Reeve knocked on the door again. If she called the police, he would probably go away, but the police were still too much of a gamble, and she wouldn't be any closer to learning the truth of the situation. For all his faults, Reeve had information, and she needed answers. And he *had* taken her to the hospital earlier. Why would he bother if he planned to hurt her? Further in his favor, twice today he'd prevented someone from abducting her, and she hadn't forgotten how much he seemed to hate the Iceman.

"The enemy of my enemy is my friend," she whispered

as she made up her mind and moved to the door. Besides, her lusty neighbors would hear if she screamed and would possibly come to her aid just so they could get back to sleep.

A brief look through the peephole revealed he was alone. She pulled the chair away and turned the knob. He stood there for a moment with his arms lifted above his head and braced over the door. The light from the hall cast him in silhouette, outlining an impressive and somewhat imposing physique. For an insane moment, she wanted nothing more than to fling herself forward to be wrapped up in the protective embrace of those strong, muscular arms. She fought the alien urge. If she allowed abject terror to destroy her self-reliance, she might as well give up and die anyway.

Jessie slowly lifted her eyes to his face and found his mouth half open while his eyes focused below her chin. She looked down to see her nipples standing up, giving him a royal welcome through her wet camisole. Mortified, she dashed back into the bathroom and slammed the door. A loud giggle trilled from next door.

"That doesn't sound like kissing and making up to me!"

CHAPTER FIVE

REEVE STEPPED INSIDE and closed the door, leaving the room lit only by the dull moonlight that managed to filter through the dingy curtains. He groped for the light switch but then pulled his hand back. A little darkness seemed prudent at the moment. That wet top of hers had left nothing to his imagination, and his body reacted accordingly. She didn't need to come out of the bathroom only to be confronted by the definite bulge in his pants.

He leaned back against the door, folded his arms across his chest, and willed his traitorous libido into submission. Convincing her to leave with him was already going to be a tough sell. She had good reason to be suspicious, and looking like a randy teenager would not help his cause.

The bathroom door opened a crack, and Jessie thrust an arm out. "I need my shirt and tote bag. They're on the dresser."

The sliver of light coming through the crack of the bathroom door only went so far. Thankful she kept her head behind the door, he found the switch on the wall and flipped the overhead light on. Quickly gathering up her shirt and bag, he placed them in her outstretched hand. She shut the door again. A glass lay on the floor, a few drops of water still clinging to the sides and solving the mystery of her wet shirt. He picked it up, placing it on the dresser before resuming his stance by the door, gradually getting himself under control.

She emerged a few minutes later, dry shirt donned and hair combed, and tossed her tote bag on the bed. Her eyes held a haunted look, and Reeve cursed himself for having anything to do with putting it there. "Are you all right?"

"That depends," she whispered.

"On what?"

"On you." She trembled, wrapping her arms around herself.

Reeve took a step forward, automatically lifting his arms to pull her into a comforting hug. He stopped cold when she took two quick steps back toward the bathroom, eyes wary and wide. "Jessie, I mean, Miss Haynes, I'm sorry about before. I won't hurt you. I promise."

"How can I trust you? I don't even know you."

"I know." Reeve raked his hand through his hair and leaned back against the door again. "I didn't help matters earlier, either. But I really thought you were working with the Iceman."

"I don't know him."

"I believe you. I didn't before, and I apologize for that." He cleared his throat. "I know an apology is not a lot to go on, but I'm going to have to ask you to come with me."

"No."

"You can't stay here. It isn't safe. If we found you, then believe me, *he* won't be far behind." Her eyes grew even rounder, and he regretted resorting to such bluntness. But if what Jake had said earlier about the Iceman's hacking skills was true, he would track her down just as they had. Soon. Much as Reeve would love to wait here to confront the bastard and throttle him with his bare hands, getting Miss Haynes out of harm's way remained his top priority.

"Who's *we*?" she asked.

"Excuse me?"

"You said, 'If *we* found you.' Who else knows where I am? I didn't tell anyone, and I paid cash."

"My whole team knows you're here. We work for a private investigation company." He pulled a card from his wallet and gave it to her. She barely glanced at it before looking back at him, waiting for him to continue. "We were able to track you down by using the hospital's outside cameras, and then working with the cab company."

"Why are you investigating me?"

"We're not. We're after the Iceman. When I saw you two together at the hotel last night, I assumed you were working with him. I was further convinced when he flew here and went directly to your house. I thought you guys were a romantic item and probably a criminal team. When you ran out of the house and he started shooting, I figured things went bad between you, and that I would be able to use you to get to him."

"So what changed your mind, Sherlock?" Her eyes, green as spring grass, glowed with defiance, and Reeve couldn't blame her for popping some attitude. He deserved it. And he liked it far better than seeing that frightened-rabbit look in her eyes.

"When I met the police—the real police—I found out there wasn't anyone named Fox on the force. And when I saw you struggling to get away from him, I knew I must have made some error in judgment."

She raised an eyebrow. "That's it? You say you made an

error in judgment, and I'm supposed to leave with you? Just like that? Are you kidding me?"

"Look, I know you don't know me, but it's important that you trust me."

A familiar creaking started up through the thin wall, followed by lewd moaning. "Oh yeah, baby, c'mon!"

Jessie bit the inside of her lip to keep a bout of hysterical laughter from bursting forth. Reeve's expression as he gaped at the wall was priceless, and she wondered if this night could become any more bizarre.

"Gimme some more, you pagan stud!" The creaking increased in tempo, and Reeve swung wide eyes back to her.

"That's nothing," she said. "Wait until they really get going."

He shook his head with a small laugh that didn't quite dispel his serious tone. "I'm afraid we can't wait. We've got to go. Now."

She bristled. "Look, just because you took me to the hospital and managed to chase that cop away, don't think you can order—"

"We really don't have time for this. If you stay here, he's going to find you."

Her stomach rolled. The mere possibility of another encounter with that man terrified her more than she could stand. "Maybe I should just go to the police."

"Bad idea. That phony cop proves the Iceman is organized and has resources. And he's going to some pretty elaborate extremes to get to you. Who knows how many real cops he may have paid off. Is that a risk you want to take?"

That thought unsettled her. Her father had police on his payroll, she was certain of it. She'd be naïve to believe no one else did. She stared hard at Reeve, wanting so badly to trust him. Her gut told her he stood on the right side of all this, and her instincts had always served her well in the past.

But that didn't make the decision any easier. Having to relinquish one iota of control over her life to anyone went against her personality at an almost primal level, and his pushy attitude set her stubborn stance to high. That he knew more about this while she remained in the dark only made it worse.

As did the simple truth that she really didn't have any choice.

"Miss Haynes..."

"It's Jessie."

"Jessie, we need to go."

She stood still, unable to bring herself to agree until the throes of passion next door reached decibels of war whoop proportions. "Yeah, well, it's not like I'll be able to get any sleep with Romeo and Juliet going at it all night," she groused, reaching for her tote bag. "I hope I'm not going to regret this."

"You won't." He helped her gather up her few belongings, and she stuffed everything in the bag.

They left the room, and Reeve led her away from the elevator. "We'll go out the back. This way no one from the lobby can tell him they saw you leave."

Irrational laughter bubbled up in her throat, and she forced it back down. Good grief, had she landed in some sort of twisted spy movie? Did other people really live this cloak-and-dagger stuff? Apparently so. She followed Reeve through the metal fire door and down the stairs, noting that his broad-shouldered frame perfectly suited him to the play the role of the hero in her personal spy movie. His tight butt was an added bonus.

She squashed back another crazy giggle. On the run

from someone called, of all things, the *Iceman,* and checking out a virtual stranger's ass. Geez, she *must* be losing it.

They reached the ground floor without incident. A man she recognized from outside her house earlier stood waiting for them. "I'm Ian Westlake," he said before falling in behind her as they walked out to the parking lot. Leading her to a black SUV, Reeve opened the passenger door. She climbed in and fastened her seat belt.

"Stay here," he said.

"Yes, commander," she snapped.

"Look, I know this is all scary and frustrating, but you have to believe we know what we're doing. Now sit tight." He closed the door and walked to the front of the other vehicle to talk to Ian.

"*Sit tight*," she mimicked. Oh, how she hated this. As the men conferred, she took the opportunity to study them, Reeve in particular. Just as she had noticed on the beach, he was tall and solidly built, his expansive chest tapering to a narrow waist and flat stomach. Those broad shoulders and muscular arms of his would give anyone under his protection a sense of security.

Still, she questioned her wisdom in trusting him. Part of her—the terrified part—took comfort in having someone with his gladiator chassis acting as her bodyguard, while common sense called her a fool to go off with a stranger instead of seeking the police. But her encounter with Fox had her leery of the authorities, at least until she had more information. Maybe she should call a cab and go to another motel.

A quick check of her wallet confirmed another motel would be out of the question. *Dammit!* Until she could get some cash, she had to depend on Reeve. She sent another text to Candy, giving her Reeve's name and the name of his agency. At least someone she knew and trusted implicitly would know she was with Reeve.

She glanced back outside in time to see him take a denim jacket from the back seat of the other SUV and shrug into it as he walked around the front of the vehicle. A lock of hair draped low on his forehead, and she could easily picture him on a billboard, modeling for a jeans ad. If they'd met under different circumstances, she definitely would have considered adding him to her so-called "booty call" list. Now, all she wanted was answers and to live to see breakfast.

"Where are we going?" she asked as he climbed into the driver's seat.

"We have a safe house not far from here. We'll keep you there until we can pick up his trail again."

"How long will that take?"

"Hopefully, not long. Ian will hang around this dive for a little while and see if the dirtbag shows up."

"Looking for me." She barely suppressed a shudder.

He reached for her hand and gave it a soft squeeze before easing the SUV out of the parking slot. "Try not to be scared. I'm not going to let him get near you."

Jessie prayed he could keep his word.

"WHAT A DUMP."

Iceman chuckled to himself as he pulled into a slot in a dark corner of the seedy motel's parking lot. His plan had worked even better than he expected. Cutting off her credit cards had limited her options for going to ground. On a hunch, he'd looked up the kind of motels in town that took cash. Then he hacked into and monitored some of the traffic cameras near those establishments and, bingo, the cab she'd gotten at the hospital appeared on the feed of one only three blocks from here. At a cesspit like this, he had no doubt a fifty slipped to the desk clerk would get him her room number.

He reached into the back seat and grabbed his duffel bag. Taser, check. Glock, check. He shoved both items into his waistband, then reached for the door handle.

A wash of light spilled over the parking lot entrance as a black SUV, followed by a second one, pulled into the lot. He slid low in his seat as he recognized the two newcomers. They got out and hurried into the motel.

Dammit to hell! Who the fuck were these guys? His search into the Haynes woman's background had divulged nothing of their identity.

He had no choice now but to wait. Perhaps the woman would send them away, though he doubted he would get that lucky. With a muttered curse, he got out of the car and walked to a dark spot behind the motel's dumpsters, not far from where the SUVs were parked.

About fifteen minutes later, the two men returned to the lot, accompanied by the redhead. She and the dark-haired man got into one of the SUVs and drove away.

The remaining man made a call. "It's Ian," he said. "Reeve just took off with Miss Haynes. He's taking her to the safe house, and I'll meet them there later with some food. I'm going to wait around here for a little while and see if our guy shows up. In the meantime, I need you or Jake to meet me here with another vehicle. Reeve and I switched because his windows were all broken this afternoon." He paused for a moment as the person on the other end spoke. "Okay," he responded. "I'll see you when you get here."

Iceman waited until the man—Ian—disconnected the

call before walking from behind the dumpster. He raised the Taser and fired just as the man whipped around. Ian cried out and dropped to his knees. Iceman administered a roundhouse kick to his head, knocking him unconscious. A search of his pockets quickly produced the phone, a wallet, and the keys to the SUV. He pulled a switchblade from his own pocket and bent down to finish off the meddling nuisance at his feet.

Headlights drew closer as a honking horn sounded from the road. A large van with heavy metal music blasting from its open windows barreled into the lot, parking directly across from where he stood. The doors opened, and several laughing teenagers tumbled out.

Oh, piss on a stick. Iceman slipped the knife back into his pocket and got into the SUV. He quickly drove out while the noisy kids were still preoccupied with each other and the cases of beer and shopping bags full of snacks they were unloading from the back of the van. Not one of them looked in his direction. If his luck held, the stupid kids wouldn't even notice the man on the ground for another five minutes. Plenty of time to get out of sight and plan his next move.

He drove out of the lot, happy to see the vehicle came loaded with a high-tech GPS. Between that and the phone he'd just stolen, he would locate the Haynes woman in moments. He looked forward to dispensing with her other pain-in-the-ass bodyguard.

And then the real fun could begin.

CHAPTER SIX

"How's your head?" Reeve asked as they drove away from the motel. "You never did get it looked at, did you?"

"It's fine. Just a couple of scratches. I washed away the blood and applied some antiseptic. They're shallow cuts, won't even leave a scar."

"You're sure? No headaches or anything?" She seemed okay, but so had Ann Marie, and he would have liked it a whole lot better if a doctor had looked at those wounds.

"I'm sure, but never mind my head. Why me? What does all of this have to do with me?"

It certainly didn't take long for her to get to the million-dollar question, did it? Reeve scoured his brain for the million-dollar answer. What the hell was he missing? "You're certain you never saw him before last night?"

"Yes."

"You didn't maybe run into him at a party or something? Or see him with another guest? Delivering drugs?"

"I don't believe this! You still think I'm working with him, don't you?" Her glacial tone grew icier by the moment. "You think I'm some kind of drug dealer or a junkie."

"No, I don't. I'm just trying to get to the bottom of this. I have to look at every angle to find the connection, including the possibility you had some other interaction with him prior to last night. Something casual, maybe, that you might not think of right away."

"I don't do drugs, casual or otherwise. Never have. No matter how hard you try, you are not going to connect me to that maniac in any sort of criminal capacity."

"I'm not trying to connect you as a criminal. But if I'm going to figure this out, I have to know everything. I really am trying to help you."

"Then listen to what I'm telling you because I'm tired of repeating myself. I. Don't. Know. Him. Got it? Candy and I were in Key West for a week, and we spent most of our time just lazing around on the beach. We didn't attend any parties while we were there. Believe me, with that hair of his, I would remember if I'd seen him on the beach."

"He used the name Dean King at the hotel. Does that mean anything to you?"

"No."

"How about before your vacation? Any chance you saw him before Key West?"

She raised her hands up to either side of her head and shook them. "Aargh! No, dammit! Don't you listen?"

"Okay, okay, I'm sorry. I won't ask again." He hadn't forgotten Ian's earlier reminder. Antagonism would only slow things down. Patience didn't come easy, though, especially when the foreboding sense that time was not on their side clung to him like a persistent rash.

"Apology accepted," she huffed.

He turned the car onto a long, twisty, narrow driveway lined with tall, densely planted evergreens. Rounding a final bend, he parked next to a sprawling ranch-style home. Once he got Jessie settled in for the night, he'd give Jake a call and see if he'd been able to find any new information online. "C'mon. Let's get inside and get some rest. You must be exhausted."

"I don't think I can sleep. Can we make some coffee?"

He nodded, although he really didn't think she needed coffee right now, not with her toes already tapping a staccato beat on the SUV's plastic floor mat. But since he'd already pissed her off enough for one day, he decided not to suggest she avoid caffeine for a little while.

His phone rang as he got out of the SUV, Ian's name flashing on the readout. "What's going on? Any sign of him?" No answer. "Ian? What's happening?" Still no answer as he unlocked the front door and preceded Jessie into the house. "I'm not hearing you, buddy. Try calling back again."

"Is something wrong?" she asked as he punched in the code to disable the alarm.

"No. The cell phone service is sketchy around here. We have a booster inside. I'll turn it on. The kitchen is this way." He led her toward the back of the house. "I doubt there's any milk or cream, though. That coffee will have to be black."

"Fine."

While Jessie filled the coffee pot with water from the tap, Reeve pulled a bag of coffee from one of the overhead cabinets and set it on the counter before heading for the utility room in the basement. He turned on the cell booster and then tried Ian's number. It went straight to voicemail. "Ian, we're at the safe house and the booster is on now. Call me back if you need me."

He returned to the kitchen just as Jessie flipped the switch on the coffee maker and started opening cabinets. As the crisp scent of coffee filled the air, he took note of how her pale pink jeans snugged sweetly across her butt as she reached up for a couple of mugs. *Not good.* He quickly turned and went into the other rooms to pull all the shades. Putting her out of sight for the moment helped some, but not entirely. If they were going to be in close proximity for a while, he'd damn well better find a way to subdue his libido and maintain his professionalism.

When he came back to the kitchen, she had poured the coffee and settled herself onto one of the stools at the end of the island. He took a seat across from her and pulled one of the mugs in front of him. She picked up the other mug and blew on the steaming liquid, fascinating him with the way her pink lips pursed together. He could imagine their taste. Sweet with just a hint of coffee.

Lord, he was in trouble.

"I still don't get it," she said. "Why were you following me on vacation? Why were you at my house?" All traces of her earlier anger were gone, and he seized the opportunity to bring his mind back to business.

"Like I said before, I work for a private investigation company. We weren't following you, we were looking for him. He's a murderer, and we want to get solid evidence against him so the authorities can put him away for a long time." He leaned back and sipped his coffee.

She raised an eyebrow. "That's it? That's all you have to say? Nuh-uh. I'm not in the mood to play twenty questions. Either you tell me what the hell is going on right now, or I'm calling a cab."

He hesitated and she whipped out her cell phone. "Okay, okay. I'll tell you everything I know. But it isn't pretty, so be prepared."

She nodded, biting her lip as she put her phone away. "Go ahead."

"The company I work for, October Armstrong Security

and Investigation Services, does a lot of work for high-end businesses. Banks, brokerage houses, insurance companies, most of the big software firms, that sort of thing. We also provide personal security and crisis management to the rich and famous. Our clients rely on us as much for our discretion as they do for results. A couple of weeks ago, we took on some new clients. Parents who were looking to get their daughter back. She'd been kidnapped."

"No offense, but why would they go to your company instead of the police or the FBI? Don't they handle kidnappings?"

"Yes, but there were a number of reasons the clients came to us instead."

"Such as?"

"Sadly, their daughter had been a repeat runaway and habitual drug user. She had finally gone through a good rehab program and gotten clean. When she was taken, her parents knew the police weren't going to give it their all, and it would take too much time to convince them she'd really been kidnapped, not just relapsed into her bad habits. So they came to us. We had done some very meticulous and sensitive work for her father's business last year. He knows what we're capable of."

"What does that mean?"

"Thanks to its upscale clientele, OASIS is very well funded. We can afford to hire the best people and buy the best software and equipment. And because we're a private company, we can operate without being bound by certain... legal constraints."

She folded her arms and stared at him. "In other words, you break the law to catch lawbreakers."

"I didn't say that."

"You didn't have to."

"Anyway, the Spencers came to us—"

"The Spencers? Are you talking about Tabitha Spencer, that rich banker's daughter who had her throat slit and was left in a dumpster? That was all over the news!"

"Yeah," Reeve bit off. "The Iceman killed her and just threw her away. Like garbage."

"How do you know the Iceman is her killer? The articles I read said there were no suspects in her death."

"That's because the police still don't believe Tabitha's murder is anything more than a teenage junkie getting in over her head. The Iceman has managed to stay off the grid. He's like smoke. Our own tech guru is a genius at locating people on the web, and even he can't find anything about this guy. We don't know his real name. I doubt the police have any idea he actually exists. And they probably never will because they're just not looking that hard."

"Then how do you know about him if there's no online information?"

"We got a tip from the accomplice who kidnapped Tabitha. The Spencers were right. Their daughter *hadn't* run away again. She was turning her life around. But that didn't erase the fact that before she got clean she spent a great deal of time mixed up with some very bad elements. She owed a lot of money to a so-called *high-class* drug dealer." He snorted. "High-class, my ass. Andy Pugliesi is a street punk scumbag through and through. He had the nerve to show up at the Spencers' home and demand they pay off Tabitha's debt. He threatened to go to the press with pictures of Tabitha injecting a needle into her arm. But Mr. Spencer didn't get where he is in the business world by caving in to threats. Especially a threat he knew was a bluff."

"A bluff? How could he know that?"

"Simple. Pugliesi is a drug dealer. If he went to the press, even anonymously, he risked attracting the attention of law enforcement. And he would more than likely lose the faith of his other rich clients. When he realized he wouldn't get a dime from Mr. Spencer, he came up with another way to get his money."

"The Iceman."

"Bingo, and even though the Iceman is like smoke, Pugliesi isn't. The Spencers were able to give us enough information to find him. He told us he'd sold Tabitha to the Iceman."

"He just confessed to such a thing? Why would he incriminate himself like that?"

"Let's just say we can be... persuasive... when we need to be." Reeve shifted a little in his chair, uncomfortable with the idea she might think he was a thug who always used his fists to get what he wanted. But it had worked, and he wasn't going to apologize for it. Besides, it had only taken one smack to get the coward to talk.

"Pugliesi also told us where he'd delivered Tabitha. But when we got there, it was too late." Reeve left out the fact that the sole responsibility of that particular fuckup, and ultimately Tabitha's death, rested with him. Not exactly the sort of thing to admit if he wanted to gain her trust.

"Why is he called the Iceman?"

"I don't know, but it's the only name Pugliesi knew for him, and he was terrified to tell us even that much. But I don't really care what the son of a bitch is called. What I really want to figure out is why he's after you."

"Could it be something random? A simple case of being in the wrong place at the wrong time?"

"I doubt it. He's after you for a reason. You don't stay off the grid as well as he has by being casual or random. Everything needs to be carefully planned to maintain that kind of anonymity."

"Then how did you know he would be in Key West?"

"The bastard must have been in a hurry when he dumped Tabitha's body. The police found a crumpled fragment of paper stuck to her shoe. The words 'Key West' and a partial name of the hotel were written on it with a date. More than enough information for Jake to identify the specific hotel. We set up surveillance and it paid off."

"Why did you think he and I were together?"

"Yeah, I'm sorry about that. But you *were* awfully close to each other, and your hat blocked your faces. I figured you were kissing, especially when he rubbed his hand on your leg. Why did you let him touch you like that?"

"It's not like he asked. He just did it. I was stunned at first, but then I was really frightened. It was one of those deer-in-the-headlights kind of moments."

Reeve put his mug down. "So what happened exactly? What did he say to you?"

"Nothing, really. He said he was looking for his little boy. It was all a lie, though. He told me there never was a little boy when we were at my house."

"What else did he say at the house?"

"Just a lot of creepy stuff. That he wanted to see me, even though he normally doesn't go for redheads."

"That's it?"

"Pretty much. Oh, he wanted me to fix myself a drink. As if that would relax me. Ha."

"How did you get away?"

Her forehead and nose wrinkled a bit. "It's kind of hard to explain. At first I froze again, but then I just got so mad. All I kept thinking about was how hard I worked to make a nice, peaceful life for myself. And how dare that slimy piece of scum break into *my* house and threaten me. Next thing I knew, I hit him as hard as I could and then ran like hell."

"Good for you. I'm glad you were able to get away."

She opened her mouth to answer, but her stomach gave a loud growl before she could speak. A light blush swept across her face, and he quickly sought to put her at ease. "Hang on, I'll see what we've got here."

He stepped into the small pantry to see if there were any cookies or anything, but the shelves were pretty sparse. Next staff meeting, he would talk to Tobie about keeping this place better stocked. His own stomach rumbled, reminding him Jessie wasn't the only one who hadn't eaten in a while. Where the hell was Ian with those groceries?

Emerging from the pantry, he pulled his cell phone out. It rang in his hand before he could dial a number. Tobie's name flashed on the screen. "What's up, boss?"

"Get out of the house right now. Someone ambushed Ian in the motel parking lot. His cell phone, wallet, and SUV are missing."

"How long have we got?" Reeve pulled out his Glock, and Jessie's eyes went wide as she hopped to her feet.

"Not long," Tobie answered. "Jake and I just found him two minutes ago. So the bastard has had plenty of time to catch up with you. Jake is on his way to the safe house, but he's still at least twenty minutes away. Don't wait."

"Got it. I'll call you soon."

"What is it?" Jessie asked as he pocketed his phone.

"Ian's been attacked." He walked around the end of the breakfast bar and took her by the arm. "We have to go right now."

"Why? I thought we were supposed to be safe here." She grabbed her tote bag off the counter and slung it over her head, snaking her free arm through the straps.

"Whoever attacked Ian took his SUV. It's a company vehicle with a GPS. We can't risk the Iceman wasn't able to access this address from it."

"It was definitely the Iceman who attacked him?"

"Either that or someone who works for him. Odds are against it being random." Flicking off lights as they went, Reeve led her back through the house. She followed him so closely the heat of her body sent a tingling sensation up and down his spine. He opened the front door a crack and peered out into the darkness. No one lurked around the driveway, but he couldn't see whether anyone hid among the trees that lined the end of the property.

"Stay inside," he whispered. "Wait until I get the car turned around. I'll open the passenger door when it's safe for you to come out. As soon as you get in the car, get down and stay down."

She nodded, her eyes wide jade pools of fear in the dim light of the moon. After another quick check of the driveway, he raised his Glock in front of him and stepped outside.

Keeping to the shadow of the house, Reeve crept over to the SUV. Ducking low by the vehicle, he took another scan of the property before opening the door. The dome light dutifully came on. "Crap!" Reeve muttered as he smashed it with the butt of his gun. He reached out and closed his door just as the crack of a gunshot barked through the night and the rear window of the SUV exploded.

Reeve ducked down low and rammed the key in the ignition. The engine roared to life, and he threw the gear shift into Reverse. He raced the vehicle back across the lawn, skidding to a stop as close to the front door as he could manage. Another bullet tore off one of the side-view mirrors.

He hadn't seen the muzzle flare of either shot, so he

couldn't pin down the shooter's position. Shit, for all he knew, there could be more than one. Much as he would rather stay and fight, for Jessie's sake they had to run. He leaned over and stretched between the bucket seats and opened the back passenger-side door.

"Get in!" he roared. Jessie burst from the house and dove headfirst into the back seat. "Stay down." Reeve shoved the gear shift into Drive and stomped his foot on the gas. The small truck rocketed across the lawn, its rear tires skidding on the dewy grass as he spun the wheel, steering back toward the driveway. Jessie screamed as a bullet shattered another window.

"Keep your head down!" Reeve hunched down low over the steering wheel as they flew down the long driveway. Only after rounding a curve did he sit up a little straighter and turn on the headlights. "Oh shit!"

Ian's SUV was parked lengthwise across the driveway. The dense line of trees along the sides left no room to go around it. Reeve slammed on the brakes and turned the wheel hard to the left. The sides of the two vehicles slammed together in a deafening crash.

"Jessie! Are you all right?" He spun in his seat, his heart dropping as he saw her lying on the floor covered in glass. For a stupefying moment, the image of another girl's body, bleeding from the head, superimposed itself over Jessie's form. He pushed the image away. "Jessie!"

"I'm okay," she said hoarsely. "Just get us out of here."

"We have to run. The driveway is blocked." He jumped out and went to her door. "Be careful. Watch the glass."

She shimmied her way back out of the vehicle and got to her feet. Reeve took her hand and hurried her around to the other SUV. He looked in the driver's window to the ignition. No keys, just as he expected. The Iceman wouldn't make such a rookie mistake. Pushing Jessie behind him, he quickly fired a couple of rounds into two of the vehicle's tires. If they were going to be on foot, so would their adversary.

He pulled her along as he dashed behind the trees. Reeve hoped the Iceman would assume they were headed for the road instead, giving them time to get away. The ferocity of this attack made it all too clear that every second counted because the Iceman, whatever his motive might be, was willing to go to extraordinary lengths to get his hands on Jessie.

Over my dead body, asshole.

CHAPTER SEVEN

JESSIE BIT back a whimper as yet another rock dug into her foot. Her sparkly pink beach sandals were not ideal for running through the woods, but there was nothing she could do about it. Even if she had a more sensible pair of shoes in her tote, they couldn't stop moving. Not with that madman right behind them. She clung to Reeve's hand and prayed she wouldn't turn an ankle.

They raced on through the woods, weaving in and out among the trees. The leafy canopy blocked most of the moonlight, and she could hardly see in front of her. Reeve seemed to have no such difficulty as he whisked her along. He slipped behind the massive trunk of an oak tree and pulled her close behind him. Gun in hand, he peered cautiously through the dense darkness.

"Can you see him?" Jessie whispered close to his ear. His scent filled her nostrils, and she detected some rough stubble against her lips. The comforting heat from his body warmed her skin.

He shook his head and raised his hand for her to be

silent. Cicadas and crickets chirped loudly, and Jessie wondered how he expected to hear anything over their constant clacking. After a few moments, Reeve turned to face her, his back against the vast trunk. Snaking an arm around her waist, he pulled her up close to his chest. He lowered his head and put his lips right against her ear. "I can't see him or hear him, but I know he hasn't given up. We've got to keep moving, quickly and quietly. Can you do that?"

All too aware of how her body draped across his from head to toe, Jessie resisted the urge to push away. There would be nothing quiet about that. Truthfully, she didn't really *want* to push away. The fear she'd experienced back at the hotel room was nothing compared to the terror coursing through her right now, and his arm around her provided the first glimmer of comfort she'd felt since this whole nightmare began. That terrified part of her wanted to close her eyes and hide in his embrace.

"Jessie? Are you okay?"

She nodded.

"All right," he continued, his mouth a soothing tingle against her ear. "We're going to move slowly now. Stay close to me and stay low. Watch your footing, and try not to step on any twigs or branches if you can help it. Got it?"

She nodded again. He released his hold on her waist and took her hand once more. They slunk through the forest, and Jessie's heart stuttered in her chest any time one of them inadvertently made a sound. No gunfire erupted from their unseen attacker, so she could only be thankful now for the incessant clamor of the insects muffling the sound of their progress. Before long, she could make out the moonlit ribbon of the road several yards ahead.

"We'll keep to the woods but follow the road," Reeve

whispered. "There's another house not too far from here. The owner is away, and there should be a car in the garage."

They snuck along the tree line, and Jessie stayed as close to him as she could without stepping on his heels. An hour ago, she didn't want to have anything to do with Reeve Buchanan, and now the thought of being more than six inches from him scared the hell out of her. As much as she hated to admit it, even just to herself, she was thankful to be facing this ordeal with him instead of going it alone. She valued her life more than her independence, and this latest attack confirmed just how precarious her continued good health had become.

They reached the neighbor's property in a few moments. No lights shone from the large farm-style house, and an air of abandonment permeated the place. "Do you think anyone's home?" Jessie asked.

"I doubt it. It's owned by an actress who only uses it when she wants to get away from the Hollywood scene. It's not even in her name. She used an alias to buy it so the press wouldn't find out about it."

"How do you know about it then?"

"OASIS thoroughly checked out all the surrounding properties before purchasing the safe house. The fact that this place would be empty most of the time was an important factor in making the purchase."

"It's the middle of the night. How do you know she's not in there sleeping? Wait, don't tell me. Your tech guru again, right?"

"Yeah. Jake looked up her schedule earlier tonight. She's in London, promoting her latest film. So unless she lent the place to a friend, which she's never done so far, the place is empty." Reeve made no move to leave the cover of the trees.

"So what are we waiting for?" The answer hit her before

Reeve could respond. "It's him, isn't it? The Iceman. You think he got here ahead of us, don't you?"

"I don't know. But it's best to be careful." He spent another few minutes carefully scrutinizing the area. Placing a finger on his full lips, he jerked his head to indicate she should follow him. They darted out from the trees and hurried toward the back door of the house.

Jessie's heart sank when she spied a keypad with a blinking red light by the door. Of course the house would have an alarm system. She could only imagine the racket it would make if they broke in. The Iceman would pinpoint their location in seconds.

"Great," she muttered. "Now what?"

"Now we enter the code and get inside." He quickly punched in a few numbers, and the blinking red light turned a solid green. He flashed a flirty little grin at her and opened the door. "OASIS has had the code ever since the system was installed here. We never planned on using it, but you never know when something like that might come in handy."

Jessie shook her head. "I'm not sure I want to know what else OASIS is capable of finding out."

They stepped into a large, vintage-country-style kitchen, eerily silent with only the light from the microwave's clock and the moonlight drifting in through the windows to relieve the inky darkness. She was glad to be out of the woods, but the pitch-dark shadows of the room made the hairs stand up on the back of her neck. Even though Reeve said no one was here, she couldn't shake the feeling someone was going to leap out at them from any of the stygian corners of the room.

Reeve dropped her hand and pulled a small Mag flashlight from a loop on his belt. He began rifling through the drawers. "Start looking in the cupboards. See if you can find any car keys."

She shivered, missing his warmth, but did as instructed and was carefully feeling around her third cabinet when he said, "I got 'em. Let's go." Jessie automatically reached for his hand, telling herself she didn't actually *need* the reassuring feeling of his firm grip but welcomed it as a nice-to-have.

They climbed into the nondescript beige sedan parked in the garage. "I guess she really doesn't want to attract attention when she's here," Jessie remarked as she buckled herself into the passenger seat.

"She's only been here four or five times in the last two years. Once she arrives, she rarely leaves the property. There's a caretaker who comes and checks the place once a week and keeps things in working order. Including this car." He turned the key, and the engine agreeably turned over. A press of the remote attached to the visor sent the garage door slowly rolling up. "Keep your head down."

She ducked over as they drove out of the garage. Reeve accelerated and headed for the main road. He spoke again after a few moments. "You can get up now. No one is following us."

She straightened and turned to look out the back window. The sight of the deserted road did little to relieve the tension strangling her nerves.

The Iceman was still out there.

Dammit!

Iceman aimed at the dwindling taillights, but they disappeared around a bend before he could pull the trigger. He swore again under his breath and raced to the garage in hope of finding a second vehicle. No such luck.

With another angry curse, he yanked out his phone, nearly flinging it against the wall when he saw he had no service out here in the fucking boondocks. He stomped into the kitchen and spotted a wooden antique phone on the wall. He picked up the bell handset, amazed to get a dial tone. With the kind of luck he'd had tonight, he would have bet money the damn thing was only a decoration.

He placed a call and made the necessary arrangements to have another car delivered. Then he called Cochran. As expected, the man was not pleased.

"You let her get away? I thought you were a professional. The best there is."

"I am a professional. You wouldn't have come to me otherwise."

"So far I'm not impressed. She should have been taken care of by now. If you can't handle the job, just say so. I'll get someone else. Someone reliable. You're not the only one who wants to buy women."

Iceman counted to three. If it weren't for the damned thumb drive, he'd tell Cochran what he could do with himself and hang up. But he couldn't afford that luxury right now. Maybe later there would be an occasion to pay the cocky weasel a visit and let him know what happened to rich little jerks who thought too much of themselves.

"I'll get her," he ground out as civilly as he could manage, "and you'll get your fee. She's using the name Jessie Haynes. Does that mean anything to you?"

"No."

"Okay. Tell me anything and everything you know about

her friends and any family members she might go to for help."

"There's no one in the family that will help her. They all know better. My mother talks to her once in a blue moon, but that's about it."

"What about friends?"

"She has a close friend named Taffy or Candy or something stupid like that. I'll find out more details and get back to you."

"Good. There's something else. Somehow or another she seems to have gotten the help of a private security team." Ian Westlake's cell phone, along with the registration in the SUV, had finally revealed the identity of her new bodyguards, as well as who they worked for.

"What? How the hell did she do that?" Cochran hissed. "She wasn't supposed to have any idea about this. How could she have hired a security team?"

The more Iceman thought about it, the more certain he became that his initial assessment had been correct. The Armstrong operatives had been after him, not the woman. That prickly suspicion he was being followed in Key West had driven him to slip the thumb drive into her tote bag. In the unlikely event he was caught, he hadn't wanted it to fall into the hands of the authorities. Now he had to get it back as soon as possible, making it even more imperative he extract the succulent redhead from her protectors.

But this idiot didn't need to know any of that. "I don't know how she hooked up with them. I just know she is, at this very moment, in the protective custody of one of their operatives. The agency is called October Armstrong Security and Investigation Services. Do you know anything about them?"

"Never heard of them."

"They're top-notch and well financed." He'd figured that much out on his own from the expensive phone and SUV he'd stolen from Westlake. The business cards he'd found in the man's wallet were also top quality. "Is there anything you can do on your end to hamper them?"

"Oh fine, I'll see what I can manage." Cochran sighed. "Is that all?"

"Yes, for now. I'll contact you in an hour or so."

"Just get the damned job done!" Cochran hung up, and Iceman again contemplated the merits of paying the man a personal visit someday.

Definitely something to consider.

SHIT! Rob Cochran lit a cigarette and paced the circular driveway in front of his stepfather's mansion. His luck had been in a downward spiral for months, and now this. He would have taken great satisfaction in telling the Iceman to go to hell and never contact him again. But the bastard had only paid Rob a partial fee in return for Judith's where-abouts. He desperately needed the rest of it, which the Iceman refused to pay before he actually had Judith in his possession. Assuming, of course, the dirty prick didn't double-cross him.

How the hell had he gotten into this fucking mess? His stepfather had finally started to trust him with business matters and had begun paying him a halfway decent salary. So what did Rob do? What he always did when he had some money in his pocket. He took his first paycheck and ran to the track with it. Hell, he'd probably run faster than any of the lousy nags he'd put money on. Then he didn't even wait for his next check. He went to a loan shark and hurried right back to the track. But his horses didn't run any faster, and now he owed a staggering amount of money to the kind of people who were not known for their patience.

He didn't dare ask his stepfather for a loan. That tight-assed dickhead wouldn't give Rob a nickel he didn't sweat blood to earn. And if the old man found out he'd gotten mixed up with loan sharks, Rob would be out on his ass in a nanosecond, cut off without a cent. Rob didn't even want to think about what his stepfather might do if he got even a whiff of Rob's involvement with the Iceman. Reputation meant everything to the reclusive Mitchell Cochran.

Rob had thought selling Judith off to the Iceman would be a smooth solution to his pressing problems—provide some quick cash he urgently needed and get the bitch out of his life once and for all. But just as she always had, Judith excelled at taking care of herself and remained a thorn in his side.

He flicked his cigarette into the fountain in the center of the driveway, not really giving a shit the groundskeeper would be given bloody hell if he didn't find and get rid of it before Mitchell spotted it. He took out his phone and called one of his old college buddies who now worked at a public relations firm. A half an hour on the phone saw Rob's efforts to discredit Reeve Buchanan and the OASIS agency well along. Now to find out about Judith's friends.

With a sigh, he went inside the house. He found his mother in her sitting room doing needlepoint. She peeked up from her canvas and smiled at him. "Is everything all right, dear?"

"Fine, Mom. Listen, have you heard from Judith lately?"

Her head snapped up from her stitchery. She leapt to her feet and closed the door to the room. "Rob! You know better than to say her name when your father is in the house."

Looking into his mother's eyes, round and wide with fear, Rob's emotions, as usual, ripped in two. Part of him hated to see that look on her face, and part of him just plain hated her for marrying Mitchell Cochran in the first place. They would have been better off on their own, even if they had been dirt poor. But Mitchell's proposal had seemed like the answer to his mother's dreams, a Cinderella story come true. But in this case, Prince Charming turned out to be the Big Bad Wolf.

"Is he still up?" Rob asked. It was well past midnight, but everyone in the house knew better than to go to bed before Mitchell retired. If he wanted to see or speak to someone for whatever reason, they had damn well better be awake and ready for him. His stepfather had always been a vindictive tyrant, and he could be downright cruel if someone displeased him. He'd been bad enough before but seemed to have gotten even worse since Judith left.

Another reason Rob couldn't stand the bitch.

But vindictiveness aside, the man did know how to attain the finer things in life, and from him Rob had developed a taste for living on easy street. He didn't want to see that end. The sooner he paid off the loan sharks, the sooner he could get back on track. So far, they had not connected him with Mitchell, and Rob hoped they never would. If they found out he was the stepson of an obscenely wealthy man, he'd never be rid of them. Which meant he had to find out what his mother knew about Judith. Now.

"So have you heard from her, Mom?"

Kim Cochran gave a nervous glance toward the door. "I

spoke to her on the phone a few weeks ago. Right before she left on a trip to Key West with her friend. I thought I told you that."

"Yeah, you did." Enabling Rob to give that same information to the Iceman. "Which friend did she go with?"

"Candy Bartlett. You remember her, don't you? They met at college, and Judith brought her here that Christmas your father was away closing that deal in Brussels."

Rob did indeed remember Candy. Tall, blonde, and stacked. Just the way he liked them. But she hadn't seen fit to give Rob the time of day during that visit. She'd taken her cue from that bitch Judith. "So the two of them are still close, huh?" he asked aloud.

"Yes, they are, as far as I know." She frowned at him curiously. "Why do you ask?"

"A friend of mine from school just called. He says he thought he saw Judith in Barbados. It made me wonder if she'd changed her plans."

"Your friend called at this hour to talk about Judith?" His mother didn't look convinced.

"Among other things. He's a night owl and knows we are too."

"Thanks to your father's insistence," Kim muttered. Her eyes popped wide again as she clapped a hand over her mouth. "I shouldn't have said that," she hissed. She ran to the door and opened it a crack. "No one's there," she said with relief as she closed the door.

"Relax, Mom. Even he can't be everywhere at once," Rob said, hating the skittery, gutless woman she'd become. If only she'd had the nerve to stand up to her husband and demand to be treated fairly, Rob wouldn't be dealing with this current hot mess.

But things were going to change. Once Judith was gone for good, he'd be back on his way to the top.

———

"Relax, Mom. Even he can't be everywhere at once."

Mitchell smiled as he sat in his opulent home office, listening to his idiot stepson over the secret intercom.

"Oh yes," he laughed quietly. "Yes, I can."

CHAPTER EIGHT

JESSIE WOKE as the car came to a stop. She blinked rapidly before sitting up straight. "I can't believe I fell asleep."

"It's the crash after the adrenaline rush. You've had it pretty rough for the last several hours. I'm surprised you held out as long as you did." His voice held only the faintest rasp of sleepiness, and she wondered how the heck he still managed to look rested and ready for anything. Even after her nap, she felt like she could sleep for a week.

Jessie tore her gaze from his tantalizing profile and looked out the window at the busy truck stop parking lot. "I thought we were going to another hotel or safe house or something."

Reeve turned off the ignition and pocketed the keys. "Call it hiding in plain sight. He was on foot, so we've got quite a lead on him. Like you, he'll expect us to go to ground immediately, so even when he gets his hands on a vehicle, he's not going to look here. And I don't know about you, but I'm starved."

The mere idea of a meal prompted a rumbling pang in

her stomach. Jessie hadn't eaten since lunchtime yesterday before boarding the flight from Key West. Right now, a plate of eggs and home fries sounded pretty darn good to her. She reached for the door handle.

"Wait," he said. He leaned through the bucket seats and began rooting around the floor in the back.

"What are you doing?" she asked, trying very hard not to be distracted when the front of his denim jacket parted and his tee shirt rode up, presenting her with a lovely view of his taut, flat stomach.

He popped back up. "This'll work. Here," he said, thrusting a worn gray baseball cap at her. "See how much of your hair you can hide under that. If by any chance he does come looking here later, we don't want people to remember you."

Jessie wound the bulk of her hair on top of her head and pulled the cap over it. She flipped the vanity mirror down and began tucking up as many stray wisps as she could. "What time is it?"

"A little before 5:00 a.m."

"Ugh. I've never been much of a morning person under normal circumstances." She made a face at herself in the mirror. "I hope the clientele here won't be offended by me walking in looking like death warmed over."

He reached over and gently tucked a wayward strand under the band of the cap. "You look great. The clientele should consider themselves lucky."

She turned toward him in surprise, his soft tone like a warm blanket. "Thanks," she whispered, blinking back unexpected tears, not at all sure why the compliment got her so worked up. Maybe it was the exhaustion. Or maybe after all this time of looking after herself, it was the unfamiliar comfort of having a man on her side. Her practical nature rebelled at that thought, but the woman who'd come home to find a psycho in her living room wanted to kick that practicality to the curb.

She stared at him, not knowing what to say. He held her gaze, and electricity all but crackled across the seats. She couldn't say for sure which one of them moved first, but as the distance closed between them, she closed her eyes and tilted her head back, knowing full well what was coming and, for some peculiar reason, welcoming it wholeheartedly.

His lips brushed hers, velvety and soft at first, but as her hand reached up and touched his shoulder, he clamped his hand on the back of her head and kissed her with an intensity that should have unnerved her but didn't. She'd known since the first moment she'd met him, guns blazing on her quiet street, that Reeve didn't do anything halfway. Nor did she believe he would hurt her. The kiss might be strong, but she never doubted his control.

She gave herself up to the warm sensation of his lips on hers. Not just a kiss, but a relief, an escape from the madness engulfing her life. She kissed him back, hard, opening her mouth and meeting his tongue thrust for thrust. A rush of desire took hold of her, the strength of its grip so powerful it shocked her more than the actual kiss.

Jessie wanted him. Plain and simple. Here and now. She didn't give a damn if they didn't even make it into the back seat. She leaned closer, and he dropped his hand from her head to her back, knocking the cap off and pulling her right up against him. He tore his lips from hers, and she angled her head as he started marching sweet nibbling kisses down her neck. Her fingers slid through his hair, its silken texture a nirvana to touch.

She missed his mouth on hers and gently guided his

head back up to her face. Their lips fused together, hot and fast. She pressed even closer to his granite chest, silently cursing the gearshift and steering wheel for preventing her from climbing directly into his lap.

An ear-splitting horn blast came from a passing semi truck, and they jumped apart as if electrically shocked. The quick rise and fall of his chest kept pace with her own quickened breathing. Her blood boiled in her veins as the impact of what almost just happened, what she so desperately wanted to happen, assaulted her brain. Heat flamed across her face, and she wished she could slide onto the floor of the car.

The look of desire on Reeve's face slowly morphed into a look of uncertainty. Jessie couldn't blame him. Goodness knew she wasn't certain of anything anymore. She'd never been shy about sex, but never had she launched herself at someone like that, and definitely not on such short acquaintance.

He blinked a few times and then shook his head as if rousing himself from a daze.

"Jessie... I mean Miss Haynes... I don't know what..." he stammered as he raked a hand through his hair. "I'm sorry. I never should have done that. I don't know why..." He trailed off and stared out the windshield.

She picked up the cap and pulled it back on. "Don't worry about it," she said as calmly as she could. "It takes two to tango, and I was right there with you, dancing up a storm."

He glanced at her for a second before turning his attention back to the dull gray view of the truck stop parking lot. "Still, I shouldn't have done that. I'm supposed to be protecting you. How can you trust me to do that now?"

Jessie didn't understand why his voice held such a note of anguish over a few kisses. Some pretty damned great kisses, but just kisses all the same, and ones she'd eagerly participated in. He acted as if he'd forced himself on her.

"I trust you, Reeve." She reached out and gently touched his arm. "I think we're both operating under sleep and food deprivation. Don't read so much into it."

Ha! Hypocrite, thy name is Jessie. It took everything she had to act as if those kisses were no big deal. They had practically set her pants on fire and had her wishing she'd need his bodyguard services every day.

But she knew better than anyone that wishing for things like that served no purpose.

Up against a foe light years beyond her skill to deal with, accepting Reeve's help made sense. Relying on him for anything more than that did not. Not even dynamite kisses. She trusted him, and kissing him certainly hadn't frightened her for her physical safety, but it had left her thirsty for more, and *that* frightened her a great deal. Until now, she'd been perfectly content with no-strings-attached relationships serving only to satisfy a physical urge. Wanting more from someone was the first step to losing independence, a step she'd long ago vowed she would never take.

Drawing up some good humor she didn't honestly feel, she rubbed her hand up and down his arm and then gave it a playful shake. "Hey! Didn't you say something about getting some breakfast?"

He smiled at her, his white teeth a stark contrast to the sexy stubble on his face. Jessie wanted to feel the rasp of that stubble against her skin, and she wanted to bolt from the car at the same time. He spared her from choosing by turning away and opening his door. "You're right, I did. Let's eat."

He got out, and Jessie blew a deep breath up from her bottom lip. She tucked her hair back up under the cap as Reeve came around the car and opened her door. The cool morning air sent a slight shiver through her. He immediately slipped off his jacket and wrapped it around her shoulders. She avoided looking directly at his face, simply falling in step behind him as he wove a path through the big rigs and the occasional car on their way to the diner. Slipping her arms through the sleeves of the jacket, she detected a musky scent that was all male and did nothing to dispel the lingering traces of their steamy kisses.

For her own sake as well as his, Jessie hoped she'd been accurate by blaming their behavior on lack of food and sleep. She didn't want to believe it could be something else. That maybe after all this time she wanted to let someone in, let someone get close. She hugged the jacket around her and firmly shook off the notion.

No. She would never, ever make that mistake.

REEVE PAUSED at the door of the diner, quickly scanning the interior for potential threats. Focus. That was what he needed right now. He really didn't believe there would be anything to worry about here, but he needed to force his brain back on his job and not on his intense attraction toward Jessie.

Miss Haynes, he reminded himself. She'd fallen under his protection, which meant he shouldn't be so familiar with her. He certainly had no business kissing her, and he called himself every kind of fool for doing it.

Even though it would be the easy excuse, he couldn't

blame lack of food and sleep. His tours of duty in the SEALs had prepared him to go for a long time without either of those physical necessities. He'd led successful raids and military campaigns on less food and less rest and had always maintained his professionalism. He got the job done.

Or at least he used to get the job done. Ego-blowing or not, he had to admit he was none too proud of his performance over the past few months. A young girl had been murdered, and another woman faced an extraordinary threat. His actions had a lot to do with both of those things.

It didn't matter that the Iceman had put Jes—*Miss Haynes*—in jeopardy to begin with. Reeve couldn't dismiss the possibility that if he hadn't been so quick to jump to conclusions, the events of the last twenty-four hours could have gone a lot differently. His rushed and reckless behavior had landed two of his team members in the hospital and nearly placed an innocent woman directly into the hands of a ruthless killer.

Knock it off. Yeah, he'd screwed up by forgetting there was a reason SEALs didn't do rushed and reckless, but dwelling on it only made it worse. Learn from it, then shake it off and get the job done without any more mistakes.

Like kissing the woman who trusted him to protect her. That couldn't happen again.

Seeing no imminent threat in the diner, he opened the door and held it wide. "Head for that booth at the back," he instructed. The corner booth had windows on each side, allowing a more expansive view of the parking lot.

She preceded him to the back of the room. His jacket did a lot to hide her sultry curves, and they made it to the booth without attracting any attention from the several truckers scattered throughout the diner. He placed a hand on her arm, silently signaling her to take the seat that would keep her back to the majority of the restaurant. He slid into the opposite seat and grabbed the plastic menus wedged between the salt and pepper shakers.

Their fingers touched briefly as he handed her a menu, and he tried not to dwell on the spark of awareness that zipped up his arm. She met his glance, and the slight lift of her brows above her jade eyes told him she'd been no less affected by the contact. He pulled his hand back as she quickly tilted her head down to look at the menu, the bill of the baseball cap shielding her face.

A middle-aged woman in a light blue waitress uniform complete with a white apron and large white collar approached their booth. "Morning, folks. What can I get you?" she asked, plunking two glasses of water on the table.

"I'll have a western omelet, home fries, orange juice, and some coffee, please," Jessie said.

"Make it two," Reeve added, closing the menu he'd barely even looked at. The waitress scribbled down their order and sauntered off.

"I'm so hungry I think I could eat two omelets," Jessie said.

"Yeah, me too." Reeve avoided her gaze and looked out the large window, scanning the parking lot for any new arrivals.

"You don't think he'd get here that fast, do you?"

"No. I doubt he'll come here at all. But letting your guard down is never a good idea." He turned back to find her looking directly at him.

"Well," she said, her eyes alive with determination, all hints of awkwardness gone, "then let's eat quickly and get out of here. I'll feel a whole lot better if we could find some-place safe and quiet so we can figure out how to stop him."

Her voice grew firmer as she spoke, its edge of fear replaced by a stern practicality. Impressive. She could just as easily dissolve into hysterics—and considering the threat, he wouldn't blame her—but he still breathed a mental sigh of relief. With someone like the Iceman on their tail, guarding her would be challenging enough. Neither of them could afford to lose their shit.

The waitress delivered two steaming cups of coffee. Jessie added cream and sugar to hers before raising it to her mouth and blowing on it. His gaze locked on her lips, and the memory of their kiss slammed to the front of his mind. *Knock it off, bonehead. Keep it professional.*

He should get one of the other operatives to take charge of protecting her. Now that she knew who they were, there was no reason he had to be the one with her twenty-four seven. He picked up his own mug and took a swallow. The black coffee just about scalded his tongue and throat. He let out a muffled curse at his own stupidity.

"Are you all right?"

"Yeah." He took a sip of water, feeling like an idiot to the millionth degree. But the episode cleared his head. He couldn't walk away from her. It was his fault Jessie—*Miss Haynes, dammit!*—was in this fucked up mess. He owed her his protection, and nothing would stop him from keeping her safe.

He'd already screwed up twice. He'd be damned if he took a third strike.

THEIR OMELETS ARRIVED, and for a few minutes they both ate with gusto, the clinking of silverware against plates the only sound at their table. Not nearly enough noise to distract

Jessie from the two images waging a visual war in her head. If she wasn't thinking about those brain-melting kisses, the Iceman took center stage in her mind. Neither image could be called soothing, and she felt as if she were ready to fly off in a thousand different directions in spite of her fatigue.

She willed herself to focus on the Iceman. Not the more pleasant of the two images, but definitely the most immediate threat. Reeve's voice broke into her thoughts. "I hate to bring up a sore subject, but I keep coming back to what happened at the beach. It's so odd that he knelt down so close to you and touched you like that. Instead of freezing like you did, you so easily could have screamed instead. Why would he risk drawing attention like that?"

"I couldn't tell you. But it turns out he was using that proximity to rifle through my tote bag. That's how he got one of my business cards and found his way to my house." She straightened up. "That's right. When we were in my living room, he told me he used my business card to track me down on the internet. See? Why would he need to do that if we already knew each other?"

"I don't know, but I still don't think it's likely he picked you at random. Not with the amount of energy he's putting into this. He must have some motive."

"Well I certainly don't know what it is!" Exasperation appeared in his sapphire eyes, and she instantly regretted her outburst. "Sorry. I know you're just trying to help."

"It's okay." He rubbed his hand over his face, where lines of frustration were growing more evident by the minute. "Think again, back to before you went on vacation. Is there any time at all you could've crossed paths with him somewhere? In your work, perhaps?"

Jessie closed her eyes and placed her thumbs on her temples, resting her forehead on her extended fingers. "I don't think so. Candy and I are consultants and run an inter-view coaching business. We help write resumes, practice interviews, give fashion advice. Our clients are mostly women. All in all, I lead a pretty dull life. I work from home most of the time and occasionally have a girl's night out with a few friends." She lifted her head and met his gaze. "If I'd seen him before, I'm sure I'd remember."

"Maybe he had on a disguise?"

"Well, it must have been a damn good one." She stopped herself from slamming the table, remembering Reeve's warning about not drawing attention. But remaining calm proved difficult when all she really wanted to do was scream her aggravation to the entire truck stop.

Reeve reached across and took one of her hands. "Try not to let it get to you. If we lose our cool, he gains the advantage. Let's pay the check and get on the road."

He rubbed his thumb over the back of her knuckles, and Jessie appreciated the tenderness that small touch conveyed. She smiled at him. "Thanks."

His eyes darkened as his grip on her hand tightened almost imperceptibly. Warmth flowed up her arm, and the urge to kiss him again was held in check only by the table between them.

Reluctantly pulling her hand from his, she opened her tote bag and dug around for her roll of breath mints. Her fingers closed over something small and hard she couldn't immediately identify by touch. She pulled it out of the bag.

"What's that for?" Reeve asked as she opened her fingers to reveal a USB thumb drive encased in hard black plastic.

"I don't know. It's not mine. I've never seen it before." She looked at it closely, but it revealed no markings that might convey ownership. She handed it to Reeve.

"You're sure it's not yours?"

"Yes. I only use them for work now and again, and mine are hot pink. And I'm sure I didn't pack one to take on vacation." A chill raced up her spine as she examined the drive. Her eyes flew to his. The spark in his eyes confirmed her suspicion. "It's his, isn't it? The Iceman's."

Reeve nodded. "Most likely. He must have slipped it into your bag when he stole your business card."

"Why would he do that?"

"I don't know, but I think we may have just found out why he's pursuing you so relentlessly. He probably wants this back. We'll have to get our hands on a laptop and see what's on this as soon as we can." He put it in his shirt pocket. Sliding from the booth, he tossed a few bills on the table for a tip.

Jessie followed him to the cash register. "I'm going to the ladies room," she said as they waited for the waitress to come and ring up their check.

"Okay. Come right back."

She bristled a little, barely stifling a biting remark that would let him know she didn't need his permission and would spend as much time in the ladies room as she liked. A sigh escaped her lips as she stalked off. She was overreacting, but she couldn't help it. Even the faintest illusion she let someone else control anything in her life rankled like nothing else.

"Focus on the big picture," she muttered as she locked the bathroom door, "and the rest will take care of itself." Removing the threat of the Iceman from her life would then eliminate any need for her beach boy turned bodyguard to issue any sort of directives. In fact, it would eliminate any need for her to see Reeve anymore at all.

Which will be fine with me, she reminded herself. She'd been doing quite well on her own before, and she would do so again once both men were out of her life. Because if those blazing kisses were any indication, Reeve might be just as hazardous to her emotional well-being as the Iceman was to her physical one.

And Jessie wanted no part of either.

CHAPTER NINE

REEVE WATCHED as Jessie headed down the short corridor to the ladies room. She slipped off the jacket as she walked, and the seductive sway of her hips pretty much glued his eyes to her backside. A soft clearing of a throat brought his attention back to the cash register. He grinned sheepishly as he handed some bills to the waitress, who barely hid her own smirk right back at him. As she counted out the change, he glanced back just in time to see the bathroom door close and three other guys turn their heads back to their food. The youngest of them looked toward Reeve, a gleam of challenge in his eyes.

Reeve straightened slightly and held the guy's stare. "Help you with something?" he asked quietly. The trucker stared back for a moment before shaking his head and turning away. It wasn't much as far as trouble went, but it made Reeve antsy to leave. With luck, the jerk would forget the minor incident by the time he finished his breakfast and got back on the road.

After collecting his change, Reeve turned and leaned against the counter, keeping an eye on the bathroom door and silently willing Jessie to hurry along. Out of the corner of his eye, he noted the truckers kept glancing toward the bathroom door as well. Great. So much for going unnoticed.

"Hey, Sally," called another trucker from the end of the counter. "Can we watch the news?"

"Sure thing." The waitress picked up a remote control lying next to the register and turned on the TV mounted in a corner near the ceiling. She found a news station and turned up the volume. The voice of a perky blonde newscaster rang vibrantly in the quiet diner.

"... and sources tell us that yesterday's mysterious afternoon shootout in Candlewood is only the tip of the iceberg. Authorities believe members of a private agency, October Armstrong Security and Investigation Services, are involved in the incident. The agency is run by this woman, former socialite October Armstrong."

A picture of Tobie appeared in the upper left-hand corner of the screen, and Reeve barely stifled a curse. Tobie would be furious. OASIS owed a lot of its success to its discretion. Being broadcast all over the news definitely screwed with their image.

Side by side pictures of Ian and Maddie replaced Tobie's on the screen. "OASIS operative Madeline Barnes was injured during the shootout and taken to Candlewood Hospital for treatment. While her injuries were not life-threatening, doctors were keeping her overnight for observation. However, we've learned that Ms. Barnes has left the hospital against medical advice. Since that time, she has remained unavailable for questioning. Her alleged partner, Ian Westlake, has also been hospitalized due to injuries sustained in a separate incident. It is unclear whether or not authorities have been able to speak with him. We do know that Mr. Westlake was injured in the parking lot of the Oak Motor Inn. He is a person of interest regarding the kidnapping of this woman, Jessica Haynes, owner of the home where the shooting took place."

A small gasp alerted Reeve to Jessie's return as her driver's license photo flashed on the screen. He thanked the stars above she still wore the cap that covered her fiery hair, and that she'd slipped his denim jacket back on, covering her curves from the greedy eyes of the truckers.

"It is believed Mr. Westlake was struck by an unidentified Good Samaritan who tried to prevent him and an accomplice from kidnapping Ms. Haynes from the motel."

Reeve cursed softly under his breath. "Good Samaritan my ass."

The screen changed yet again to a video of the clerk from the motel, a microphone thrust in front of his face. "These two big guys came in, asking about a redheaded woman. I wouldn't tell them anything but one of them went upstairs anyway, so I called the cops. They must have gone out the back way. I would have tried to help her if I'd seen them taking her."

"You lying little puke," Reeve muttered. "You never called the cops. You sold her out for two hundred bucks."

The screen went back to the perky blonde. "Authorities believe Ms. Haynes is in grave danger and are asking anyone who may have seen her to call the number on the screen. Her abductor has not been identified, but is believed to be a member of the OASIS organization and is considered to be armed and extremely dangerous. Citizens are urged not to approach him. Please, folks, don't take any chances. Just call the number on the screen."

The newscast mercifully moved on to traffic and weather. Not that it really mattered. A hell of a lot of damage had been done in that broadcast. They needed to get out of sight as soon as possible.

"Turn around, keep your face down and walk straight out the door," he instructed Jessie quietly.

She spun and nearly collided with the young trucker who'd been staring at her ass. Startled, she looked up into his face. Reeve glared at the man as he took Jessie's arm and led her around the guy and out to the parking lot.

As he hurried her back to the car, his phone vibrated against his hip. He knew without looking at the readout Tobie would be on the other end of the line. "Hi, boss."

"What the hell is going on?"

"I've got it under control."

"Under control? Have you seen the news? Our names and pictures are all over the place. They think we've kidnapped the woman!" Tobie's decibel level rose a fraction, a sure sign of the battle she waged to hang on to her temper.

"Yeah, I saw that. It's not true." He opened the car door and practically stuffed Jessie into her seat.

"I know it's not true! But the police and the media think it is, which means we're going to be the center of attention now. The press is already setting up camp outside the building. I'm sure I can expect a visit from the cops any minute. Where are you? Wait, don't tell me. After the Fox incident, we can't trust the police. If they ask me where you are, I can honestly tell them I don't know. Call Fitz and tell him where you are and where you're going."

"All right."

"In the meantime, I'll have Jake work his magic and find out who's feeding this garbage to the media."

"It's got to be the Iceman." Reeve jogged around to the driver's side and got in.

"You're probably right. But in order to do this, he's got to be well-connected. There's no way he could have done this alone. There's got to be a trail somewhere."

"Agreed."

"One more thing. When this is all over, we need to talk about why you thought Miss Haynes and the Iceman were partners to begin with." Tobie disconnected, and Reeve sighed. At least she hadn't come right out and accused him of screwing up the operation, but she'd probably get around to that eventually. Not that he could blame her. So far he'd done nothing to prove her initial reservations wrong, and he knew she would continue to watch his every move.

Speaking of watching, Reeve spotted that leering trucker from the diner. He stood in the parking lot now, staring at the back of their car and talking on his cell phone.

"Dammit!" He started the engine.

"What's the matter?"

"That guy from the diner, the one you almost ran into? He's on the phone to the cops right now."

Jessie whipped around and looked over the back of the seat. "Why would he be calling the police?"

"He was paying a lot of attention to you when you went to the ladies room. And he got a good look at your face right after your picture came on television. He thinks I'm kidnapping you."

"But you're not. Why don't we wait for the police? I'll tell them I'm with you willingly."

"Because they might not believe you. Not at first, anyway. They might think you're too scared to tell the truth. They'll insist we go to the station with them to sort it all out, and they'll separate us." Hell would host the next Winter Olympics before Reeve would allow *that* to happen. "What if Fox wasn't the only fake cop in the Iceman's employ? It's not a gamble I'm willing to take."

She whirled back around. "Me either. Let's go."

He sped out of the lot and got on the highway, heading back the way they came.

"Don't we want to go the other way?" Jessie asked.

"Yeah, but I want our friend from the diner to see us go this way." A quick glimpse in the rearview mirror showed the guy still talking on his phone while frenziedly pointing his finger in their direction. "We'll turn around at the next exit. And we're going to have to ditch this car."

"Will one of your coworkers bring another one?"

"We can't risk it. After that broadcast, they're going to have their hands full dealing with the authorities for a while. We'll have to borrow one."

"From who?"

"It doesn't really matter."

Her heated stare burned into him like a laser beam. "You mean we're going to *steal* a car?"

"Borrow. We'll definitely return it. Or replace it if necessary." Her angry snort let him know she saw right through the hair being split. "Hey, you didn't object when we borrowed this one."

"That was dif... I mean, he had a gun... He kept shooting at us... I... We..."

"Look, I don't like it any more than you do. But our number-one priority is keeping you safe. That means keeping you away from the police for now, and it definitely means keeping you away from the Iceman. And if that means we need to steal a car, then that's what we'll do."

"Can't we just rent one?"

"Not without providing identification. I don't want to leave any kind of a trail he might be able to pick up."

She tugged her hand from his and folded her arms. "I can't believe I'm committing a felony. Twice."

"Yeah, well..." Reeve let his voice trail off.
Better a live felon than a dead victim.

"You idiot!" Iceman hissed. "What were you thinking?"

"You said hamper them."

"Hamper them. Not spread them all over the news! Now every cop in the state will be looking for them. How can I get near them?"

"Look," Rob snapped, "you were supposed to get rid of her quietly. It's not my fault you slacked off. You asked me for help when I shouldn't even be talking to you."

"You'll do as I tell you! You're in this up to your neck. If I go down, so do you."

Rob didn't respond, and Iceman knew he'd made his point. Good. The little shit needed to be kept in check. "Did you find out about her friends?"

"Yeah. She's still really tight with her friend from college." He rattled off a name and address. "So what do you want me to do now?"

"Nothing for the moment. Don't give any more information to the media or the police."

"The police?" Rob yelped. "You don't think they'll connect me to this, do you?"

"You just plastered her face on the morning news. How long do you think it's going to take them to find out who she really is? Do as I say and keep your mouth shut."

THE LINE WENT DEAD. Rob slowly pocketed his phone and lit a cigarette. He stared down the sloping lawn of the estate without really seeing it as an avalanche of dismay crashed over him.

How could he have been so stupid? He'd been in such a hurry to get the money, he hadn't stopped to think his plan through. Story of his life.

Now, not only was there the likelihood the police would figure out Jessie Haynes's real identity, if his stepfather saw her picture on television, he would definitely recognize her. And if he found out Rob had anything to do with it, there wouldn't be a hole on earth deep enough to hide in.

Fucking Judith! This was all her fault. Why couldn't she just disappear? But of course not. In the underlying, crapbag theme of his life story, Judith easily eluded misfortune while he always landed in the thick of it.

He stubbed out the cigarette and headed straight for his bedroom. He opened the safe in the back of his closet and removed his Walther PPK. He'd purchased the handgun last year, right after his last girlfriend broke up with him. Just thinking of Tiffany boosted his temper another notch. He'd been all set to marry her, but when he'd brought her to the estate to meet his mother, his stepfather had arrived home unexpectedly and joined them for dinner. Mitchell had totally humiliated both Rob and his mother throughout the entire meal.

Instead of Tiffany offering any kind of sympathy or support, the unfeeling bitch dumped him the very next day. Rob had been so angry he'd never been able to decide who he wanted to shoot more—Tiffany or Mitchell. In the end, of course, he couldn't bring himself to shoot either of them. He'd done nothing more than buy the gun and take a few lessons on how to use it before he locked it away in his safe and cursed his own cowardice.

But he wasn't afraid now. He couldn't afford to be, and

with each passing moment he grew more certain the Iceman definitely planned to screw him over. Rob shoved the gun in the back of his pants and filled his pockets with spare ammunition. He would catch up with the Iceman at Candy's house and follow him until he found Judith. Then Rob would do whatever he had to do to save his own neck.

He'd come up with a new plan, a better plan. One that didn't involve anyone else. Other people only made things more complicated. Look at what had happened already. He would have been better off if he'd never gotten involved with the Iceman to begin with. But it wasn't too late. He could still fix this.

Judith, the Iceman, Candy. Rob just had to make all of them disappear—and anybody else who got in his way.

CHAPTER TEN

WHAT A DIFFERENCE A DAY MAKES.

This time yesterday, Jessie had been relaxing on the hotel patio, enjoying the final breakfast of her vacation. Today she found herself standing on a street corner in a questionable neighborhood, serving as a lookout while Reeve broke into a maroon Cadillac Eldorado of a late 1980s vintage. They'd prowled around the neighborhood in the early morning stillness looking for just the right vehicle. Reeve had been very specific in his requirements for the perfect car to... borrow.

"It's got to be older, and it would be ideal if it were a convertible."

Much to Jessie's surprise, they spotted the Eldorado after a mere fifteen minutes of driving around. It was old, all right, rust spots dotting the dull paint like malignant freckles. The tan convertible top appeared intact, but it was stained with large, black, greasy splotches.

Reeve parked the sedan several blocks away, and they walked back to the Caddy. Along the way, he quietly rummaged around in the various trash cans they passed, explaining he needed tools. Jessie wondered if he really expected to find a toolbox in someone's trash simply because he needed one. She didn't know what to think when he pulled a couple of large, ratty-looking bras out of the fifth or sixth can he looked in.

"Underwire," he said, as if that explained it all. He removed the underwire, and when he twisted the pieces together and made a small loop at one end, it finally made sense. The wire would lift the inside lock on the car door.

"What, you don't carry one of those slim jim thingies?" Jessie asked.

"Never took a car off the street before. Never thought I'd have to."

"Well, now I know what to get you for Christmas."

"Ha, ha. Do me a favor and let me know if you see anyone coming." With a pocket knife, he slit a small opening in the convertible top, then pushed the wire loop through it.

Jessie scanned up and down the block, praying no one would happen along and catch them in the act. Fortunately, the area remained quiet, their only company an orange striped cat slinking along under the cars on the opposite side of the street. She heard a faint click just before Reeve whispered a hasty, "Let's go."

He slid behind the wheel and leaned over to open the passenger door. Jessie climbed in and buckled her seat belt as Reeve pulled an oblong metal object from a small nylon pouch clipped to his belt. It looked like a cross between a pair of pliers and a Swiss Army Knife. He leaned over the steering column, and with what looked like just a few flicks of his wrist, the engine sprang to life.

"What?" he asked as she stared at him.

"Nothing. I'm just beginning to think you had an extremely misspent youth."

"Nah. Just a little too much time watching old MacGyver reruns." He winked at her, and Jessie pretended she didn't get a little flutter in her stomach.

"Where to now?" she asked as he pulled into the street and headed back to the highway.

"Now we get the heck out of Dodge before somebody sees us. Then we find someplace else to hide out while we sort out our next move."

"Another motel, I suppose. Sounds like a great idea. I enjoyed the last one *so* much."

"Try to hang in there. We're going to get him." He gave a quick rub to the back of her neck, and her shoulders relaxed in an instant response. She kind of wished they hadn't. In a very short time, his presence and helpfulness had grown very appealing. Not what she wanted right now. Or later.

Her life before, the one she'd walked away from, had taught her the folly of needing anyone. She'd watched helplessly as her father's increasing demands and constant need to dominate had drained her mother's quiet strength, eroding her spirit day by day. Her mother had told Jessie that in the early days of the marriage, she had liked her husband's take-charge attitude because it made her feel safe.

But over the years, that take-charge attitude had morphed into something evil and merciless as he abused and debased his wife without a flicker of remorse. Her mother had ultimately been reduced to a broken shell of her former self, all because she'd let someone else take over, giving up the notion of taking care of herself.

Definitely not the life Jessie planned to live. Ever.

She shifted in her seat, away from his hand. "When are we going to find out what's on the thumb drive?"

"I've been thinking about that. We could wait a couple of hours for the stores to open and buy a laptop. I've got enough cash. But I'd rather not do that. The fewer people we have contact with, the better."

"Agreed. And I don't want to wait that long."

"Neither do I." He pulled out his phone and tapped a button on the screen. "Maddie, are you okay? Why did you leave the hospital?"

Jessie couldn't understand the words, but she had no problem hearing the woman's harsh tones as Reeve pulled the phone away from his ear.

"All right, already. Knock it off, Maddie. I just asked," Reeve said loudly before putting the phone back to his ear. "Listen up. I need to get my hands on a computer. Some-place safe and off the grid. You know anybody around here that can help us out?... Okay, text me the address and we'll meet you there in a little while."

Reeve hung up. "With the media buzzing around her at the hospital, Maddie took off and spent the night at a cousin's house. She's still there and says we can use her cousin's computer."

"Who is Maddie?"

"A fellow operative at OASIS. She grew up around here."

"Are you sure we can trust her?"

His eyebrows shot up. "Of course."

"Don't act all outraged. I've got a right to ask. It's my ass on the line here. And she didn't exactly sound stable just now."

"She's touchy, I'll admit it, but I trust Maddie with my life... regularly. And for your information, she's the woman who took a bullet outside your house yesterday, trying to make sure *you* didn't get hurt. I don't know her cousin, but if Maddie trusts him or her, so do I."

A frosty silence descended, further fraying her nerves. Jessie leaned over and turned on the radio, fiddling with the buttons until she found an all-news station. After a brief traffic and weather update, the lead story reported their being sighted at the truck stop.

Reeve swore under his breath. "We've got to get off the road as soon as we can."

"But we've changed cars. They won't be looking for us in this one." For all of her initial misgivings about stealing cars, Reeve had made a good call.

"Yeah, and that will slow them down. But we're still too hot a topic. We've got to get out of sight." His fingers were clenched tightly around the steering wheel, and there were dark circles under his eyes.

"When's the last time you slept?"

"Doesn't matter," he muttered.

"Oh yes, it does. I'm placing a lot of faith in you. What good is that going to do me if you collapse from exhaustion?"

He sighed deeply. "It's been about twenty-seven hours. But I've gone without sleep longer than that."

"Pull over."

"What?"

"Pull over. I've already gotten some sleep. I'll drive."

"I'm fine."

"You're not fine, you're exhausted. Besides, I need to do something." The old, familiar feeling of being kept prisoner, marching its way into her soul like an invading army, ate at her like a cancer. In response, the need to contribute to her own safety grew stronger by the minute. "Look, either you pull over and let me drive, or I promise you the next time we stop I'm going to start screaming my head off. Somebody will call the cops. They can't all be in on this thing."

"That would be foolish, and it could get you killed."

"So can driving around with somebody about to fall asleep at the wheel. I mean it. Pull over."

"You don't even know where we're going."

"You can tell me. Or I can ask someone. I don't mind asking for directions," she snarked. "I'm a woman, remember?"

As if he could forget. Not with the lingering memory of her lips blending with his. But her lips were now set in a firm line, her jaw tight and her arms crossed, mutiny radiating from every pore. "Why does this mean so much to you?"

"Try to understand it from my end. I can't be a passive bystander in this. I'll go crazy."

She had a point. Unlike most of their regular clients, she'd been forced into this through no fault of her own, and that had to be messing with her head. Their destination wasn't far. Letting her drive the short distance made sense, especially if it would keep her compliant.

He pulled over, the light, early-morning traffic no impediment as they made the switch. Once back on the road, he opened up an online map service and gave her turn-by-turn directions. They found the address, located in an older section of Candlewood, and pulled into the driveway. Maddie waited for them inside the door of the empty one-car garage that looked as if it hadn't seen an upgrade since the 1950s. She waved them in and then winced as she started to pull the garage door down.

"Dammit, Maddie!" Reeve swore as he got out of the car. "You're going to ruin your shoulder. Let me do it."

"My shoulder's fine," she grumbled, but she stepped back and let him close the door.

"Yeah, sure it is," he muttered as he took a good look at her face. "I've seen milk with more color than you."

She said nothing, and that in itself told him all he needed to know. Maddie in top form would never hold her tongue. He shook his head as he gently took her elbow and towed her toward the door he assumed led into the house. Jessie followed them into a small, cheery kitchen.

He steered Maddie toward the dainty, oval dinette table in the center of the room and planted her in one of the chairs. "Any news on Ian?" he asked.

Impressively, Maddie's scowling expression turned even more sour. "Six stitches to the back of his head and a mild concussion. Tobie benched him for the next few days. He's pretty pissed."

"I'll bet."

Maddie gave a ghost of a smile. "Serves him right. He wanted to keep me out of action. See how he likes it now."

"Put a lid on it. He was acting under my orders. And until your shoulder's better, your job now is to assist Jake in whatever research he needs. No field work for you."

She rolled her eyes but didn't argue. Another sign her shoulder hurt more than she would ever let on.

"How long can we stay here?" Reeve asked.

"It depends. After you called, my cousin Janie left for work and said she'll stay at her boyfriend's place for as long as we're here. But if the news story stays hot, there's a chance the press may start sniffing around here. So we should keep the shades down and stay out of sight of the neighbors."

"Why would they come here?"

Maddie's cheeks grew pink. "I sorta made headlines here in town before I moved away. Sooner or later they'll figure out Janie and I are related."

"Headlines?"

"I don't want to talk about it. As long as we're careful, no one will know we're here." She pointed to the counter. "That's Janie's laptop. It's all booted up and ready to go."

He put the laptop on the table and sat next to Maddie. Jessie pulled an empty chair closer and took a seat on his other side. She peered over his shoulder as he plugged the drive into the laptop. Her breath sighed along his neck, and his mind flew back to the kiss. Automatically, his hand went behind her chair, and he had a tremendous impulse to stroke the back of her neck. He stopped himself, leaning back a bit and extending both arms. Maddie shifted in her chair and looked at him with a raised eyebrow. He dropped his arms and looked back at the screen.

"Let's hope he didn't put a password on it," Jessie said close to his ear, her breath teasing his lobe. He shifted uncomfortably and knew without looking Maddie was probably smirking at him. *Great, she'll never let me live this down.*

"I doubt it. Something tells me he's too arrogant for that. It never would have occurred to him you would escape him. He never expected anyone but you to have the drive, and it's obvious he had every intention of getting it back before you even knew you had it."

He clicked on the most recent of the many jpeg files contained on the drive. His stomach plunged to the floor as Tabitha Spencer's smiling face filled the screen. A caption across the bottom of the picture read, "Lot #7854. Starting bid $10,000."

"Was... was... he planning to *auction* her?" Jessie's voice shook with a mixture of horror and indignation.

Reeve closed the picture and called up another one. Another young girl's face appeared on the screen with another lot number and dollar amount. Several other files revealed similar photos. He scrolled down and discovered some video files. He hesitated, certain that whatever images those videos contained would be unpleasant to say the least, and Jessie's state of mind had been battered more than enough for one day. Hell, more than enough for a year. "I should look at this alone."

"Absolutely not. I need to know why he's after me, and if those videos hold the key, then I need to see them."

Recognizing the same steely determination in her voice as when she'd insisted on driving, he reluctantly clicked the first video file. A bird's eye view of a large room came into focus. About a dozen men, most of them dressed in business suits, were seated before a raised platform.

Young girls in various states of undress were dragged up to the platform one at a time. Some of them were obviously drugged and could barely stand up. Others did not appear to be drugged and were crying or screaming as they were hauled up and crudely displayed before the audience. Not that it seemed to matter to any of the men. They leered at the poor creatures and occasionally nudged each other in the ribs with a laugh as they proceeded to bid on each girl.

As the hideous auction appeared to wind down, some of the winning bidders stood up and seized their purchases by the wrists, or even by the hair, and dragged them out of the room. Reeve didn't want to think about what happened to the girls after that.

Unfortunately, he wasn't given any choice. A few clicks on some of the other files showed not only some additional auctions, but also some appalling footage of those same men savaging the girls they had just purchased. Sadistic domination seemed to be the norm for these degenerates, and Reeve could stand no more of it. He exited the video file and slammed the laptop shut. He closed his eyes, trying unsuccessfully to erase what he'd seen.

There had been one bright spot to the atrocities he'd just witnessed. The Iceman had been glimpsed at one of the auctions. He'd briefly passed underneath the camera, but there had been no mistaking his haughty face and the white hair. It would be enough to identify him in court. Exactly the kind of proof they'd been hoping to get their hands on. Now all they had to do was catch the cockroach.

The quiet scrape of a chair reminded him the others had been subjected to the filth on those videos. He opened his eyes. Maddie stared at the closed laptop, the feral look on her face clearly stating she would rip those men to shreds with her bare hands if given the opportunity. Good. Situation normal.

A delicate sniffle turned his attention to Jessie. Tears streamed down her face, and her complexion had gone ashen. "Those girls," she whispered. "Those poor girls." He placed an arm around her shoulder. She leaned into him for a brief moment before she pulled away and swiped at her eyes. "I can't believe what I saw. How can human beings treat each other like that?"

"Some people are just wired wrong."

"But how do they hide it so well?"

"What do you mean?" As far as Reeve could tell, those sick lowlifes hadn't been hiding anything.

"Didn't you recognize any of those men? Two of them are Congressmen, and another one made the cover of Time Magazine last month."

"Son of a bitch," Maddie said. "She's right. I saw that article. He developed some new communications software that's supposed to revolutionize the industry. Jake raved on and on about it too."

"You would think men of such supposed intelligence wouldn't allow themselves to be filmed doing something like this," Jessie said.

"They probably didn't know they were being taped. I'll bet the Iceman planned to use these files for blackmail." Reeve thought for a moment. "You know, that's not a half-bad idea. We can use this stuff to our advantage."

"Shouldn't we just turn it over to the police? Couldn't they use it to find those girls?" Jessie asked.

"We will turn it in. The authorities will need it to put those men behind bars. But that'll take time." Not to mention Reeve doubted any of those girls were still alive. Men like that wouldn't want to leave any eyewitnesses to their violent proclivities. But Jessie didn't need to know that yet. That information could only make her feel worse.

Maddie leaned back. "So what do you have in mind?"

"First, we're going to get these files to Jake. He can start matching the faces of the bidders to their names. Same for the girls. Some of them, at least, had to have been reported missing. Next, we contact as many of the bidders as we can and see if they can help us find the Iceman."

"Why would they help us?" Jessie asked. "If they know we have this footage, won't they want to try and make us go away?"

"Yes and no. We have no power to arrest them, but what if we can catch them off guard with a blackmail scheme of our own? Threaten to turn the drive over to the police unless they tell us what we want to know. They may be more inclined to give up the Iceman in order to save their own skins."

"You mean you'd let them get away with what they've done if they tell us where the Iceman is? That's... no, we have to..."

Reeve met her indignant stare. "Hell, no. Even if they hand deliver the Iceman to us, I'm still turning this in. Those scumbags don't deserve the sanctity of an honest deal."

"Damn straight," Maddie said as she pulled the laptop toward her. "I'll send these files to Jake and Tobie and let them know the plan. Why don't you two go get some rest? You both look like hell. Especially you, boss man."

"Gee, thanks."

"Anytime. Miss Haynes, you can use the guest room at the end of the hall. Hot Shot here can use the pullout couch in the living room."

Reeve followed Jessie down the hallway. "She certainly has a... way about her, doesn't she?" she remarked as they stopped at the door to the guest room.

"Yeah, tact isn't one of Maddie's strong points. But she's a good operative. We can both rest easy while she's on watch."

"I don't think I can sleep. Not after what I just saw."

"Me, either. But we should try anyway. We need to stay sharp."

She nodded, her eyes haunted and distant, her lips a solid, grim line. All the sparkle and mirth he'd seen in her in Key West was gone. A mantle of failure cloaked his conscience. His mission going wrong had brought her to this, sleeping in a stranger's home after seeing repulsive images of a practice she'd have been better off not knowing about. In that moment, Reeve had no greater desire than to somehow help her forget those damn files. Maybe help himself forget too. His jaw clenched as he fought the sudden need pulsing through him.

"Reeve? Is something wrong?"

"No. Get some rest." He turned and walked away before he did something stupid, like give in to the urge to kiss her again. Because kissing her would be a mistake.

And he'd made enough mistakes already.

CHAPTER ELEVEN

Jessie sat up and yawned. The lavender potpourri in a crystal dish on the nightstand lent a soothing aroma to the room and should have helped her to relax. But her nerves were too damn rattled. She swung her feet to the floor.

Amid several hours of tossing and turning, she'd managed to get some sleep, but it had hardly been restful. The terrified faces of those girls haunted her as she dozed. The brutality of it chilled her to the bone, and she still had a hard time processing the fact that she had somehow gotten mixed up in it all.

After escaping her own awful past, she'd done everything she could to create a simple, peaceful life. She briefly touched base with her stepmother every couple of months, mainly to try to convince the woman to leave for her own sake. Other than that, Jessie refused to have anything to do with her old life, especially her father. She worked hard at her job, and even harder at surrounding herself with a few good friends and enjoying quiet, drama-free days.

But what was the point? No matter how hard she worked to keep her life calm and serene, it could all be smashed to pieces by forces beyond her control. If finding that lunatic in her living room hadn't been enough to remind her the cruel whims of fate would do as they pleased, viewing those video files had certainly done the trick.

She stepped into the bathroom and splashed cold water on her face before taking a good look in the mirror. There were still circles under her eyes, and her whole face drooped with fatigue. But her eyes themselves were the worst. They held the same fearful, haunted look she'd seen in them years ago. The same look she'd seen in her mother's eyes before she died. The same look that had stolen into her stepmother's eyes so soon after she'd married Jessie's father.

No!

She couldn't let it happen. She *wouldn't*. Death would be preferable to a life lived in a miasma of oppression and fear. And what about those girls? What if they were still being held somewhere? This wasn't just about her own personal safety anymore. Between her fitful bouts of sleep, she'd thought long and hard to figure out a way to find the Iceman because she didn't believe for a second the men on those files would help them one iota.

She'd come up blank, though, and it tore at her conscience. Perhaps it was irrational, but she felt guilty, as if her escaping the subjugated life her father planned for her had somehow contributed to the fate of those girls.

Desperate to shake off the gloom and fatigue, she headed to the kitchen to make coffee. She found Reeve already there, sitting at the table and staring at the laptop, the late-afternoon sun casting long shadows across the floor.

"Maddie's gone," he said without looking away from the screen. "She went to the office to help Jake put together names with the faces on those files. I've been reviewing them too. I'm looking for any clues that might tell us the location of the auctions. So far, no such luck."

The files. She couldn't look at them again. Not now. Not when she already saw them every time she closed her eyes.

She took a hesitant step into the room. Reeve looked up and gave her a brief smile before turning his attention back to the laptop. The circles beneath his eyes were less dark now, and his clothes were a little rumpled, so she assumed he'd managed to get some sleep. The stubble on his face had grown darker, but instead of making him look unkempt, it drew her closer.

"There's not a lot of food on hand," he continued, "but there's enough to make some sandwiches. Are you hungry?"

She didn't respond as she stepped behind him. Carefully avoiding the images on the screen, she placed her hand on the base of his neck. His muscles jumped beneath her fingers before he stiffened.

"What are you doing?" he whispered.

Taking control of her life for now. She'd wanted him since the moment she'd first laid eyes on him at the beach and, dammit, she was going to have him. And it was going to be good. She would make sure of it.

Her other hand joined the first and she rubbed her fingers on both sides of his neck, seeking to ease the tension beneath his warm skin. He leaned back a little, not facing her, his hands dropping from the keyboard to the top of his thighs.

"Miss Haynes, really, we shouldn't be doing something like..."

He stopped talking when she leaned down and kissed her way along the back of his neck. Good. She didn't want talking. She wanted to erase the memories of the last forty-eight hours. The Iceman, the gun fights, the thumb drive, all of it. If she didn't get it out of her head for at least a little while, she'd go mad.

She looped an arm around the front of his magnificent chest as she continued kissing and nibbling his neck. Her hand slid lower, skimming across those washboard abs she'd glimpsed earlier, his muscles tightening in response to her touch. She dropped her hand even lower, and Reeve covered it with his own, halting her inquisitive progress.

Sliding the chair back, he rose and turned to face her. She shivered at the intensity in his eyes. They'd turned an even deeper blue, a midnight sky that blanketed out all the ugliness invading her life. She leaned in, and he seized her about the waist, pulling her hips against his. The evidence of his arousal sent heat rocketing through her, furthering her determination. She wanted this. She wanted *him*. Now.

"Reeve," she whispered. He didn't let her say more, claiming her mouth for a searing kiss. Her body seemed to float upward as the pure male scent of him filled her head. His hands roved up and down her back, blazing a sizzling path for her desire to follow. She ran her fingers from his shoulders to his waist before sliding them under his shirt, relishing the feel of hot skin and hard muscle.

Reeve broke the kiss, but before she could protest, he hoisted her up by her hips. She wrapped her legs around his waist as he strode to the guest room. Still locked together, they fell to the mattress. He buried his face in her neck, and starbursts of delight ricocheted through her as he worked his way back to her face with maddening little kisses. His hands slid under her shirt and found their way to her breasts as his lips closed over her mouth. His thumbs on her nipples sent her pulse into overdrive.

This time Jessie broke the kiss so she could pull off her shirt. Reeve took the opportunity to remove his own shirt, flinging it across the room before taking hers from her hands and giving it the same treatment. He bent down, taking a nipple into his mouth, and a fire exploded in the pit of her stomach, its scorching heat consuming her from head to toe. She thrashed beneath him like a wild thing as he let go of one nipple only to lavish the same attention on the other.

She clutched at his hair, whimpering with pleasure as he licked and teased her breasts. His hands found the snap of her jeans, and she lifted her hips as he slid them down her legs. Her panties followed, and he cupped his hands underneath her backside, pressing her closer to his hips. The sensation of his arousal through his jeans sent her to new heights, and she knew she couldn't wait much longer to get him naked and inside her. Hell, she wouldn't wait, not one more minute.

She reached down and unsnapped his jeans, pleased when he quickly stood up and shucked them off, removing his wallet before tossing them aside. Producing a condom from the wallet, he quickly covered himself and returned to her, entering her in one smooth motion. She grabbed his shoulders and snaked her legs around the back of his.

He held still, stretching her, filling her. His eyes locked on hers, and in them she saw the same need that had driven her to this in the first place. That need to forget, that desperate desire to prove they had the power to create good no matter how hard outside forces worked to create evil.

Seeking the perfect rhythm, they moved slowly at first, deeply, thoroughly, savoring every movement, treasuring every kiss. But their passion built with each thrust and soon their motions reached a frenetic pace, faster, harder. Jessie abandoned herself to his touch as delicious pressure mounted inside her, her mind filled with nothing but the organic, primitive instinct of their bodies and the pleasure they incited. A powerful climax possessed her, ripping a mewling cry from her throat. The muscles in his arms and shoulders tightened as he plunged into her with a final thrust, a low, wordless cry accompanying his release.

He collapsed on top of her and slid off to the side, pulling her close against his chest as they sought to catch their breath. She hugged him back, still craving the physical contact, the reassurance of his large, powerful body. She wrapped her legs around him, needing to touch as much of her body to his as she could.

If it were at all possible, she would have climbed inside his skin.

FOX ANSWERED HIS PHONE, blinking sleep from his eyes.

"Go to this address," the Iceman ordered. "The Barnes woman might be there."

"What makes you say that?"

"It seems she has something of a checkered past. The address is that of a relative. She might go there to hide."

Barnes. Of course! That explosion a few years ago. It had taken up local headlines for weeks.

"If we pick her up there, she might lead us to the Haynes woman," the Iceman continued.

"Okay." Fox disconnected, squinting an eye at the bedside clock. What he wouldn't give for another few hours of sleep. He flung the covers off and got to his feet. If a giant hole opened up and swallowed the Iceman, Fox wouldn't be sorry. The man was nothing but a pain in the ass.

But he was a very lethal pain in the ass, and Fox knew

better than to disobey. He yanked on his clothes and headed out.

"DIDN'T you say something about a sandwich?"

Reeve smiled as the breath from her words tickled his neck. "Yep, last evening. I got the feeling you weren't hungry."

"Mmmm, well, it seems I've worked up an appetite since then. I can't imagine why."

"I hear a night of hot sex can do that to you." He turned and brushed his lips against her forehead.

"Oh, no you don't, mister. No more of that until you feed me." Laughing, she rolled away and tugged the sheet off the bed, leaving him alone and naked on the mattress.

"Hey! Give that back."

Her giggles were like music in the pre-dawn darkness. "Here's your pants," she said just before his jeans landed on his chest.

"Thanks a lot," he muttered good-naturedly. He sat up and tugged them on as she headed toward the bathroom. "Don't turn the lights on. We don't want anyone to know we're here," he reminded her.

"Okay."

Just enough of the sun's early rays filtered through the windows to keep him from banging into the furniture as he walked to the kitchen. He closed the kitchen shades and then opened the refrigerator, quickly removing the sandwich fixings. His hands moved automatically to prepare the food while his mind wandered back over the last several hours.

On a practical level, he knew he'd screwed up. Sleeping

with a client definitely went against OASIS corporate guidelines. If Tobie found out, she'd probably fire him faster than a politician forgets campaign promises. The fact that, technically, Jessie wasn't a client wouldn't make one bit of difference because, in this case, that loophole totally missed the point.

Since she'd returned from Key West, Jessie had been threatened, attacked, shot at, nearly kidnapped, and subjected to the contents of the thumb drive. Her level of vulnerability had to be at an all-time high. That alone should have kept him from sleeping with her.

THERE WAS MORE to it than that, though, more to *Jessie* than that. When he'd faced her in the kitchen earlier, her eyes had been haunted and troubled, true, but they'd also held that unyielding look of resolve he'd come to expect when she planned on taking initiative. When he looked at her, he hadn't seen a vulnerable, defenseless victim, but rather someone fighting to regain control of her life, and somehow he knew she needed that more than oxygen.

His conscience gave him a nudge, reminding him he hadn't done it just for her. He'd had reasons of his own, reasons that lacked any shred of nobility. From the second they'd accessed the thumb drive and seen Tabitha Spencer's beautiful, innocent face, followed by those gruesome acts of depravity, his sense of failure had roared back with a vengeance. He hadn't been able to do anything for Tabitha, and he'd let the Iceman slip through his fingers twice now. Who knew how many other women he'd indirectly let down when the mission had imploded?

So in that moment when Jessie sought his help—the only help she'd ever actually asked him for—he'd been powerless to say no, for his own sake as well as hers. He needed to do as she wanted because maybe if he could put the life back in her eyes, he would know he could still do what needed to be done. If that made him a selfish bastard, he'd just have to learn to live with it because he knew this was the first really *right* thing he'd done since Jessie had gotten dragged into this whole mess.

He couldn't bring himself to call it a mistake. Not when he knew he'd helped her. He already heard it in her voice and expected to see it in her eyes. He'd helped himself too. For the first time in weeks, months even, his confidence wasn't whimpering in some dark box in a corner of his soul. How could something that productive be a mistake?

Tobie probably wouldn't see it that way, of course. He'd just have to keep his fingers crossed she never found out about it.

Speaking of Tobie, he should check his messages. He picked up his phone from the counter where he'd left it plugged in and charging overnight. Nothing from Tobie, which he took as a "no news is good news" sort of thing. But Jake had sent him an email with Jessie's name in the subject line. He clicked it open and scanned the contents, his mood morphing from content to irritated to seething by the time he'd finished reading.

Apparently, Jessie Haynes had some pretty damn big secrets after all.

CHAPTER TWELVE

JESSIE LOOKED in the bathroom mirror and raked her fingers through her hair. Even in the near darkness, she noted with satisfaction that the timid look in her eyes had left. Her lips curled into an impish grin. *Yeah, that was you last night, brazenly seducing a man you've known for barely two days.*

She wasn't sorry she'd done it. Great sex couldn't solve all her problems, but it had helped put things in perspective. She had *not* lost control of her life. The shock of it all had made her look at the situation from the wrong perspective. So far, her actions had all been reactive, running away from the threat and cowering in fear.

Well, no more of that crap. No one would make her run away again. The Iceman presented a dangerous disruption to her life, but just like any other obstacle she'd faced in the past, she would remove it.

She turned on the shower and stepped under the warm spray. She was still afraid—she'd be a fool if she weren't—but she couldn't let that get in the way. No more sitting around, waiting for the next pile of crap to hit the fan. Starting today, *she* would be the one chasing that reject from a bad vampire movie, not the other way around. With Reeve's help, she would come up with a plan.

Reeve didn't join her in the shower, and she mildly chided herself for being a little disappointed as she toweled off. They weren't a couple, and last night had served its purpose. Time to move on and deal with her troubles.

Wrinkling her nose, she dressed in her now unquestionably dingy clothes. Quickly stripping the bed, she replaced the sheets with clean ones she found in a hall closet. She made up the bed and wished she had time to launder the used sheets. When this ordeal ended, she'd have to find a way to make it up to Maddie's cousin for her hospitality.

She headed for the kitchen with a slight sense of trepidation. With the night's passion behind them, she had no idea what to expect. Reeve could be one of those guys who behaved as if nothing happened, which would be fine with her. But what if he was on the other side of the spectrum and thought they were in some sort of relationship now? That could whip up its own set of problems, although a surprising little voice in her head kept telling her a dinner date with the guy might be nice once they were on the other side of all this.

She stopped walking. *A dinner date?* Where the hell did that come from? She didn't date. Not really. Over the years, she'd accumulated a few male "friends with benefits." But she never actually dated any of them, not beyond the occasional let's-meet-for-a-drink-before-getting-down-to-business sort of thing.

Those booty calls you indulge in are going to get old pretty soon.

Candy's words echoed in her head, and Jessie had a niggling little feeling her friend might be right. Still, the mere thought of committing to any kind of relationship, even something as simple as a dinner date, gave her the heebie-jeebies. Relationships could turn ugly. Fast.

Yet the thought of having dinner with Reeve still appealed.

She shook her head and got moving again. Analysis of that ambivalence would have to wait. If the Iceman had his way, then dating Reeve, or anyone else for that matter, would not be in the cards.

Screw that. She and she alone would decide her future.

Reeve stood in the middle of the kitchen, the first rays of dawn dancing in golden ripples across his bare chest. She wanted to wrap her arms around him, the urge to hold the coming day at bay for just a little while longer creeping up again, but she fought it. Avoidance wouldn't resolve anything, no matter how tempting that wickedly muscled avoidance might be.

She raised her eyes to his face and took a step back. His eyes blazed blue fury, his mouth pinched in an angry scowl. "What's wrong?"

"You tell me, *Judith.*"

"What? Wait, how did you—"

"How did I find out you've been lying to me all along?"

"I didn't lie. I'm not Judith. Not anymore."

"You should have told me!" he thundered. "Do you know how much time you've wasted?"

"I don't understand. What does my name have to do with any of it?"

He rolled his eyes. "You're kidding me, right? You're the daughter of one of the richest men in the country. That makes you an obvious ransom target. If you'd been honest with me, I would have known the Iceman's motive from the beginning."

"I thought we already knew his motive. He wants the

thumb drive back. And I don't know about you, but from what I saw on those files, I don't think the Iceman is into kidnapping for ransom."

"There's a first time for everything. With the kind of wealth your father has, the Iceman could see you as a quick means to a lot of money."

"I disagree. It's not like my father is running around on a reality show, flaunting his wealth. He's a recluse, and he's got an iron grip on his privacy. Most people don't even know Mitchell Cochran exists, let alone that he has a daughter."

"We found out. Who's to say the Iceman doesn't know who you are?"

"It doesn't matter. I don't have anything to do with my father, and he's got nothing to do with me. We might as well not even be related."

"That doesn't mean the Iceman wouldn't try."

"He'd be wasting his time."

"No, he wouldn't. How do you think it would make your father look if he didn't pay a ransom? Recluse or not, Mitchell Cochran's name would be front-page news, and he'd be finished in the business world. No one would have anything more to do with him."

"Don't kid yourself. You saw the animals on those files. That's exactly the type of men my father does business with. Do you think any of those vermin would care what happened to me? If my father decided not to pay a ransom, he wouldn't lose a single deal nor a wink of sleep over it."

"Decided *not* to pay a ransom? Your own father? You can't be serious."

"Oh, yes I can. Don't assume because of my father's wealth, I must have led a fairytale kind of life. I didn't. Money and power are the only things he cares about. Family means nothing to him."

A lump rose in her throat, but she swallowed it back. Perhaps the pain of having a father who cared nothing for her would never fully go away, but she refused to spend any more time feeling sorry for herself, and she certainly didn't want anyone else to, either. Except for Candy, no one in Jessie's acquaintance knew her father's identity or what sort of hellish relationship they had, and that was precisely the way she wanted it.

"You had no right to poke into my private affairs," she seethed.

"Well it's a good thing we did. Why would you keep something like that from me?"

"Because it's none of your business."

"None of my business? I'm trying to protect you. How the hell am I supposed to take care of you if you lie to me?"

"I never asked you to take care of me. And you know what? I don't *need* you to take care of me." She stalked past him and he snagged her arm. "Let go!"

"Where do you think you're going? How long do you think you'll last on your own? He's already been inside your house. He tracked you to the motel and the safe house. You go off on your own and it's only a matter of time until he finds you again. Is that what you want?"

"No. Of course not. But I'm not going to be a prisoner. And I'm not going to stick around while you and your people do whatever the hell you want and hack into my personal life without consulting me. I'm pretty sure I could sue you for that."

He took a deep breath and dropped her arm. Taking a step back, he raised his hands to shoulder height, palms outward. "We were trying to find out who you were because we thought you were working with him. Jake was only doing his job. We all were. It's not like we did it just for the hell of it."

She counted to five, cooling her flaming temper. "Okay, I more or less get that. But no more, do you understand me? No more investigating my background without my permission, and no more making any decisions on my behalf. You talk to me first."

"We'll talk to you, but we'll have to do what we believe, with our experience, is the right—"

"No! Look, I'm frightened by all of this, terrified actually. And that's okay. It's allowed. But I will not be just a useless bystander. That is most definitely *not* allowed. I will not let myself think that way or act that way. Nor will I allow you or anyone in your organization to treat me that way. If you can't agree to that, then I'm leaving. I'm sure you're not the only security outfit in town. I'll hire my own team."

His glare screamed his frustration, but that was just too damn bad. If he thought sleeping with her gave him the upper hand, he had another think coming. Thanks to several years of hard work and careful spending, she had a decent nest egg saved up, and she'd blow every nickel of it on her own security team before giving up one ounce of control.

"Fine," he bit off finally. "We won't do anything without your consent. But it's a two-way street. You have to tell us everything we need to know from now on. You can't hold back information and expect us to be able to operate in the dark. Believe it or not, we do have more experience in this sort of thing than you, especially in the face of a direct threat. So if things get really hot, like it did at the safe house, you need to do what I say when I say."

"Didn't I do that already? You don't have to talk down to me, you know."

"I just want to be sure you understand there may not always be time to discuss every move. You can't stop to question everything. Not when it could cost you your life!"

"Why are you yelling at me?"

"Because you need to understand how dangerous this is!"

"You think I don't?" Her own voice rose. "After all that's happened, you think I don't realize I'm in a boatload of trouble? I'm not stupid, and for your information, you big lummox, I don't have a death wish. If I think it's prudent to follow your instructions, I'll do it."

"That's not good enough."

"It has to be, because I'm not changing my mind. Trust me, you're lucky I'm agreeing to that much."

His phone buzzed in his hand before he could respond. "It's Tobie," he said before answering.

While he spoke to his boss, Jessie used the time to rein in her temper. Reeve had only her well-being in mind, and she had to try to remember that.

"Got it. I'll check in with you again in a little while." He ended the call. "There's good news and bad news," he said, and Jessie was almost afraid to ask.

But she would ask. Fear would no longer dictate her decisions. "Let's hear it."

"The good news is that the media, for the most part, seems to have moved on to another story. There's barely a mention of us today. Just a few local reports that the police are still looking into everything. And they didn't even bother with pictures."

"And the bad news?"

"There's a couple of items in that category. First, one of my partners, Fitz, is back from Phoenix with his report about the Key West alias. Turns out the name Dean King was a stolen identity. The real Dean King is bald and weighs three hundred and forty pounds. He and his wife said they never heard of the Iceman."

"And Fitz believes them?"

"Yeah. Plus, Jake did a full background check on them. No red flags."

"Okay, what's the rest of the bad news?"

"We have to leave here as soon as possible. A local reporter called the office asking to speak to Maddie. After seeing her name in the news yesterday, he said he wanted to do a follow-up on where she's been the last several years. I'm not sure what that's all about, but if reporters are poking around about Maddie for whatever reason already, they'll be showing up here sooner or later. I'm betting on sooner. Not only that, if the media figured it out, the Iceman probably will too. Tobie has secured a new safe house not far from here. We'll meet the rest of the team there and figure out our next move."

Jessie's stomach rumbled, but she ignored it. "Okay. Let's go."

He blinked at her in surprise.

"What? I told you I would do as you asked if I thought it prudent. This move qualifies." She didn't wait for a reply but headed back to the bedroom to collect her tote bag. She picked up his shirt from the floor and tossed it to him when she arrived back in the kitchen, along with the gray baseball cap he'd given her yesterday.

"You can use that. I found this pink one in the closet." She put it on and began tucking her hair up. "Remind me to buy Maddie's cousin a new one when this is all over."

Reeve put on his shirt and pulled the cap down low over his forehead. He gathered up the laptop and slipped it into a carrying case. Reaching into his pocket, he pulled out an enormous roll of cash, peeled off several hundred-dollar bills, and stuffed them into an envelope. He propped the envelope between the salt and pepper shakers on the table.

"That should more than cover the cap and pay for the laptop in the event we don't get to return it. We're only going to be using cash so we don't leave an electronic trail." He handed her a thick stack of hundreds along with a cell phone. "Just on the very remote chance we get separated. Don't use your credit cards or your own phone. Use this one to call our office as soon as you possibly can. It's disposable and can't be traced."

While not exactly gruff, the tone of his voice indicated he was still mad she hadn't told him about her father. *Yeah, well, get over it, tough guy.* But she had to admit she missed the low, sexy rumble that soothed her fears. She crammed the bills in her front pocket, trying very hard not to think about the fact that he'd just handed her a wad of money after a night of sex.

She followed him out to the garage and climbed into the passenger seat. They pulled out to the quiet street, and Reeve muttered a brief curse under his breath.

Jessie's heart pounded. "What is it?"

"Get down. Now."

She obeyed immediately, sliding off the seat and crouching down. "Is it the Iceman? Has he found us?"

He spoke quietly through his teeth, barely moving his lips. "I don't know. There's a red Mustang parked across the street."

Her stomach somersaulted as the hair stood up on the back of her neck. "Officer Fox?"

"I don't know. And he's not a police officer." Reeve turned the car and drove slowly up the street. "There's no one in the car. I can't see the license plate. It's parked too close to the next car." He turned the wheel again, taking them around the corner.

Jessie watched him anxiously as he checked the rearview mirror. "Is he following us?"

"No, not yet. Stay down."

Her heart galloped in her chest, hampering her ability to remain calm.

Two more minutes passed before Reeve spoke again. "You can get up now. We're not being followed."

"Do you think it was him?" she asked as she sat up and fastened her seat belt.

"I don't know, but it really isn't likely. Especially since no one is following us. Probably just a coincidence." He cast another glance in the rearview mirror.

"You don't really believe that, do you?" she asked. He shifted slightly in his seat, confirming her suspicion. "You don't think it's a coincidence."

"I don't like it," he admitted. "But he didn't try to come into the house, and he's definitely not behind us, so if it was him I can't figure out what his plan might be. I'll call Tobie and have her send someone over there to check it out."

While Reeve made the call, Jessie looked through the back window. No red Mustang, but what about the other cars? She scanned the other drivers. Moms in minivans, businesspeople on their morning commute, courier drivers racing along to make their early delivery deadlines. They all looked legitimate.

But so had Fox.

"Could someone else be following us?" she asked Reeve when he hung up.

"Did you see something?" Reeve checked all the mirrors.

"Not really. I'm just paranoid, I guess."

"No, you're not. I don't see a tail, but we'll keep watch."

She resumed her vigil, her pulse hammering any time a car came too close. Images of a window rolling down to reveal the barrel of a gun invaded her mind, coating her heart with a fear so strong she almost shrieked. *Screw it, enough is enough!*

She faced forward in her seat. "Forget the new safe house. Let's go get him."

Fox crouched behind the hedge. A small break in the leaves allowed him to see the driveway of the house the Iceman had ordered him to watch. There'd been no activity all night, and he desperately wanted to leave. His stomach growled, and his need for a bathroom grew more acute by the minute. But the Iceman was already pissed at him, so he didn't dare screw up again. For the millionth time, Fox wished he'd never even heard of the jerk-off.

The garage door opened, and a man in a gray baseball cap retreated back into the darkness a moment before an old Eldorado emerged and headed down the driveway to the street. The rising sun cast a bit of a glare on the windshield, but Fox thought he saw a flash of pink in the passenger seat. As the old car rolled past he saw no sign of pink, only the man. The cap sat low on his head, but Fox still recognized him as the man with the Haynes woman at the hospital.

Cautiously, he stepped out from behind the hedge as the car turned at the end of the street. He should follow, but if he did, they would recognize his Mustang. Reluctantly, he pulled out his cell phone.

"What's going on there?" the Iceman said without preamble.

"Someone just left the house. That same guy helping her at the hospital yesterday."

"And she's still with him?"

"I think so."

"Where are they headed now?"

"It looked like they might be headed for the highway."

"Aren't you following them?"

Fox braced himself. "No."

"Why the hell not? Wait, don't tell me. You didn't get rid of your car, did you?"

"I can't! My father gave me that car. It's the only thing we—"

"Spare me your sentimental sob stories. I'm not interested in hearing about your useless old man." The icy venom in his tone turned Fox's stomach to lead.

"Never mind about that now," the Iceman continued. "Meet me at your office. I'll arrange for you to have another car to use. We'll talk about the Mustang once we get hold of the Haynes woman."

The line went dead. Fox slid into his car and headed for the highway, tossing his cell phone into the first sewer he passed. His shabby little storefront sat in a strip mall a few exits to the north. He took the entrance ramp going south. The Iceman had no intention of "talking" about the car. Fox wouldn't live to see the sun set if he went to his office. He might not be the sharpest tool in the shed, but he wasn't *that* stupid.

New England winters sucked. Maybe it was time to find out what living in Florida might be like. Or he could go west. He'd never been to Arizona or California. At this point, he didn't give a crap where he went.

As long as it was nowhere near his office.

CHAPTER THIRTEEN

Forget the new safe house. Let's go get him.

Did she really just say that? "What are you talking about?"

"Officer Fox, or whatever his name really is. Let's catch him. I'd rather be looking forward than over my shoulder."

Her voice held a level of excitement Reeve didn't particularly like. She was serious about this. "No way. It's too dangerous."

"Didn't you just get through telling me you had lots of experience with this sort of thing? Can't you handle it, or are you one of those guys who just likes to brag?"

He snorted. His time in the SEALs had provided him with several life-threatening experiences. "Honey, you have no idea. *I* can handle it. You're the one without the experience. I can't put you at risk like that."

"You're not putting me anywhere. I'm the one who suggested it."

"No. Tobie will send someone."

"Seriously? This guy is the one connection we've got to the Iceman, and you don't want to go after him? You know what? I think I will get my own security team after all. One that won't waste time. One with some balls."

Okay, that stung a little, mostly because her idea meshed with his own desire. He'd promised the Spencers he'd find their daughter's killer, and now here he was driving away from a tangible lead. By the time the rest of the team got here, Fox would be long gone. No wonder she thought he didn't have any balls.

He drove another few seconds before making up his mind. *Fuck it. Might as well give Tobie another reason to fire me.* "Hang on." He spun the wheel hard and executed a tight U-turn. "Okay, we'll go back and see if he's still there. But under absolutely no condition are you to approach him."

"What if—"

"No! No *what if*s. If you can't give me your word on that, then we don't go back."

"Okay, fine. I won't approach him. But could you hurry it up? If it's him he's probably going to leave soon, if he hasn't already."

"Bossy, bossy."

"Damn straight. I want my life back." Her skin glowed a light pink, whether from anger or excitement he wasn't sure. But he liked the way it looked on her.

His own heart beat a little faster with the thrill of the hunt and maybe, just maybe, with the idea he might be impressing her after the "no balls" remark. Although why impressing her should matter, he didn't want to think about at the moment.

They made the turn back on to Janie's street just in time to see the Mustang turning the corner at the other end.

"Look! He's leaving right after we did. It's got to be him!" Jessie practically cackled with nervous excitement.

"Yeah, I think you're right. That's just one coincidence

too many." He accelerated, the sense of doing the right thing settling over him for the second time that morning.

"How are we going to get him to stop?" Jessie asked.

"We're not. We'll follow him and see if he'll lead us to the Iceman." Putting his phone on speaker, he called Tobie. "Listen, boss, I've got a new lead but I'll need backup. Tell the team to head for the highway. I'm pretty sure we've got a bead on the fake cop who tried to snatch Jessie at the hospital."

A brief silence from Tobie confirmed her displeasure at the change in the arrangements. "Hold on," she said tightly, and they could hear her talking to the others. "Okay, Fitz and Maddie are on their way. What's your plan?"

"We're just going to follow him for now and see where it takes us."

"Can you see his license plate?"

"No. I don't want to get too close. It might spook him. We're coming up on the highway now. He's taking the south-bound ramp."

Tobie relayed this information to the team. Reeve easily kept the bright-red vehicle in sight even while staying several car lengths behind it. A few minutes later, their quarry pulled into a rest area. Reeve followed and parked one row over from the Mustang.

"It's him!" Jessie said as Fox exited his car and headed for the main building almost at a trot.

Reeve got out and stepped one foot onto the floorboard, looking over and then reeling off the Mustang's license plate number to Tobie. "He went inside. I'm going to follow him and see what he's up to. I'll call you right back. Send the team this way."

He hung up before Tobie could object and bent down to speak to Jessie. "Stay here. Keep the doors locked."

"Oh, don't even start. I'm coming with you."

"Jessie, listen—"

"Save your breath. I'm not staying here by myself. Where you go, I go." She unclipped her seat belt and got out.

"Dammit!" Reeve slammed his door and met her at the front of the car. He took her hand in a firm grip. "All right, stay close to me."

They walked into the large gray rectangular building housing the restrooms, a few fast food counters, and a gift shop. As they passed through the glass doors, they spotted Fox hurrying into the men's room. Reeve led Jessie into the gift shop across the hall. Once inside, he steered her through the display racks to a spot just past the window facing the restrooms. "Keep away from the window," he said as he yanked his cap lower on his forehead.

"Okay," she agreed.

Keeping a surreptitious watch on the restroom entrance, Reeve feigned interest in a display of mugs sporting a picture of an American Robin, the state bird of Connecticut if he remembered properly from his Boy Scouts days. He idly picked up one of the mugs, pretending to check the price. A quick glance at Jessie showed her remaining in place, her eyes questioning, and he shook his head slightly.

He put down the mug and fingered the tee shirts on a nearby rack. A minute later, a familiar shape exited the men's room. Reeve waited until Fox passed the window and headed for the exit before motioning to Jessie. "Okay, let's go."

They followed him back outside. As he approached his car, a flashy yellow Jeep whipped into the lot and parked next to the Mustang, nearly rear-ending the car in the next row. Three men in their twenties popped out of the car and started running in Fox's direction. One of them tossed a football toward the other two. "It's the Rest Area Bowl!" he shouted with a laugh.

One of the others jumped up to deftly snag the ball out of the air, but he collided into Fox as he landed, sending both of them to the ground. "Oh, geez! Sorry, dude! I didn't see you." He popped up and reached a hand out to Fox. "You okay, dude?"

"Yeah." Fox accepted the helping hand and got to his feet. He brushed his pants off and looked up, staring straight at Reeve and Jessie. His eyes bugged and he bolted to his car.

"Shit!" Reeve hissed.

"What do we do?"

"Follow him. Hurry!"

They ran to the Eldorado and jumped in. Reeve ignored his seat belt as he started the car and raced out after Fox. He dug in his pocket and tossed his phone to Jessie. "Call my boss. She's on speed dial one. Put it on speaker."

Jessie tapped the screen. Tobie barely had time to speak before he overrode her. "Listen, we're heading south on 95 again. He spotted us."

"Reeve, I want you to stop right now. Fitz and Maddie are northbound and almost to the rest area. They'll turn around and pick up his trail."

"No. We can't afford to lose him. He's the only lead we've got." A blue Honda cut Reeve off, and Jessie squeaked as he swooped onto the left shoulder to avoid a collision.

"Dammit, Reeve! You've got a civilian in the car! I want you to disengage pursuit right now or so help me—"

Jessie turned off the speaker and pressed the phone to her ear. "I'll stay on the line, but if it's all the same to you, I'd rather you weren't yelling at him while he's driving like this."

Reeve barely held back a snort. If Tobie heard him laugh, her already inflamed temper would go through the roof. Hell, his current actions were already tantamount to writing his own pink slip. But he wasn't about to stop pursuit. Not with the prospect of catching Tabitha's killer so close at hand. He would not fail this time.

Fox peeled off the highway at the next exit, leading them into an area of mostly abandoned factories. Jessie relayed their location to Tobie. He could hear his boss's frenzied response before Jessie covered the mouthpiece.

"She says Fitz and Maddie can head him off. Fitz is going to cut him off at the next intersection and force him to turn right. Maddie will block the end of that road. He should have no way out." She pressed the speaker button on the phone. "Tobie's conferencing everyone in."

"Everyone's on," Tobie said.

"I'm in position," Fitz reported. "I see him coming."

"Send that sucker to me. I'm ready," Maddie added.

Fox reached the intersection, and a black SUV charged out in front of him. The Mustang swerved to the right, narrowly avoiding Fitz's front bumper. Fitz accelerated after him, and Jessie hung on for dear life as Reeve hurtled them around the corner. Fox headed straight for Maddie's SUV, the two of them playing a lethal game of chicken. Jessie's heart lodged in her throat, but at the last moment, Fox swung the Mustang to the left, driving into the parking lot of one of the empty factories. Fitz and Reeve followed. Jessie looked back to see Maddie pull up to the entrance and angle her vehicle across it so Fox wouldn't be able to slip out again.

Fox led them down a long row of loading docks toward a wood fence. "What's he doing?" Jessie asked. "There's no exit down there, is there?"

"None that I can see."

"Is he going to try and crash through the fence?"

"Let's hope he's not that stupid."

The words barely passed Reeve's lips when Fox swerved to the left. The Mustang rotated all the way around and started back, Fitz right on his tail. Reeve moved the Eldorado a bit to the left before swinging the wheel hard to the right and slamming on the brakes. The now sideways behemoth Cadillac left no room for Fox to get past. Jessie couldn't fully see around Reeve, and a sickening screech of tires on pavement filled her ears. She braced herself for impact, but Fox managed to stop before hitting them. Fitz closed in behind him, preventing any opportunity for the Mustang to back up.

Fox bolted from his car and ran, but Reeve jumped out and tackled him before he'd gone five yards. Fox fought to shake him off but couldn't gain any advantage. Fitz, a tall man with longish, shaggy blond hair and a matching scruffy beard, got out of the other SUV. He walked over to the two men on the ground and calmly pointed a gun to Fox's head.

Fox immediately ceased his struggles. "Shit, shit, shit!" he muttered.

Jessie slipped out of the Eldorado as Maddie pulled up and got out of her truck.

"Where is the Iceman?" Reeve demanded, hauling Fox to his feet.

"I don't know."

Reeve shook him back and forth. "Don't give me that bullshit! You've been working with him every step of the way! Now where is he?"

Blood drained from Fox's face. "I swear I don't know! He didn't tell me anything except where I should go and what he wanted me to do. That's how he always operates."

"So you've worked with him before? How long have you known him?"

Fox clammed up and Reeve smacked him in the head.

"Hey! You can't do that, that's police brutality!" He looked beseechingly at Fitz and Maddie. "Get him off me!"

"I got news for you, asshole, I'm not with the police. And neither are my friends."

"That's right, nimrod," Maddie added. "If you don't start talking, we might just take over smacking you around when his arm gets tired."

Reeve smiled evilly and raised his hand again.

"All right, all right! Don't hit me! I've known him since we were kids. We were in the same foster home together."

"What's his name?"

"I don't know."

"You just said you grew up with him. How can you not know his name?"

"He was at the foster home first, along with two other foster kids, Cheryl and Frannie. He introduced himself as the Iceman when I got there, and that's all I ever knew to call him. I learned pretty fast not to ask him any questions and just do whatever he said. We all did. It was less painful that way."

"Someone must have called him by his real name. Your foster parents, the social workers."

"I never saw a social worker make a visit for him. Whenever mine bothered to show up, the Iceman made himself scarce. I don't think she had any idea he even lived there. I sure as hell never told her."

"But your foster parents," Maddie chimed in, "they must have said his name."

"Ha! Our foster parents were only interested in the checks they could collect. They fed us, gave us some clothes, and made sure we showed up at school so they wouldn't get any hassles from social services. Other than that, they didn't give a damn about anything but getting high. I could go for days without even seeing them."

"Where did he go to school?" Jessie asked. She looked at Reeve and the rest of the team. "The school would have his records, right?"

"I doubt it," Fox said. "Only me and the other kids went. He never did."

"Oh come on! The social workers didn't know he was at the house? The school didn't notice he never went to class? How stupid do you think we are?" Reeve demanded.

Fox shrugged. "He's always been a genius with a computer. Back then, he hacked into databases just for fun. He manipulated the school records so his absences were never noticed. Mine, too, when he wanted me to play hooky and do something for him."

"Like what?"

"Nuh-uh," Fox said. "I've already told you too much. He made me swear I'd never tell anyone his business. Said he'd kill me if I ever did, and he meant it."

"All right, never mind what shit the two of you pulled when you were kids. Where is he now? Where does he live?"

Fox shrugged. "I don't think he ever stays in one place very long. And he certainly never shares his whereabouts with me. I only see him when he wants something from me."

"Call him. Tell him you need to meet him," Reeve ordered.

"No! I fucked up when I didn't get rid of my car. If he gets anywhere near me, he'll kill me."

"We'll protect you. Help us nail him and you'll be free of him forever."

"You can't help me. He's too smart. No matter what you do, if he wants to get to me he will." Fox nodded his head toward Jessie. "And he'll get to her too. Count on it."

Jessie took a step back as if he'd slapped her, alarm replacing the rapidly evaporating adrenaline rush from the car chase. She'd sort of believed once they caught Fox, they'd find and neutralize the Iceman pretty quickly. Listening to Fox only confirmed she'd been locked into the crosshairs of a clever and relentless madman, and there would be nothing easy about catching him.

"Don't listen to him, Jessie," Reeve said. "The Iceman's not going to get anywhere near you." He faced Fox again. "And if you help us, we won't let him hurt you, either."

"Forget it. I know him. He'd torture me before he killed me. I lived with that psychotic fuck for eight years. You don't want to know what kind of nasty shit I've seen him do. To animals. To the rest of us kids..." Fox's eyes went hazy for a second before he shook his head and looked at them with a desperate expression. "You've got to let me go. If I leave now while he's focused on getting his hands on her, he might forget about my screwup with the car."

"After everything you've just told us, do you really believe that?"

"No, I'm a dead man walking," he muttered thickly. His face crumpled, tears streaming down his cheeks, and Jessie actually felt sorry for him.

Fitz nodded to Maddie, who pulled her own weapon and trained it on Fox. Taking Reeve's arm, Fitz led him toward his SUV, raising an eyebrow as Jessie joined their little huddle.

"It's all right," Reeve said. "Say whatever you have to say in front of her."

"Okay. Look, we need to get out of here. If anyone called

in that car chase, the cops could show up any minute. Let Maddie and me take Fox back to headquarters and see if we can convince him to help us." He reached into the passenger seat, pulling out a plastic shopping bag and thrusting it into Reeve's hands. "Here. We brought you some extra burner phones. Take Miss Haynes to the new safe house like we planned. We'll call you as soon as we know more."

Reeve shook his head and passed the bag to Jessie. "You take her. I want more time with this jerk-off. I'm not buying his sob story. He's no angel in this. Hell, he tried to snatch her at the hospital!"

"Which is exactly why you can't question him. You're too angry to conduct a proper interrogation."

Jessie shoved the bag back to Reeve, taking perverse satisfaction at the woof of air he elicited as it hit his midsection. "Not to mention I'm not going anywhere with someone I've just met."

Reeve glared at her. "You need to go where it's safe."

"Agreed. But I'll be the one deciding where that is, exactly. I'm not going off with someone I don't know." She held his furious stare as her own temper rose. What would it take to get through his thick head that she would call her own shots?

"Jessie, listen, please. You can trust anyone on my team. I promise."

"Wrong. *You* can trust anyone on your team, but at this stage of the game, I'm not giving anyone the benefit of the doubt. So like it or not, I'm sticking with you." She threw a sparing glance at Fitz. "No offense."

"None taken." He shot Reeve a smirky look, and Reeve never felt more like putting his fist in a friend's face.

"Hey!" Maddie called out. "What are you guys doing

over there, reciting the phone book? We've got to get out of here."

"All right, let's go," Reeve grumbled, walking back. "The Eldorado's probably been reported stolen by now. We'll take Fox's car."

"No, wait! You can't!" Fox's tears doubled and they all looked at him as he dropped his chin to his chest. "It's all I have left of my old man," he sobbed. "He couldn't raise me alone after my mom died. I tracked him down when I aged out of the system. He was dying of cancer, but we got to spend some of his last months working on the car together."

Maddie rolled her eyes. "Stop whining. They'll bring it back." She bound his hands with zip ties, stuffed him into the back of her SUV and slammed the door. "What a load of crap. Can you believe the bullshit these guys sling?" she muttered as she stomped around to the front of the car. Without waiting for an answer, she started the vehicle and sped off.

Reeve, Jessie, and Fitz all looked at each other. "I'm not so sure that was bullshit," Fitz said.

"Me, either," Jessie whispered hoarsely.

"Jake will go through his records and find out soon enough," Reeve said. "In the meantime, let's clear out. Fitz, have the Eldorado towed and the roof repaired. When it's ready, we'll drop it off somewhere and leave some cash in the glove box for the owner's trouble."

"You got it. I'll call you if we get anything useful out of Fox." Fitz slid into his SUV and took off after Maddie.

Reeve wiped down the Eldorado for fingerprints before they got into the Mustang. Jessie opened the glove compartment and pulled out the registration. "Let's go check out his house. We might find information about the Iceman. I find it hard to believe they grew up together yet Fox has no idea how to locate him."

He looked at the paper in her hand, that familiar tingle rising up inside him. The one he always felt when he discovered a promising new lead. "Are you sure you weren't a PI in another life?"

She smiled, and his heart melted a little. "I just want to get this finished."

"We can't keep deviating from the plan. It's not fair to the team."

"And I told you before, no plan is final without my say-so. I never agreed to go into hiding, and I'm confident you'll keep me safe. You know your team is going to get around to searching Fox's place sooner or later. Why don't we just go do it now and save time?"

Her ability to zero in on what needed to be done was impressive. No wonder being included in decision-making was so important to her. She would be one of the smartest people in any conversation, and most likely knew it. And her faith in him boosted his bruised ego. She could see him as the professional he was, and that knowledge was like a break in the clouds, reminding him he'd had more successes than failures on his resume.

Knowing he really should take her to the safe house, he hesitated a second longer. Just long enough to realize it might be hours before they got anything useful out of Fox. Who knew what information might be at his residence? Hiding out would yield nothing constructive to the investigation. And he knew himself well enough to know he would be climbing the walls of the safe house in no time. He started the ignition.

"You're right. Let's go."

CHAPTER FOURTEEN

WHERE THE HELL is the little dweeb?

Iceman had arrived quickly and parked his boring gray rental car down the street from the strip mall where Fox kept a two-bit storefront office. None of the other local businesses were open yet, and passing traffic remained light. Iceman anticipated no obstacles to concluding his business here in a swift and, more importantly, unnoticed manner.

That was if Fox ever showed up.

With an impatient sigh, Iceman set his laptop on the passenger seat, opened the lid, and clicked on the vehicle-tracking software. The street map opened up, and the blip for the Mustang flashed red on the screen. Only three blocks away. *It's about time.* As soon as the idiot arrived, he'd follow him inside and then do what had to be done.

Normally, Fox knew better than to keep him waiting, but lately—and quite unexpectedly—the little worm showed signs of independent thinking. That, coupled with Fox's recent and monumental mistakes, made it necessary for him to disappear. Still, he had been a good little foot soldier over the years, despite being a spineless wretch. And they were sort of family. So Iceman would make it quick. It was the least he could do for family.

He screwed the silencer onto his Beretta 92FS.

The Mustang appeared from around the corner and parked in front of Fox's office. *What the hell?* Reeve Buchanan and Jessie Haynes got out of the car.

Damn, damn, damn! If they had his stupid car, they had Fox. Who knew what the idiot had blabbed to these people?

Buchanan entered Fox's storefront while the woman waited at the door. Iceman reached for the door handle, the red haze of his fury demanding he snap Buchanan's neck and seize the woman this instant. His lifelong practice of self-preservation fought the blinding urge and insisted he stop and think.

As far as he could tell, the couple had come here alone, but others from the agency could be right behind them. Plus, the morning traffic grew a little heavier with every minute that passed. Too many potential witnesses, especially since instead of just Fox, he now faced two targets, one of them a former SEAL and trained as a professional bodyguard. No longer the quick in-and-out task he'd anticipated.

Frustration buffeted his normally patient nature. Between Fox and that other moron, Rob Cochran, too many mistakes had been made on this job. He closed his eyes and breathed deeply, regaining his calm after a few moments. Thrumming his fingers on the steering wheel, he assessed the significance of the couple's arrival.

Since they'd come here to check out the office, Fox probably hadn't told them very much of anything. How could he? Iceman never told him more than the bare necessities just so the jerk wouldn't be able to reveal anything useful if questioned. Which meant the couple still didn't know exactly who they were after and had come here looking for answers. Answers they were never going to find.

Perhaps his idiot foster brother had actually done him a favor. He looked over to his laptop, still open to the software that tracked Fox's car, glad now more than ever he'd installed the tracking device on the Mustang a few years ago. That satisfying little red blip blinking on the screen gave him all the advantage he needed. While they chased their tails trying to track him down, he'd be able to follow them from a discreet distance. It would only be a matter of time before the opportunity to get rid of Buchanan and take the woman presented itself.

The woman entered the storefront, and he quickly drove around the corner and parked out of sight.

Nothing to do now but wait.

THEY FOUND the address on Fox's registration with no trouble. It was a small storefront office in a washed-up strip mall that had obviously seen better days. Most of the establishments were vacant, windows soaped up or broken. It appeared a check cashing business and a bodega were still in operation, though neither were open at this early hour.

They approached Fox's shop, a faded sign above the door proclaiming "Sly Fox Private Investigations" with a cartoon picture of a fox wearing a trench coat and fedora. Reeve rolled his eyes. "Really? The mope's a PI?"

"Not a very good one, if this office is any indication," Jessie remarked.

He snorted his agreement and cupped his hands around his eyes as he looked in the window. "Okay, it looks empty, but until I'm sure, you are not to set foot inside. That's nonnegotiable."

"Tell me three more times, why don't you?" The slight touch of humor in her eyes softened her sarcasm. "I said I would wait here, didn't I?"

"And if you see or hear even the slightest thing, you will...?"

"I will run like hell, screaming and yelling at the top of my lungs, and I will call OASIS right away." She waved one of the burner phones at him. "I've got it. Let's do this."

He ignored her impatient tone, recognizing both it and the sarcasm for the bravado they were. She reminded him so much of Ann Marie, a similarity that warmed him yet terrified him at the same time. His sister had never been one to back down from anything. From the time she could walk, she went after any challenge, even ones that filled her with fear. Her determination to be strong sometimes led to foolish behavior.

And it cost her in the end.

He didn't want to lose Jessie like he had Ann Marie. That Jessie exhibited more common sense than Ann Marie ever had was at least a small comfort. Still, he needed to make his message a thousand percent clear and didn't give a rat's ass how often he repeated himself as long as Jessie understood and accepted what she needed to do.

Testing the keys on Fox's key ring, he opened the door on the second try. He pulled out his Glock and stepped inside. The small office offered little in the way of hiding places. A beat-up black metal desk with a duct-tape-spotted office chair on one side and two metal folding chairs on the other took up most of the space. In one corner, a dented brown filing cabinet stood next to a mini refrigerator, and a closed door broke up the small expanse of the back wall.

He walked over and pressed his ear to the paper-thin door. Silence. He tried the knob. It turned easily, and the door opened with a mild squeak, revealing a short hallway.

After a quick glance back at Jessie, Reeve raised his gun and stepped into the hall. Another door on his right opened into a minuscule bathroom. The end of the hallway led to a small area meant for storage, but it was obvious Fox used it as a living space. A single mattress lay directly on the floor, and a skinny closet with its door hanging open on one hinge revealed a few flannel shirts, two pairs of jeans, the phony police uniform, and a pair of generic gray workman's coveralls. A small, ancient television set balanced on a rickety stand at the foot of the bed, and a narrow chest of drawers had been tucked in the corner behind the door.

Satisfied the room held no dark areas concealing the Iceman, Reeve returned to the front entrance. He drew Jessie inside and locked the door. "Okay, you look in the desk drawers while I check the filing cabinet."

They worked in silence for a few minutes. Both the desk and filing cabinet revealed nothing but thin files and a stack of bills, several of them stamped as overdue. "Looks like the only thing he's current on is the insurance for the car," Jessie remarked as she flipped through some of the envelopes.

"Yeah, well, it's hard to keep up with your bills when your few clients don't bother to pay you." He slid the last of the folders back into the cabinet. "It looks like he sent out as many overdue notices as he received. C'mon, let's see if we have more luck in the back."

In the back room, Jessie headed for the closet while Reeve opened the top drawer of the chest. Four pairs of socks and some ratty-looking underwear. He pulled open the next drawer. A rumpled pile of tee shirts concealed a small plastic bag containing weed. The last drawer revealed a stack of porn magazines and a ridiculously ambitious number of condoms. At least the putz believed in practicing safe sex.

"Reeve? I think I found something."

He closed the drawer and joined her. "Look," she said, pointing down toward the back of the closet. "There's a small door in the floor, but it's locked."

Reeve pulled out Fox's key ring and found the right key. The door opened to a small chamber containing a battered metal strongbox. He lifted it out and took it to the desk in the front room. Using the last key on the ring, he opened the box and removed the contents one at a time. A handgun, a lighter with the name *Roger* engraved on it, a few concert ticket stubs, and a large assortment of fake badges and IDs.

"I guess impersonating a police officer isn't the only scam he operates," Jessie said, fingering a gas company ID card bearing Fox's picture.

"I guess not. That must go with the coveralls in the closet."

He picked up a small stack of photographs, the final contents of the box. He flipped through them as Jessie looked over his shoulder, her florally scented hair refreshing in the stale office. The first photograph showed a young couple holding a toddler about three years old. Reeve flipped it over to see the words "Me, Mom, and Dad." The next picture showed an adult Fox standing in front of the Mustang, his arm around an older version of the man in the first picture. Time had not been kind to Fox's father. He was shriveled, bent, and wearing an oxygen mask.

"That must be Roger, the smoker," Jessie said, picking up the lighter.

There were a few more pictures of Fox and his father and the car as well as one of Fox's mother in what must have been her senior year high school portrait. The last photo showed Fox as a boy around twelve years old, standing next to a teenaged boy in front of a decrepit-looking farmhouse, neither of them smiling. In fact, Fox looked as if he might be ready to throw up.

Jessie gasped. "The Iceman."

Reeve looked closer at the teenager. He wore a baseball cap in the photo, hiding his hair, but there was definitely something familiar about the features. "I think you might be right."

"I know I am. Those eyes. I'll never forget them." She shuddered and looked away.

Reeve understood her revulsion. The darkness of the eyes did give the young man a sinister, otherworldly appearance. Fox's nauseous look of discomfort confirmed the story he'd told them earlier. The Iceman's sociopathic and aggressive tendencies had revealed themselves at a very young age.

Reeve studied the rest of the picture. The Iceman stood next to a mailbox, his arm draped casually along the top and his hand dangling a bit over the front. There were numbers and a street name on the box, but Iceman's fingers blocked most of the address. Reeve could make out a 4 and the letters i-e-w. Not enough to identify the location of the house.

Reeve shoved the contents back into the box and then tucked it under his arm. Outside, the enticing aroma of coffee filled his nostrils as he locked the door to the storefront. The lights were on in the bodega, and the parking lot had a few trucks parked there now as early-morning laborers stopped for their wakeup shot of joe.

He took Jessie's arm and steered her into the bodega. As he'd suspected, the establishment also specialized in hot breakfast sandwiches. They placed an order for way too much food and took it back to the car.

Jessie unwrapped her big, drippy bacon, egg, and cheese sandwich and took a bite. Reeve forgot all about his own food as he watched her close her eyes and chew with a rapturous expression on her face. She swallowed and then opened her eyes and poked around in the bag for a home fry. She ate one, licking the salt off her fingers and ratcheting his heart rate up another few notches. Her eyes met his, and she flushed a little.

"I normally don't eat stuff like this, but every once in a while it's just so damn good."

He laughed as she took another big bite, obviously relishing it as much as the first. She opened her eyes again and nodded at him. "You better eat before I devour it all."

"Not likely," he said as he unwrapped his own sandwich. "We ordered enough to clog the arteries of ten people."

"Today, I really don't give a damn. With everything else that's going on right now, I refuse to worry about cholesterol or calorie counting."

"Works for me. Besides, I can definitely attest you've got nothing to worry about as far as counting calories goes." The words were out before he thought to censor them. But he couldn't help it. With aching clarity, he remembered the feel of her silken contours in the dark as he'd explored every inch of her. She was deliciously curvy, but there wasn't an ounce of unnecessary fat on her.

Her skin grew pink but she met his gaze with darkening eyes. Heat simmered in the small confines of the car, and he knew it wouldn't take much to push them both into a passionate frenzy in the back of the Mustang.

His phone rang, breaking the spell. Fitz calling as promised. "Hey. Any luck getting information out of Fox?"

"No. He just keeps telling us the Iceman is a master computer hacker and not even the Witness Security Program would be able to protect him. He's certain the Iceman will track him down. Nothing we say otherwise is getting through."

"Friggin' dirtbag."

"I don't think that's it. Not entirely, anyway. The guy's paler than a coal miner and shakes all the time, but it's not us he's scared of. At least, not as much as he's scared of the Iceman."

"Damn. Keep working on him. He's got to know something we can use."

"Yeah, we'll keep at it."

"Has Jake come up with anything?"

"Yeah. Jake hacked into the foster care system. There's a record of Fox being placed with a childless couple named Berger. Two other children were fostered there as well, both of them girls about the same age as Fox. But that's it. So if the Iceman was placed with the Bergers too, someone deleted the records. Unless Fox is lying about the whole thing, and that's not how he knows the Iceman."

"No, I don't think he is. We're at his office right now and we found a picture of him with another kid in front of an old house. It's the Iceman."

"Are you sure?"

"Yeah, no doubt about it. I can read a partial address on the mailbox in the picture. But I have no idea what town or state."

"Hang on a second." Reeve heard Fitz shuffling some papers. "Okay, the last known address for the Bergers is 41 Oldview Road, Sandy Hollow, Maine. There's no record of them having any other foster children besides Fox and the two girls he mentioned. But Jake looked into the utility bills. All are current and still in the Bergers' name."

"They're still there? Great. Maybe they can help us. I don't care what Fox said. Junkies or not, they must have been given the Iceman's real name when they took him in. I'm going to head up there right now."

"Do you think it's a good idea for you to go? I mean with Ms. Haynes in tow? Tobie won't like it. Let's send Maddie while you take Ms. Haynes to the safe house."

"No, Maddie needs to stay in the office and rest that shoulder. Besides, this takes out two birds. I can track down a lead and get Jessie out of sight like Tobie wants."

"Yeah, all right. I'll let Tobie know. Check in as soon as you get there."

Reeve disconnected and met Jessie's expectant stare. "I've got the address where Fox and the Iceman grew up."

"Really? So fast?"

"Yeah. I've got the foster parents' name too. Want to go see if they know where to find that scumbag?"

"Absolutely. Let's go."

They finished eating and hit the road. "Do you think they'll tell us anything?" she asked.

"We won't know until we get there."

"Can we threaten them with anything? Tell them we'll report the abuse Fox suffered from the Iceman because they weren't looking out for him?"

"We could, but I doubt that will make a difference. After all this time, it would be very hard to prove, and they probably know that. We'd be better off threatening them about the drug use, assuming they're still using."

"How long will it take us to get there?"

"About six or seven hours."

"That long?"

"Afraid so. There aren't really any shortcuts."

She slumped in her seat. "You're right. But the delay is killing me. I just want it over."

"You and me both."

As much as she wanted to pretend otherwise, the finality with which he uttered the phrase hurt a little. Was he that anxious to be rid of her? Maybe she hadn't made his job easier with her demand to approve of all decisions, but just now, when he'd asked her instead of ordered her to go on this road trip, she'd thought they'd turned a corner.

Guess not. For all she knew, he still chafed at letting her have any say in the proceedings and looked forward to his next case, where he could call all the shots.

She tried to keep in mind this whole thing couldn't be much fun for him, either. From the few conversations she'd overheard, it sounded like Reeve and his boss weren't exactly getting along. Worse, with Tabitha Spencer's murder weighing on his mind, Jessie had no doubt he'd rather be going after the Iceman full bore without having to worry about her safety.

The feeling of being a burden rankled like a pebble in a shoe. If she was holding him back, how could she expect him to like being with her? Out of bed, that was. He'd definitely liked being with her in the sack. Typical guy.

Geez, could she be any more high school drama queen?

She shook her head. When all this was over, she'd take a long hard look at herself. Hadn't she always been the one who wanted no bond with men outside of sex? Maybe she needed to reevaluate her stance on relationships, or maybe she just needed to realize all these recent cocktails of terror spiked with adrenaline were making her crazy. Whichever it might be, she couldn't let it rule her thinking. She needed to thicken her skin and stop reading so much into everything he said.

Surprisingly, she managed to catch some sleep during the uneventful drive to Maine. When she woke, she offered to take the wheel again so Reeve could grab a nap, but he insisted he was fine. He did look more rested than last time, so she didn't push it.

Just outside of Sandy Hollow, they pulled into the lot of a small diner refashioned from an old railroad dining car and painted a cheery red. Gold cursive lettering spelled out "Betsy's Down East Diner" underneath the black-framed windows lining the upper half of the car.

"Hungry again?" Jessie asked.

"Not really. But this looks like the kind of place where the locals hang out. I want to see if we can find out a little information about the Bergers before we head to the house. If they have a propensity toward violence, I'd like to know that before we get there."

Her spirits plummeted as she unbuckled her seat belt and got out. Why had she been so naïve as to assume questioning known drug users would be simple?

With a deep breath, she followed Reeve to the entrance, shrugging into his denim jacket once again. Maybe Lady Luck would smile on them, and they'd discover the Bergers had kicked their drug habit. Having mended their ways, they'd be happy to share whatever information they could. She walked past Reeve as he held the door and wondered why she persisted in kidding herself.

From the moment the Iceman had approached Jessie in Key West, Lady Luck had left the building.

HE GLIDED UP THE HIGHWAY, humming to himself. Thanks to the happy little blip on his laptop, things were back on track. Buchanan and the woman cruised up the interstate, the stretches of sparsely populated areas growing longer and longer as they all headed north. They were making it easy for him. He'd have the Haynes woman in his possession in no time.

His phone beeped and flashed Rob Cochran's name. He debated not answering but then thought better of it. Until he was safely out of the country, he still might need the little maggot for his connections. He grabbed the phone from the console. "I told you to wait for my call."

"I didn't want to wait. I thought I'd find you at Candy's. What's going on? Have you taken Judith yet?"

"No, but it won't be long now."

"Where is she?"

"She and the bodyguard are heading north on I95."

"Where are they going?"

"Why do you ask?" Rob's incessant questions were growing tiresome.

"Because I want to be there when it goes down. I want to see that this gets done right."

Iceman's temper flared, but he clamped down on it quickly. Maybe it wouldn't be a bad idea for him to meet up with Rob. The man's irrationality intensified by the second, and irrational people could not be trusted. Perhaps the time had come to eliminate him altogether after all, and screw his stupid connections.

"I don't know where they're going exactly, but I've got a tracker on their car, so I'm following them and will know exactly where they wind up. You're not far behind. Start heading north if you want. I'll call you if we change highways or reach a final destination." He ended the call without waiting for a response. It would be better if Rob thought he didn't give a damn whether he showed up or not.

A muffled thumping sounded from the trunk, and he chuckled quietly. It seemed his guest had woken up. Tightly bound and gagged, she could thump around all she wanted. Her fruitless struggles amused him.

He hadn't originally planned on taking another woman, but adaptability accounted for a large portion of his successes. He'd need the woman in the trunk to make his plan work. And once he had the tantalizing Miss Haynes in his possession as well, he'd have some fun with both of them before selling them off.

Pleased with his new plans, he resumed his happy humming as the miles flew past. His guest gave a few more mild thuds before releasing a barely audible groan of frustration.

He laughed out loud.

CHAPTER FIFTEEN

THE HOMEY SCENT of meatloaf and gravy greeted them as they walked in the diner. A line of booths took up the wall opposite the long counter. A few old men sat in one of the booths, two of them playing chess as the others looked on. At the counter, silver swivel stools with red vinyl seats happily beckoned, and Reeve and Jessie accepted their invitation.

A waitress approached, sliding a cup of coffee in front of each of them. "Here. You two look like you could use this. It's on the house, assuming you're going to order some food."

"Thanks," Reeve said. "We'll take half a dozen of those," he added, nodding to a large cake stand piled high with frosted doughnuts.

She sacked up the order and placed the bag by Reeve's cup before pulling out a pad and writing up the bill. Reeve pulled out his wallet and smiled at her. "By the way, we're hoping you can help us with something. Do you know the Bergers? They live on Oldview Road."

"You mean up at that old farm?"

"Yes, that's them."

"Sweetie, nobody's seen them in years. They cleared out a long time ago. Took those lousy foster kids with them too."

"You knew the foster kids?"

She leaned her ample hip against the side of the counter, all ready to give them an earful. "The Bergers were junkie trash, but they kept to themselves. High as a kite most of the time. Those kids they took in were nothing but bad news." She sighed. "I shouldn't think ill of the younger ones, I guess. But there was an older kid, and you could see they were scared to death of him. He was always nearby whenever the younger ones were doing something like egging the principal's house, or stealing from the church collection box. But he was smart enough not to do it himself, and those kids would have cut off their own arms rather than rat him out. He was a creepy, nasty little mongrel, and most folks around here gave him a wide berth. Still do whenever he shows up."

Reeve jerked back. "Shows up? You mean he still comes around here?"

"Not too often, but yeah, sometimes. None of the local kids will go near that house. They think he haunts the place." She shuddered. "Can't blame 'em, really. He looks like a damn ghost with all that white hair."

"Do you know his name?"

"Nobody ever asked him, far as I know."

"When's the last time you saw him?"

She tilted her head and stared out the window, obviously wanting to get it right. "It had to be about a year ago."

"It was ten months ago," one of the old men called from the booth. "Ayuh, I remember because it was my granddaughter's birthday, and he passed me and the missus on the road when we were driving over to Sally's party. Why do you want to know all this anyway?" he asked.

"We're conducting a private investigation, so I can't tell you anything other than he's a part of it. But when we find him, we plan to turn him over to the police."

The man fell silent and the waitress's expression went from friendly to frightened to shuttered in the blink of an eye. "I thought you were looking for the Bergers. I didn't know you were after him. We don't want any trouble around here. We ignore him and he ignores us. We'd like it to stay that way. What if he finds out we told you anything? Wouldn't put it past him to set a torch to this place, or worse," she said.

"He wouldn't hear it from us. We want to see him in prison for the rest of his life."

She folded her arms across her ample bosom, pressing her lips so tightly together they practically disappeared. The old man got up and shuffled toward the counter, extending his hand to Reeve. "I'm Morton Green. Used to be the deputy chief of police around here. That wily punk was a pain in my ass back in the day. Evil as the day is long. Never could pin anything on him, though. Like Betsy here told you, he got the other kids to do all his dirty work."

He released Reeve's hand and gave him a long, piercing look. "No, you ain't regular law, but you've been in the service, haven't you? And you strike me as a decent guy. If you think you can rid us of that poor excuse for a human, I ain't afraid to help you." He pulled a napkin from one of the shiny silver dispensers on the counter. "Betsy, gimme a pen."

She hesitated a second but then handed him a pen from her apron pocket. Green scribbled down a crude map. "You go two miles west of here and then turn left on the county road. Then you take the third right onto Oldview Road. It's not marked and there's a ton of weeds and overgrowth, so you really have to watch for it. And take it slow with that Mustang of yours. That road ain't paved and is as rocky as they come."

He slid the napkin across the counter and looked at the clock hanging above the swinging doors to the kitchen. "You guys ain't back here in an hour, I'm gonna call my friends over at the Sandy Hollow PD's office and have them send someone over there to check on you."

"That won't be necessary."

"I ain't asking you, sonny, I'm telling you. You look like you can handle yourself, but that little pissant was hellish enough when he was a teenager. I can only assume he's gotten worse as he's gotten older. The only reason I ain't sending someone from the police department's office with you now is I figure you've got the element of surprise on your side. But if he's in the neighborhood, that won't last long. So you've got an hour. If you're able to get rid of him, one way or another, none of us will lose any sleep over it. In fact, you'd be doing this little town a favor. But I *would* lose sleep if I sent you up there and you never came back and he still walked around here like he was king shit. One hour. Take it or leave it."

"We'll take it." Reeve tossed some money on the counter and took Jessie's hand. "Let's go."

"That was weird," Jessie remarked as they buckled up and headed west.

"Yes and no. I'm guessing Green knows the Iceman is a menace to everyone here whenever he shows up."

"But if girls keep disappearing whenever he's around, wouldn't they have arrested him by now?"

"I doubt he takes anyone from here for that very reason. If a lot of local girls went missing, he'd be the first suspect. I can't imagine he'd invite that kind of scrutiny. Green might not know about the kidnappings and auctions, but I think he knows the Iceman is most likely a sociopath, and just because he hasn't hurt anyone here so far doesn't mean he won't. You saw how afraid of him they all were. You heard what Green said. Hell, he just about begged me to execute the Iceman."

"Could you do something like that?"

Reeve didn't answer right away. A couple of weeks ago, he would have said no. But a couple of weeks ago he hadn't seen those auctions, hadn't seen Tabitha Spencer tossed away like so much trash. Maybe the world would be better served all around if he could just put a bullet through that sicko's brain.

"Reeve?"

"I don't know. I've always known I could kill a man if he threatens my life or someone else's. I'm a firm believer in self-defense. When I was deployed, I killed eight men. I'm not proud of it or happy about it, but that was war, and they were firing on me and my men. But here in the real world? All I can say is I've never been tempted to kill someone I know is a murderer and a threat to society. I've always been content to let the courts handle it. Until now."

"Meaning?"

"Meaning this son of a bitch is pure evil. Has been for years. Since birth, probably. What if he gets off on a technicality? Or some bleeding heart parole board lets him out in a couple of years? There's no rehabilitating this guy. He'd be back at his old tricks in no time. How could I live with myself?"

"So you would be judge, jury, and executioner?"

"Maybe. I've never wanted to be a vigilante, but for the Iceman, I might make an exception."

They made their first turn before she responded. "I can't say I agree with you. But in all honesty? After what I've seen him do? I can't say I disagree, either."

Silence fell between them as they drove along, looking for their turnoff. Green hadn't been kidding about the road. Reeve nearly missed it amid the thick growth of weeds and wildflowers.

Spindly trees grew along either side, forming a dismal canopy over a dirt path rutted with rocks and potholes. He could only imagine what it must have felt like to those kids as they came home along this road. A road with ghostly shadows that led to a home dominated by a real-life monster. Reeve's own childhood had been far from perfect, but at least he hadn't spent it living in abject fear and misery. Fox's paranoia made much more sense now.

They found the house, and it didn't look all that dissimilar from the picture. The windows were dark, and an air of abandonment permeated the place. Yet an invisible and distinctly sinister miasma clung to the property. Reeve could almost feel the dread and despair that must have haunted Fox and his fellow foster children.

He parked the Mustang near the mailbox. Removing his Glock from his waistband, he confirmed he had a fully loaded magazine. He carefully scanned every inch of the property he could see.

Jessie sat stock-still in her seat, her arms wrapped tightly around her middle as she glanced about the property. "Do you think he's here?"

The tremor in her voice tugged at his heart. She felt it too, the evil misting about the house, and it scared her as much as it made him uncomfortable. There was just something off about this place.

"No," he answered. "But he's proven to be a wily bastard,

so it just makes sense to be prepared." Jessie remained motionless in her seat. "You can stay here, if you'd rather."

She shook her head as if clearing it from a trance. "No. This is not a place I want to be alone. At all. I'd feel safer going with you."

Manly pride surged through him, further bolstering his battered self-esteem. He took her hand and gave it a reassuring squeeze. Her fingers were ice-cold and trembling.

"I know Betsy and Morton said the Bergers are gone," she said, "but why does it feel like someone's here? Like *he's* here?"

"I don't know. Some people believe houses hold on to their old ghosts. This one certainly appears to. But ghosts are made of nothing but mist. They can't hurt you." He kissed her freezing fingertips before getting out.

"Stay behind me and stay close," he said as she joined him. She nodded, slipping her shaky fingers inside the back of his waistband as he moved ahead. He walked slowly, keeping the Glock in front of him as he kept a careful eye on either side of the path leading up to the rickety steps that stuttered up to the equally rickety front porch.

Sunlight filtered through the leaves, casting dappled shadows on the porch, reinforcing the eerie feeling of the place. No lights shone from inside, and all the windows were shut. No telltale hum of an air conditioner or generator filled the air, further convincing him no one lived here. Disappointment swallowed him. It was one thing to hear the folks at the diner say the Bergers were gone and another to have it confirmed. "Shit."

"So what should we do? Can we get out of here now?"

"Not yet. I want to look inside. There still might be something useful."

Her eyes widened into jade circles of dismay. "Inside? Really?"

"You can go back to the car. I won't be long."

"No. I'll go with you. But let's hurry. I can't take much more of this place."

A large, rusty doorbell jutted from the wall beneath a laminated sign proclaiming *No solicitors! Just turn around and take your sorry ass and your sorry products with you. That includes all you pint-sized cookie-sellers and freeloading donation-seekers. You have been warned.*

Reeve ignored the notice and pressed the button. A sickly voice came from a hidden speaker. "I guess you're a moron who can't read. Now you're going to be a dead moron."

A spark flashed from the doorbell. Reeve whirled around and yanked Jessie from the porch at a full run. They barely cleared the bottom step when an enormous explosion pelted them forward, and they hit the ground hard.

Heat roared across his back. He dragged Jessie closer and shoved her beneath him as burning debris showered down around them. An ancient washing machine landed two feet from where they lay. Reeve tucked her tighter beneath him, covered his head with his arms, and prayed they wouldn't be crushed by a refrigerator or something.

A moment passed, maybe two. A few bits of debris hit his back, and something that might have been a toaster bounced painfully off his arms before the missile shower of rubble came to an end. He lifted his head and looked over his shoulder. A ferocious inferno completely engulfed what was left of the house, and the hungry flames spread quickly as they tasted the dry, waist high weeds surrounding what used to be the front porch.

"Jessie!" he gasped as he rolled off of her, the acrid smoke searing his throat. "Get up! We have to move. Now!"

She pushed feebly at the ground, and his breath locked in his chest. His eyes raked her from top to bottom, unable to see an injury. She lifted her head, and he rolled her over. The muscles in her neck contracted as she tried vainly to draw air into her lungs. He helped her to a sitting position. "Okay," he rasped, looking into her panic-filled eyes. "Try to relax and take a breath. Use your stomach."

She strained a moment more before finally drawing in some air. She coughed violently as she inhaled some smoke too. He hauled her to her feet. "Let's go." With his arm wrapped firmly around her waist, they hurried back to the Mustang. Ignoring his own racking coughs, he jammed the gear shift into Reverse and backed down the rocky dirt path as quickly as he dared without breaking an axle. Once they reached the paved road, he shifted to Drive and raced back toward the main road. He stopped at the intersection. "Are you all right? Do you need a doctor?"

"No," she spit out between a last few sputtery coughs. "I just had the wind knocked out of me. I'm okay."

"Are you sure? Did you hit your head?"

He ran one hand over her scalp, feeling for any kind of bump or laceration. She pulled her head away. "I told you I'm fine."

He nodded and turned the wheel, taking them away from the town.

"Shouldn't we report the fire?" Jessie asked.

"Not necessary. I'm sure our friend Morton Green heard the explosion, along with everyone else in town. I guarantee you, the local firefighters are on their way." The words had no sooner left his lips when a siren shrieked in the distance.

A quick glance in the rearview mirror showed several red flashing lights racing toward Oldview Road.

"But shouldn't we tell them the place was rigged? What if there's another bomb?"

"We can't stay here. There's nothing to stop them from thinking we were the ones who set the explosion. I doubt there's another bomb. There's nothing left to blow up. But I'll have Tobie get in touch and tell them about it."

He called the office and relayed what happened. "I'll call again when we settle in for the night," he told his boss.

"Okay, so now what?" Jessie asked. "Other than confirming Fox's story, this trip hasn't yielded anything beyond a near-death experience."

The irritation in her voice echoed his own sentiment. What the fuck *were* they going to do now? Unless Jake could find something useful in the foster care database, they were back to square one.

"Who does that, anyway?" Jessie went on. "Rig a house to blow up a salesman? Or a kid selling cookies?"

"With his warped mind? He probably did it just for kicks."

"That doesn't sound like him. And now that I think about it, the whole thing seems like a scam."

"What do you mean?"

"Well, all those people at the diner said how they and everybody else in town had no use for the Bergers, or the kids. And they were all afraid of the Iceman."

"Right. So?"

"So none of the locals were going to go ringing that bell. As for salesmen? You saw what the place looked like. What salesman in his right mind would waste time calling on that house? And I don't doubt for a second the Iceman knew all of this. He didn't care about solicitation. He wanted to make sure people like us, people who might actually be looking for *him*, didn't get into that house. He's hiding something there."

Although now impossible to verify, her theory made a lot of sense. Hot damn, but she had some set of smarts on her. "What do you think he might have been hiding?"

"Don't nut-jobs like him keep trophies of their atrocities? Could be he stored them here, and that's why he comes back every now and then. To visit his sick mementos."

"Serial killers keep mementos, but we don't know that he is one. So far, we only know he's a sadist."

"What do you think happens to all those girls when the Iceman and his friends are finished with them? You think they just let them walk away?"

"No. I'd bet the bastard either sells them off to someone else or kills them. Probably some combination of both."

"And how many girls were on those videos? Dozens at least. Sounds like he's a serial killer to me."

"You're probably right. But serial killers usually keep their trophies closer to them, so they can look at them and relive their twisted fantasies whenever they want. From what Green and Betsy told us, he doesn't come around here that often."

"Since when has anything he's done so far been *usual*?"

He nodded. "Good point. And it's possible the house contained some concrete information about his true identity. We know he doesn't want anyone getting their hands on that."

"Well, whatever it may have been, it's blown to smithereens now."

They fell into a frustrated silence. The Mustang ate up the miles as Reeve hurried to put lots of distance between them and Sandy Hollow. Local law enforcement would all too easily connect them to the gunfight in front of Jessie's house. He couldn't risk them being detained.

His aggravation grew as the miles rolled away. For most of the day, he'd felt as if he were so close to catching Tabitha's killer. Now, he and the team were going to have to start all over again. Worse, with no other leads to follow, he had no choice but to take Jessie and keep her hidden.

He stifled a sigh, not wanting Jessie to pick up on his exasperation. Hiding out would piss her off, not that he could blame her. Sitting still while others did the heavy lifting wasn't at all how he liked to do things, but he'd find a way to deal with it.

Hell, he'd glue his ass to the sidelines before he let another woman die on his watch.

CHAPTER SIXTEEN

"So where are we going now?" Jessie asked when the silence in the car got on her nerves.

"There's a bunch of small towns along the coast of Maine. We'll find a motel and get some rest while we figure out our next move."

"I've been thinking about that. We should go back to Candlewood. I could go back to my house, make it easier for him to find me. Then we can trap him."

"You want to set yourself up as *bait*? Absolutely not."

"But—"

"Look, I admire your courage, but you have no idea how hairy something like that could be. If we are going to activate that kind of plan, we'll disguise Maddie or Tobie to look like you."

"Won't that put them in harm's way? He's already hurt two members of your team, including Maddie." Guilt seeped into her bones at the thought of those who had already been injured on her behalf. "Using them as bait isn't right. I'm the one he wants. Why shouldn't it be me?"

"First of all, this is our job. It's what we're paid to do. Second, we all have extensive training."

"Hmph. How much training do you need to be bait?"

"A lot more than you think. Let's not forget who we're talking about here. You've already seen how lethal he can be."

"Agreed, but let's also not forget I got away from him once already. I can do it again."

"Do you really think he'd underestimate you a second time? Of course he won't. And he knows you're not alone in this anymore, so he'd be suspicious of a trap. If he even went for it, which is a long shot, he'd do some kind of a blitz attack on you. Something up close and personal. I'm willing to bet our self-defense skills are a lot more developed than yours."

"But if we work out a plan with your team, I'll be safe. I won't do anything stupid or take a foolish chance. I promise I'll follow—"

"No. It's not going to happen. And it's not just me saying that. No one at OASIS will agree to it either."

"Reeve, I can't let him drive me into some hidey hole. I have to do *something*. Why can't you understand that?"

"I do. Honestly, I do. But why can't you understand there are other avenues to explore that don't require you being bait?"

"Such as?"

He gave her a brief glance before focusing back on the road. His thumbs beat a lively tattoo on the steering wheel as the strong set of his jaw with its sexy little scar grew tight. Foreboding filled her. She wasn't going to like whatever he had in mind.

"I hate to bring up a sore subject, but I need to know more about your issues with your father. I know you don't think he's involved, but we need to explore every probable angle."

"You can't be serious! Not that again."

"Look, you said you wanted to be involved. Unless Fox starts talking, our one and only good lead just got blown sky high. Crappy as it is, we have to start over, and this is an angle the agency needs to investigate. Do you want to help or let us do it ourselves?"

Irritation and resignation warred within her. She avoided the topic of her father at all costs, but Reeve was right. They were at a dead end and would have to explore all possibilities. "How much do you know about me already?" she sighed.

He gave her a nervous glance, then turned his eyes back on the road. *Crap.* If he was this uncomfortable speaking about it, their investigation into her background must have gone deep. Very deep. "Go ahead. Spill it."

He sighed before speaking. "Okay. Your real name is Judith Margaret Cochran. You're twenty-nine years old, birthday May twenty-first. You were raised in Greenwich, Connecticut and went to Notre Dame University, where you graduated summa cum laude, seventh in your class.

"Your father, Mitchell Cochran, age fifty-one, is the fourth-richest man in Connecticut, the ninth-richest in the United States. He's a self-made billionaire who first struck it big in the financial industry and has since branched out to several other endeavors, such as the electronics and phar- maceutical industries. He's a full-fledged recluse. He never gives interviews and has somehow managed to avoid being publicly photographed in over thirty years—that alone is a pretty amazing statistic in this day and age. Your mother, Elizabeth Mannion, married your father when she was eighteen years old. She died in a boating accident at age thirty-seven, right after you graduated high school."

He paused and a lump rose in her throat while tears burned the back of her eyes. "Go on," she said hoarsely. She needed to hear what else he knew. "Please. Say it all."

"Your father remarried two months after your mother's death, to a woman named Kim Rottenger, now aged thirty-nine. You gained a stepbrother, Rob, from that marriage. Rob, age twenty-three, still works with your father while you, his only daughter—his only blood relative as far as we can tell—appear to have no contact with him whatsoever."

Her hands shook, and bile rose in her throat. She'd worked so hard to put that life in her rearview mirror, and Reeve spouted it all off as if it were nothing. Of course, to him those were all facts, just dry bits of data. Which they were, and one hundred percent accurate. But mere facts didn't truly convey the sinister reality of living in Mitchell Cochran's house, and Reeve would ask about that next. She wasn't ready. "How did you find all that out?" she croaked, stalling for time.

"You may have changed your name, but you didn't change your Social Security number. Once Jake had that, he was able to find out just about anything he wanted to know about you."

"I didn't think I would need to change it," she muttered dully. "As you've discovered, my father has always kept his private life extremely private. I mean, even his so-called 'public' persona isn't well-known by the masses. Very few of the bigwigs in the finance world are widely known. Since just about no one outside of my father's inner circle even knew I existed, I figured changing my name would be enough. It's not like I wanted to conceal a criminal past."

"For most people, just changing their name would be

enough. But you are the daughter of an exceedingly rich and powerful man. That makes you a target."

"So you're back to thinking the Iceman wants to ransom me? I thought we agreed he's targeting me because he wants his thumb drive back."

"That's a possibility. Hell, maybe that's all it was about when he slipped it into your bag. But why was he in Key West when you were, and why did he slip it into *your* bag in the first place? Random? Possible, but I don't think so. But even if that were the case, we'd be foolish to assume the only information he hacked from your business card was your address. He probably knows as much about you by now as we do."

The thought turned her stomach, and the fact that it made sense didn't help. "It doesn't matter. Like I told you before, he'd be wasting his time trying to ransom me."

"I find it hard to believe a father would abandon his child to a monster like that, no matter what they disagreed about."

"Mine would."

"So you've said, but I need to know why. I can't keep working in the dark."

The truth of his statement broke through her reluctance. Reeve needed to know everything, if for no other reason than to be able to do his job effectively. He couldn't rule out a connection to her father if he didn't know the truth. Her knee bobbed up and down like a jackhammer. She'd rather chew barbed wire than discuss anything about the man who'd been nothing but a tyrant for as long as she'd known him, but she'd have to get through it.

She took a deep breath. "My father is a control freak."

"So are a lot of people."

"That's true, but my father takes it to the extreme. As far

as he's concerned, he's the only one who can make decisions. No one else is allowed to even have an opinion."

"Not that I'm saying it's right, but a lot of successful men are like that. It's very cutthroat in the world of business."

"Also true, but he's like that in all aspects of his life, not just the business arena. He's incapable of loving or caring for anyone." Her vision blurred as tears threatened to fall, but she hurriedly blinked them away. She would *not* shed one more tear over her miserable childhood. "My mother and I were just pawns to be used in his never-ending quest to make the next big deal."

"How so?"

"He met Mom when she was very young. He wined her, dined her, and basically swept her off her feet. They had a storybook wedding. But it turned out he only married her because she was the daughter of a wealthy business associate. He used the marriage to gain the trust of his new father-in-law. He got himself a spot on the board of directors of the family's investment company and quickly managed to take over. According to my mother, losing the company ruined my grandfather. He lost most of his fortune and his health began a long downward spiral."

"That must have made your mother angry."

"She didn't know about it at the time. When they were first married and up until a few years after I came along, my father treated my mother and me fairly well. She didn't notice that over time he'd slowly isolated her from her family and friends. When my grandfather was in his final days, he sent a note, asking to see his daughter. My father refused to allow it. He hired"—she raised her fingers to air quote—"*bodyguards* who were nothing more than prison wardens. Mom couldn't go anywhere without one of those men in tow, and they reported her every move back to my father.

"But Mom wasn't so easily put off. She started a small fire in the kitchen and managed to slip away in the ensuing chaos. My grandfather told her everything. She came back to the mansion determined to get me and go back to her family. My father was furious she'd defied him. He told her if she tried to leave and take me away, he'd see to it that she never saw me again. He pulled out a stack of affidavits signed by men swearing my mother had been sleeping with them all, sometimes in front of me. He had records from doctors, swearing she was addicted to painkillers and was therefore an unfit mother. He even threatened to have her committed, and he'd bought off plenty of doctors who would back him up."

"Un-friggin-believable."

"Yeah, I know. Mom was terrified. After that, his gloves were off. He didn't even pretend to be nice to her anymore. Not a day went by that he didn't belittle her in some way. She tried to keep it all from me, but as I got older I could figure out what the words meant, the dreadful things he would say to her. And cosmetics can only cover so much. I saw the bruises."

"Did he hit you too?" he growled, low and deep.

"No. Mom kept me out of his path most of the time, and I did my best to behave as he wanted. Never made any mischief at school, always got good grades. As long as I didn't make any waves, he barely seemed to notice me. He focused all his venom on my mother. And for her sake, I was petrified. I wanted to confide in a counselor at school or something, but I couldn't. I thought he'd kill her. Not that it made a difference."

"What do you mean?"

She wrapped her arms around her middle, but it failed to ward off the familiar cold feeling of despair that enshrouded her whenever she thought about her mother.

"When I was eighteen, my father took Mom out on his yacht. She never came back. The authorities barely even looked into it—something I'm certain my father had a hand in—and they declared her death an accident. I never believed it, especially since he remarried so soon."

"I'm surprised you didn't run away."

"I wanted to, but the day my mother died, my father shifted all those so-called bodyguards to me. Those men scared me. And Kim was nice to me. I missed my own mother so much and I had no one else, so I clung to her. In a very short time, she came to mean a great deal to me. My father knew it. The day I left for college, he took me aside and told me that if I even thought of trying to run away, he would make Kim pay for it."

"Holy shit."

"Yeah. But for the most part, things were fine during the college years. I did my schoolwork, kept my nose clean, showed up at home for the holidays. I even brought my friend Candy home once, when I knew for sure my father would be away on business."

She smiled briefly at the memory. "That was the one time I felt like a normal college kid, laughing with family and friends over the holiday dinner. Kim may have been in denial about what kind of man she'd married, but she was great at putting on the façade and making things seem normal. She always tried to make things happy for me and Rob—as much as she could, anyway.

"But it all ended on the day of my graduation. My father actually deigned to show up for the ceremony. Not out of paternal pride or anything, but because he wanted to lay down a new set of rules for me. He'd brought Kim with him, and while she and I were getting ready for the ceremony in my room, I saw her bruises. I realized then and there that my behavior, good or bad, would never have any effect on how my father treated her. While I felt bad for her, for me it was as if someone finally opened the prison door."

"What did you do?"

"Immediately after the commencement, my father announced he had arranged for me to be married the following week."

"What?" Reeve sputtered. "He *arranged* a marriage for you? Is he still living in the Dark Ages?"

"No, he just believes everyone should bend to his whims."

"Who did he want you to marry?"

"A man named Tony Wallace. He's thirty-five years older than I am and the owner of yet another company my father wanted control of. I refused, of course."

"What happened then?"

"Needless to say, my father doesn't like to hear the word *no*. He told me if I refused to marry Wallace, he would disown me. Cut me off without a cent. I told him that was just fine with me. I'd never seen him so angry. I don't think it ever occurred to him I would disobey."

"Did he hurt you?" Reeve's knuckles grew white on the steering wheel.

"No. I'm sure he wanted to, but there were too many people around. He settled for putting me out of my dorm room, still wearing my cap and gown. Said everything in the room belonged to him since he'd paid for it."

"So you had nothing but the clothes on your back."

"That's all I needed." She remembered that day with satisfaction, marching proudly out of the dorm, off the campus grounds, and never looking back. The only thing of value, true value, her father had ever given her was something he could never actually take away—an education at one of the finest schools in the country. Not so she could make something of herself. Her father couldn't care less about that. But so she could hold her own during conversations at the lavish private dinner parties he liked to throw from time to time. Mitchell expected his wife and daughter to be knowledgeable and charming, little more than trained dolls he could show off to his exclusive guests.

With each stride she took away from all that, her self-confidence had grown. She'd changed her name, the very first step she took to create her own life—and to send a not-so-subtle nose thumbing to her father. Just as she didn't need or want his money, she didn't need or want his name.

"So you don't think there's any way at all he has anything to do with this? Does he still want you to marry this Wallace guy?" Reeve asked, outrage simmering under every syllable.

"No. A few months after graduation, I read in the news that the merger had gone through. It probably cost my father more than he had planned, but he still got his deal in the end."

"But not the way he wanted to do it, right? Would he seek revenge? I mean, from what you're telling me, it sounds as if he let you go almost too easily."

"I thought so too at the time. I mean, a few well-placed phone calls from him, and I would have been virtually unemployable. And when Candy and I started our business, the thought occurred that he might try to sabotage it. But nothing ever happened, and as time went by, I assumed he more or less forgot about me. I mean, why would he bother jeopardizing his reputation by calling attention to the fact that his daughter wants nothing to do with him? My whole life, his vitriol was focused on his wives, not me. I figured once the initial anger had worn off, he moved on. Maybe I was kidding myself."

"Well, it is a long time to hold a grudge. I think most people would have come to the same conclusion. That he'd given it up."

"Yeah, but I should know better. I know *him*. Of course he's going to want revenge. If not now, then someday. But even so, Reeve, I can't imagine him getting involved with human trafficking."

"Not even as a client?"

Her stomach dropped. She had never given a thought to her father's sexual propensities. Worse, now that she did think about it, she couldn't put such an act past him. Power and domination were the two things her father thrived on. Literally owning a frightened young girl to do with as he pleased would be right up his alley.

"I suppose it's possible," she said quietly, turning to look out the window as tears spilled down her face. It sickened her to know she shared her father's genes. Logically, she knew a person couldn't choose their blood relatives, but she couldn't help feeling guilty by association anyway. The thought of her own flesh and blood perpetrating such heinousness filled her with excruciating shame.

Dammit! Why couldn't she let it go? Why, after all this time, did a small part of her still want more than anything to be the daughter of a kind man who loved her? A man she could turn to during this crisis? *No!* She swiped angrily at her tears. She'd worked so hard to be stronger than that, prided herself, even, on not needing *anyone*.

On that fateful graduation day, she'd made the deliberate choice to keep everyone at arm's length, even Candy to a degree, no matter that Jessie loved her like a sister.

And her lovers? Forget it. Having seen firsthand how dangerous trusting the wrong man could be, she shut down any relationship she suspected might be getting serious. She would rather be alone, but she'd known it would be a trade-off, so she had no right to feel sorry for herself now.

"Let's say you're right," she said quietly, "and my father is a client. What would it have to do with me?"

"Maybe that's how the Iceman found out about you to begin with. I would imagine he would do extensive research on any prospective clients. He's not going to let strangers off the street participate in those auctions."

"Then he would know my father and I don't speak to each other, right?"

"Possibly. But he still might try to extort money from your father through you. We can't rule it out. Maybe we should talk to your father."

"No!"

"But—"

"What purpose would it serve? Even if my father does know the Iceman, he's never going to admit it."

"I still think we should talk to him. You don't have to be there. Tobie can do it. Even if he doesn't admit anything, she can learn a lot by reading his expression."

"No, put it out of your head. He probably wouldn't see her anyway."

"Jessie, we have to try."

"Well, try coming up with something else." He opened his mouth, but she plowed on before he could say anything. "Look, if we can't think of any other possibilities, I'll reconsider. But until we've exhausted all other avenues, we stay away from my father."

He blew out a frustrated sigh. "All right, but we can't wait too long. Whether he wants to ransom you or sell you, the Iceman's not going to waste any time."

"Sell me?" She blinked rapidly as she took that in. "Like those girls on the thumb drive?" She shuddered but then shook her head. "No, he wouldn't. I'm at least ten or twelve years older than those girls. Those psychos want teenagers they can terrify and dominate. They don't want a full-grown woman."

"Actually, I don't think they really care how old their victims are. I watched a few more auctions after you went to lie down. Two or three of the victims were around your age. I think it's more important to those men to be dominant. It's most likely easier with young girls, but they would probably get an extra special sick charge out of dominating an older woman. Especially in a way they could never get away with in acceptable society."

She stared out the window, unsuccessfully trying to keep the horrific auction images from her mind. "I think I'd rather he kill me," she whispered.

"Don't say that. Don't ever say that. It's not going to happen, Jessie. I won't let it. He's not going to get anywhere near you."

His unwavering protectiveness chipped away at the wall she'd built around her heart, and she couldn't remember why she'd ever been opposed to letting him help her. He was one hundred percent committed to her, and that loyalty endeared him to her like nothing she'd ever experienced before. The sensation was heady, and she sought his reassurance like an addict. "How can you know that? How can you be so certain?"

"I know because even though it may not seem like it at the moment, we have the advantage after all."

"How do you figure that?"

"The thumb drive. As long as we don't go public with it, he's got to assume we don't know about it. But he's also got to assume we'll find it eventually. He's going to want to get to you before that happens, which means he's got to act fast. He'll make a mistake."

She wanted to believe him. He sounded so sure. "I hope you're right because I can't take much more of this. I want it to be over."

"It will be. I promise. Before you know it, you'll be back home and you'll be rid of all of us. You can pick up right where you left off."

His words should have made her happy. Only... once the Iceman was gone, Reeve would be gone too. Of course he would. He'd move on to his next case while she settled back into her old routine. *Which is exactly what I want,* she reminded herself.

Except... maybe it wasn't.

CHAPTER SEVENTEEN

"I NEED to call the team and tell them everything you just told me. Is that all right?" After all she'd shared, her vehemence about having a voice made sense. But if she objected, he had to come up with a way to convince her.

She gave the barest of nods as she stared out the window. With that assent, he made the call. After some discussion, Tobie decided she and Fitz would follow up with the Sandy Hollow Police Department to find out more information about the house and the explosion.

"There's not too much else to tell you," Tobie said. "The Candlewood police were here. They know Ms. Haynes is really Judith Cochran, but apparently they aren't releasing that to the media. In fact, there seems to be quite the cover-up about it all now. I suspect her father has something to do with it."

"I'm sure you're right. But until we figure this out, we need to stick to the plan and keep Jessie out of sight."

"*Jessie*? What happened to *Miss Haynes*?"

Dammit! He hadn't meant to let that slip.

"You're letting this get too personal, aren't you?" Tobie asked.

"No. I've got everything under control."

"You'd better. If anything happens to her, there'll be hell to pay. Mitchell Cochran will eat us alive if anything happens to his daughter on our watch."

"I don't know about that."

"Well I do. I heard everything you just said, so I know he's not going to win any Father of the Year awards. But if anything happens to his daughter, the media will make the connection to him pretty soon. He'll have to kiss his reclusive anonymity goodbye and be forced to play the devastated yet outraged father. If he's as vindictive as she's saying, he'll make sure someone pays for that. And if it's not the Iceman, then you can bet your ass it will be us."

Reeve couldn't blame Tobie for the sharp edge in her tone. If OASIS went down in flames, she had the most to lose. "Nothing's going to happen to her."

"See that it doesn't. Call back when you've settled yourselves safely."

"I will." He disconnected and looked over at Jessie. The slump of her shoulders made her dejection evident. He could only imagine how humiliating it must be to hear people discussing her father's contemptible habits, even if they were estranged. That he could do nothing to ease her discomfort just added to his guilty frustration.

If it weren't for his missteps, the threat would have been neutralized by now. They should have had the Iceman back at her house. But he'd wanted to wait before going in because he'd wanted to catch Jessie too. He'd been so sure of her involvement, and that had been a costly mistake.

What the hell was wrong with him? Up until the Spencer

case, he'd been good at his job. Now he was losing people he'd been hired to save and engaging in inappropriate behavior with someone he should be focusing on protecting. Maybe he ought to start thinking about getting into a new line of work. One that didn't have other people's lives on the line.

Images of Jessie laughing on the beach taunted him. He wanted to see her smile and laugh like that again. Of course, thinking of her on the beach led to thinking of her generous curves in that sexy bikini, which in turn led to thinking of her warm and passionate in his arms last night. He had to find a way to keep those intoxicating memories at bay. They diluted his focus.

Which was why he never should have slept with her.

He liked her. A lot. She possessed a combination of exceptional intelligence and rare strength. And he certainly couldn't deny the physical attraction. He'd wanted her from the moment he'd laid eyes on her in Key West. Only then it had been in a schoolboy, lustful, ain't-never-gonna-happen kind of way. But now it was more than that. Not only had it definitely happened, he wanted it to happen again... and again... and again.

Yeah, he really never should have slept with her.

Several more miles passed in gloomy silence. The road narrowed to a single lane in each direction as they entered a small town. He stopped for a red light and glanced over. Jessie continued to stare out the window, that glum set still weighing down her shoulders. His eyes traveled down. Her cream-colored tee shirt had small, protozoan-shaped stains of dried blood, most likely from her scalp lacerations, on one shoulder. Thanks to the house explosion, her pink jeans were now streaked with dirt and had a ragged tear below the left knee. A far cry from the attractive way she'd looked in those clothes when she'd entered her house two days ago.

Two days ago. Hell, maybe he could do something right now to put a smile on her face after all. "What do you say we stop and get some new clothes?"

She looked at him, the shine of tears in her eyes twisting a knot in his stomach. But a small smile appeared on her lips, loosening that knot and filling him with a rich warmth that he didn't truly care to analyze at the moment.

"I'd like that," she said. "But will it be safe? I mean, after the explosion, won't we be news again?"

"We'll make it quick. Keep your hat pulled down low and try not to lift your face. That way the security cameras won't get a good look."

Her smile faded. "Maybe we shouldn't bother."

"It will be all right. And I don't know about you, but I don't want to have to put the same clothes back on tomorrow."

"All right. If you're sure."

The light changed, and in less than two blocks they found a strip mall with a medium-sized department store at one end. The full lot indicated a fair number of shoppers. Good. More customers meant they wouldn't stand out to the employees.

They put on their caps and pulled them low. Reeve got out and waited for her at the front of the car. He put an arm around her shoulders, pulling her close. She looked at him with a question in her eyes.

"We're just an average couple doing a little shopping together." He walked toward the store entrance, smiling down at her the whole time. "Relax. Smile if you can."

Her lips curved upward into more of a grimace than a smile.

"Jessie, I've seen better smiles on kids heading for the dentist's chair."

She blinked in surprise before letting out a giggly laugh, an authentic grin lighting up her face and caressing his heart.

"That's better."

They reached the store entrance, and he held the door. They headed straight for the women's department. "Pick out enough stuff for a few days."

She nodded, efficiently picking out clothing without a lot of fuss. There was a brief moment of awkwardness as she approached the lingerie department. "I promise not to peek," he said, dramatically placing his hands over his eyes.

Jessie laughed and swatted him on the arm. "I guess it's a little late for me to be worrying about you seeing my underwear." She quickly selected the necessary articles and then accompanied him to the men's department. He, too, made his choices quickly, and they were soon in the cosmetics department, picking up a few toiletries.

"We'll find a motel soon," Reeve said as they exited the store with their purchases. "We can grab a shower and get into our clean duds."

"Sounds like paradise." She wore the same genuine smile he'd seen on her face in Key West, and he felt ridiculously thrilled at how the little shopping detour seemed to snap her out of her doldrums. The knot in his stomach unraveled altogether.

As they walked to the Mustang, a gray sedan passed the strip mall. Something about it tickled his memory, and Reeve stared after it as it approached the intersection. A flash of white hair caught his eye, but the car raced through the light and around the corner before he could get a good look. "Get in the car. Now."

Her eyes bugged and she yanked her door open. "What is it?"

"Probably nothing, but I want to check it out."

"Check what out?" she asked as she fastened her seat belt.

He pulled into traffic. "I saw a gray car parked near Fox's office this morning, and one very much like it just drove by here."

"A gray car? Really? Aren't there like, I don't know, a million of them on the road?"

"Yeah, but I think the driver had white hair, and he or she seemed to speed up when I started looking that way. It's probably nothing, but I want to be certain."

He turned at the corner. A small crowd stood clustered to one side of the road, several people on their cell phones and gesticulating wildly. A young man wearing a neon blue bike helmet sat on the ground a few feet away from his mangled bicycle. His expression was dazed as another man pulled off his tee shirt and pressed it to the blood flowing from a long gash on the cyclist's leg. Reeve slowed to a stop next to a group of teenagers snapping pictures with their phones.

Jessie stuck her head out the window. "What happened?" she asked the nearest one, a young girl with black hair dyed pink at the tips.

"This old guy ran over the bike rider. Didn't even stop."

"No, it was an old woman," the boy next to her said. "They shouldn't let old people drive. Bet that old woman can't even see anymore. She shouldn't have a license."

"She was really old, huh?" Jessie asked.

"Yeah, like forty or fifty or something."

Reeve choked back a snort. "Did you get a picture of the license plate?"

"No, she drove away too fast. Crazy old lady driving an ugly old gray car."

Sirens sounded in the distance as the flashing lights of an ambulance appeared in the rearview mirror. "We need to go."

"Okay." Jessie pulled her head back in, banging it on the car frame as she did. "Ouch! Watch me get a headache now." She rubbed the back of her head

"You have a headache?" Unease marched through him, remembering she could have bumped her head during the explosion. "Let's find a hospital." He maneuvered around the gaping crowd and hurried away.

"A hospital? For a headache I don't even have yet? Don't be ridiculous."

"Head wounds are nothing to mess around with."

"Head wound? Geez, I just bumped it a little. What is it with you and head injuries?"

"What do you mean?"

"I mean, you're always asking me if I hit my head or if I have a headache. You insisted on going to the hospital the other day for a couple of scratches. Now you want to go again because of a little bump. There's a reason. What is it?"

"Nothing."

"Uh-uh, not buying it. You don't get to go all strong and silent type on me. Spill it."

"Sorry, but it's personal."

"You're kidding, right? You know everything there is to know about me. Weren't you the one who insisted there be no more secrets?"

He shifted in his seat. She had a point, but he still didn't want to talk about it.

"How do you expect me to trust you when you're hiding some kind of trauma?" she persisted.

"I'm not hiding a trauma!"

"Like hell. Look at you. Your shoulders are practically

covering your ears, and if you were gripping that wheel any tighter, you'd break it in two."

He drew in a deep breath, relaxing his shoulders and loosening his grip on the steering wheel, but his voice still stuck in his throat.

"Talk to me, Reeve. I've already got enough unknowns going on in my life. I can't have you be a mystery too."

Guilt tugged at him. He didn't want to add to Jessie's worries, but he didn't want to talk about Ann Marie's death. When he'd gone back to work shortly after the funeral, everyone at OASIS had offered a sympathetic ear, but he hadn't taken any of them up on it, preferring to think about the job instead.

But that hadn't exactly turned out too well, had it? Tabitha Spencer had borne a slight resemblance to Ann Marie. If he wanted to be honest with himself, he needed to admit he'd thought of his sister quite a bit while working Tabitha's case. Maybe he should have talked to the others when he'd had the chance.

Jessie's stare bored into him like a laser, blasting its way through his natural instinct to clam up and ignore the pain. Fragments of something his father used to say poked at his brain. What was it? Something about repeating the same action and expecting different results being the definition of madness.

Ah, hell, just start talking.

"Okay. Eleven years ago, my parents and little sister were in a bad car accident. My parents died instantly, and Ann Marie spent over two weeks in the hospital. She was only fifteen, and from that point forward she had a full-on phobia of hospitals. I was twenty-two and in the military. While I was deployed, she stayed with our aunt, but whenever I came home, she stayed with me, and I spoiled the heck out of her, always trying to make her happy. She loved adventure, so we traveled whenever we could. Even after she graduated college and started her own life, we saw each other as often as our schedules would allow.

"A few months ago, we went hiking in the Adirondacks. On our way down, she tripped on a tree root and hit her head on a rock when she fell. I wanted to take her to the hospital, but she laughed it off, calling me a complete wuss. I didn't push it because I knew how strongly she feared hospitals, and it really hadn't been a bad fall. She never lost consciousness and she was laughing all the way back to our hotel. We had a quick bite for dinner and then called it an early night. She never showed up for breakfast the next morning. I got the manager to let me in her room."

His voice caught. "We found her on the floor next to the bed, still wearing the same clothes from the night before. We rushed her to the hospital, but she never came out of the coma. She died that afternoon. Epidural hematoma, a brain bleed."

"Oh, Reeve. I'm so sorry."

"Yeah, thanks." Silence descended. He fought to shove the pain and guilt back into the locked box in his mind where he usually stored them, but they obstinately refused to be shut up. His fingers tightened on the steering wheel again, and he bit his lip to keep from screaming at the top of his lungs.

"Let me guess. You think it's your fault she died."

"It *is* my fault! I should have insisted she go to the hospital right away. I was the big brother, the one who should have known better. I had some basic medical training—I used to be a damned Navy SEAL, for Christ's sake. Instead, I indulged her just like always. She was so young when the car accident happened, and I always felt sorry that she didn't get to spend more time with Mom and Dad. So I never wanted her to do anything she didn't want to do. Nothing that would make her the least bit unhappy."

"You couldn't have known how bad it was if she didn't tell you. Maybe *she* didn't even know how bad it was."

"Doubtful. The doctors said she must have had a wicked headache. But she didn't tell me because she knew I would have made her go to the hospital right away. She covered it well. She smiled and laughed the whole time. Laughing, when she was already dying."

"I bet that pisses you off."

"What? No! How could I be angry at her? I'm the one at fault, not Ann Marie."

"Wrong. It was an accident, a tragic, meaningless accident, and neither one of you is to blame. Even so, it's all right to be angry at her. It happens a lot. As much as I loved my mother, I've always been a little angry at her, too, for not leaving my father before it was too late. I know it's not a hundred percent rational, but it is what it is. I'll bet you're furious with Ann Marie for not telling you the truth about her headache. I would be. But we have to remember we're only human. You, me, my mom, your sister. We all make mistakes, big ones sometimes, but we have to try and move on. Some days it's easier than others, but we have to try."

How did she do it? He'd never told anyone about his anger toward his baby sister. He barely admitted it to himself, always crushing the thought whenever it nudged at his conscience. Yet somehow Jessie knew. And she didn't think he was a piece of shit because of it, her words like a soothing balm to his conscience. "Maybe you're right."

"I'm really sorry about your sister, but I'm glad you told me. If I do actually get a headache, I promise you'll be the first to know."

"Thanks." His body relaxed a bit. Not until that moment did he realize how much he really needed to know for certain she wouldn't keep something like that from him.

"Are you okay?"

An ache with his sister's name on it still sat on his heart, but not nearly as sharp as usual. "Yeah, I'm good."

"At least we know it was an old woman in that car, not the Iceman," Jessie continued.

"You're probably right, but I'd feel better if we'd seen for ourselves. Those kids weren't the most reliable witnesses. They think forty is old."

"Don't we all think that when we're teenagers? But I think they can tell a man from a woman."

"I hope so." He scanned the side streets as they passed them but didn't see the gray car. No doubt the driver had hurried to get out of sight after the accident. Reeve really wanted to get a look at the driver, but they couldn't linger any longer, especially since the local police would be looking for the gray car too. Time to get moving. "Let's head for the next town and then look for a place to stay."

"Okay. How long do you think we'll have to stay out of sight?"

She asked the question lightly, but he didn't doubt she wanted a serious answer. "I don't know. We're doing everything we can."

Dammit, he needed to put an end to the Iceman. Moving her to a safe location was the right thing to do, but he couldn't keep her hidden for long. That kind of life would be torture for someone like Jessie. Just these few short days were already taking a toll on her, and sooner or later the constant stress and feeling of helplessness would break her. Hell, he'd seen trained and seasoned military men crack under such pressure.

Jessie deserved her quiet life back, coming home from her job to her sweet little bungalow. He'd greet her with a glass of her favorite wine, two juicy steaks grilling in the back yard...

What the hell?

He must be losing his mind. As soon as this case wrapped, he *would* follow Tobie's advice and take some time off and get his head screwed on right. Because this case would end. When it did, Jessie had a life to get back to. But a life that was her own, and he had no business insinuating himself into it. As if his job would let him, anyway. He would move on to another case, and another. Cases that could take him who only knew where.

All of which meant he and Jessie would have to part company. Hardly a newsflash, but the fact that it bothered him was much more of a revelation. For the last several months, his guilt over Ann Marie had devoured him until he'd been deadened to anything else.

But now? The need to enjoy life seemed to be regaining its appetite and was nudging gluttonous guilt away from the table.

CHAPTER EIGHTEEN

By LATE AFTERNOON, they reached the outskirts of the next town and pulled into the parking lot of a dreary-looking motel. Jessie stared at the squat rust-colored building, its row of dull brown doors looking as inviting as a tax audit. She accompanied Reeve into the lobby, not at all surprised to find the place as dismal on the inside as it was on the outside.

A skinny young man in a dingy white tank top and black jeans sat behind the front desk. He sported electric purple hair—the only spark of color in the lackluster beige room—and something resembling a car bolt jutted through his pierced lower lip. A sleeve of dull black tattoos coiled up both his scrawny arms.

"Help you?" he muttered, boredom oozing out of his pores as he rose to his feet, tossing a crinkled car magazine to one side.

"We need a room," Reeve said.

"How long?"

"Just for tonight."

"The whole night?" Purple Hair blinked in surprise, and

Jessie's heart sank. Despite its tired appearance, she'd hoped this establishment would be a step or two above those places that charged by the hour. Apparently, no such luck. With a small sigh, she longed for her own bed.

Reeve pulled out a wad of cash. "Yeah, the whole night. How much?"

Purple Hair blinked again at the roll of cash, and then looked at Reeve and Jessie, a wrinkle of bewilderment appearing in his forehead. "You really gonna do it all night? We don't even get teenagers in here who wanna go all night. But those poor suckers gotta be home by curfew, don't they?" He snorted at his own questionable humor.

Reeve leaned in close over the counter. "Don't you worry about that," he said softly. "How much?"

Purple Hair swallowed. "Uh, I'm not sure. Eight hours?"

"Make it twelve." Reeve's sardonic scowl proclaimed his virile pride, and Jessie bit her lip to keep from laughing. Men. Never question their libidinous stamina.

Oblivious to Reeve's glower, Purple Hair laboriously did the calculation on a notepad. "Nobody ever wants more than an hour or two," he muttered as he scratched and scribbled, stalwartly determined to beat this tricky multiplication problem into submission. Finally, he reached a number with which he appeared satisfied, and Reeve counted out the necessary bills. Purple Hair slid a plastic key ring sporting an actual key across the counter. Reeve picked it up, raising an eyebrow.

"Yeah, the boss keeps saying he's gonna upgrade to key cards and a computer system, but he never does," Purple Hair remarked. Without another word, he gathered up the cash and stuffed it into a metal cash box. He returned to his chair and picked up his magazine.

"Someone should nominate him for employee of the month," Jessie said as they stepped outside.

"Yeah, he'd get my vote," Reeve grumbled.

She stifled another giggle, quite certain Reeve wouldn't understand what she found so funny. They drove to the end of the lot and pulled into the space in front of their room. Jessie gathered up her tote bag while Reeve collected their purchases and then unlocked the door.

The room continued the established decor of numbingly dull beige but appeared to be fairly clean, much to Jessie's relief. Between the obvious lack of money spent on employees or on upgrading from keys to keycards, she'd been expecting a pigsty. She peered into the bathroom, pleased to see it as clean as the rest of the place. She took the bag with her new garments from Reeve. "I can't wait to rinse off and put on clean clothes."

She did just that. The simple scoop-necked yellow tee shirt and khaki Capri pants she'd bought gave her spirits a much-needed lift. Reeve wrapped up a phone call as she returned to the bedroom. The dark expression on his face tanked her refreshed mood. "What is it?"

"That was Jake. Fox didn't have a phone on him, he claims to have thrown it away. So Jake hacked into his phone and email accounts. The Iceman sent Fox a message, threatening him if he said anything to us. He mentioned OASIS by name."

"What? How could he know we'd gotten hold of Fox?"

"Exactly. And what's more, if he knew we had Fox, he had to know we would intercept the message. He's taunting us."

Jessie sank slowly into the room's only chair. "He can't know where we are. And if he knows we have Fox, maybe taunts are all he can resort to now. Maybe he figures I'm not worth the effort anymore."

"I wish I could believe that." Reeve stalked over to the window and closed the drapes with an angry jerk. "He's not giving up," he said hoarsely, "and there's not a damn thing I can do about it. He's one step ahead of us at every turn."

"We'll beat him," Jessie said. "He's not omnipotent. He'll make a mistake and we'll beat him."

Yanking off his shirt, Reeve walked into the bathroom as if he hadn't heard her, but came back out almost immediately. "He wants that thumb drive. He wants you. And he's making it pretty clear he's not afraid of us." Reeve marched back to the window and pulled one of the drapes aside just enough so he could peer out with one eye. "He won't give up," he repeated, his agitation growing by the second.

"He's not going to get what he wants. Not this time."

Reeve continued to stare out the window. "I hope you're right," he muttered, his body shaking as he spoke. That scared her more than anything that had happened so far. Up until now, he'd been the poster child for calm, cool, and collected.

"What is it, Reeve? What haven't you told me?" She stood and wrapped her arms around his waist, laying her cheek against his bare back. His warm skin offered little comfort as his slight tremors chilled her to the bone. "Tell me," she whispered.

Silence stretched so long she thought he wouldn't answer, but finally he spoke. "I told you how the Spencers hired OASIS to find Tabitha."

"Yes, because the authorities weren't taking it seriously due to her frequent runaways."

"Right. But I didn't tell you that we screwed up. Or more

accurately, *I* screwed up." His voice dropped to a near whisper. "I'm the one who got Tabitha killed."

She hugged him tighter. "I don't believe it. The Iceman killed her, not you."

Reeve turned and pulled her close to his chest, resting his chin on her head, his voice flat as he spoke. "But maybe he wouldn't have if it weren't for me." He took a shuddery breath. "Pugliesi gave us the address where he'd delivered Tabitha to the Iceman. We weren't very far away. I told Maddie to stay with Pugliesi while Fitz, Ian, and I took off to get Tabitha. Unfortunately, I underestimated just how much fear and desperation the Iceman inspired in people. As soon as they were alone, Pugliesi managed to overpower Maddie and escape. He called the Iceman, tipping him off. The bastard slit Tabitha's throat and just threw her in the trash. She was still warm when I got there. I missed saving her by minutes."

Jessie hugged him fiercely, the agony in his voice stirring a protective ache in her heart. "You have to stop blaming yourself, Reeve."

"I can't. Ever since my sister died, I've been acting like an idiot, making rash decisions that have gotten people hurt or killed. I was in such a hurry to save Tabitha I didn't want to waste a second, didn't want to take the time to formulate a plan. I just went charging off."

"You couldn't have known what would happen." She pulled back and took his face in her hands. "Are you listening? Not. Your. Fault."

Tears filled his eyes. "I should have taken the time to think it through. If I'd waited just a few minutes, if I'd left Ian or Fitz with Maddie or called Jake in for backup—"

"If, if, if. Reeve, you can't beat yourself up over all the *what if*s. You don't know the outcome would have been any better if you acted differently. Things could have been even worse. Maybe you or somebody from your team would have been killed as well as Tabitha."

She rubbed the wetness from his cheeks with her thumbs. "Listen to me. I've seen you in action over the last few days, up close and personal. I know you did everything you could to help that poor girl. And I know you would have put your own life on the line for her, just like you're doing for me."

"I shouldn't have—"

She pulled his face to hers and pressed a warm, brief kiss on his lips. "You can't help Tabitha by beating yourself up, but you can get justice for her. *We* can get justice for her. You are not invincible, but you are also not alone. I'm with you on this, one hundred percent. I survived my father, and I will survive this too. *We* will survive this." She kissed him again before moving onto his face, kissing his salty tears away.

His arms came up around her and he moved his lips back to hers. Their kiss grew passionate, and his tremors ceased, the tension easing from his muscles as she ran her hands over his sleek, sinewy torso, memorizing every bit of him by feel. Molten strength radiated from his perfect body as she touched him, exciting her and comforting her at the same time. As he held her close, the knowledge of all that power bent on taking care of her made her light-headed. For the first time in her life, Jessie knew what it was to be protected and cared for. The sensation was the most potent aphrodisiac she'd ever experienced.

He steered her toward the bed, and together they sought the release from the nightmare, the same exquisite release they had found together before. There was no darkness this time when they shed their clothes. Jessie took full advantage, admiring his rock-hard physique and exploring every inch of it with her hands, lips, and tongue. Reeve responded in kind, taking his time looking at her, touching her, tasting her, driving her wild until she exploded beneath him as he delivered thrust after piercing thrust. His climax quickly followed her own before he collapsed on top of her.

Sweaty and sated, Jessie listened to the sound of Reeve's breathing grow deep and even as sleep overtook him. She took comfort in the simple act of caressing his back, stroking her hand slowly up and down its length. Gently shifting her position so she could see him better, she couldn't help but smile at his handsome face. How peaceful he looked. Definitely a whole lot more appealing than the angry man who'd once accused her of being a criminal. And a far cry from the anguished man who blamed himself for the senseless deaths of two young women.

It would take time, but she'd do everything she could to convince him he wasn't responsible for what happened. She needed to believe Reeve could stop blaming himself, because she wanted him in her life. Her need for autonomy bristled at the thought. Yet for the first time in years, she disregarded the voice of caution reciting its automatic litany of reasons to fear commitment.

Terrible as the last few days had been, they had brought with them the stark reminder of life's brevity. And on the heels of that awakening came the simple realization that she didn't want to live her life all alone.

Her gaze shifted to his arms, arms that could easily crush her with their strength. The thought should have made her nervous. But not all men used their strength and power to hurt and intimidate. A warm glow spread over her as she thought of how safe she felt within his arms, not trapped and frightened. She moved her hand from his back, unable to resist touching his beckoning bicep. *Yes, these arms are heaven.*

"Oh!" she gasped as one of those arms suddenly snaked around her waist and pulled her flush up against Reeve's chest.

"Hey there," he said in a sleepy growl. "Is there something I can do for you?"

"I certainly hope so. But as someone pointed out recently, you're not exactly a teenager," she teased, meeting his lips for a sizzling kiss. "Give it your best shot."

He rolled her beneath him, pressing her back into the pillows.

"I always do, ma'am," he murmured between kisses, "I always do."

"I'll be right back," Reeve said, wrapping his arms around her and dropping a kiss on her forehead. "Don't open the door for anyone, no matter what they say."

"I won't."

He gave her a quick hug and then went out, waiting until he heard the deadbolt click and the chain lock rattle before moving away. He didn't want to leave her, not even for just a few moments, but they had to eat, and the diner across the road refused to deliver. The road was deserted as he crossed it, noting the few cars in the diner parking lot had all seen better days. He pulled out his phone and called Jake for an update.

"Here's what we've got so far," Jake said. "There's some preliminary information from the explosion site. Some human remains have been found. No positive ID as yet, but what do you want to bet they'll turn out to belong to the Bergers?"

"Did they die in the explosion?"

"Not according to the guy we're talking to. He couldn't say exactly how long yet, but he was confident they'd been there several years."

"Well, that would mesh with Fox's story. The Bergers and the other foster children were probably the bastard's first kills. That's probably why he came back to the house every now and then. To visit his trophies. I wonder why he didn't kill Fox, too."

"Who knows? Maybe he already knew he wanted to keep Fox as his trusty foot soldier. Fox did tell us that on his eighteenth birthday, he came home from school and found the Iceman waiting for him on the front porch. He told Fox he wasn't the state or the Bergers' problem anymore. The Iceman gave Fox a duffle bag with his clothes in it and a couple of hundred bucks and told him to get lost. Fox left and says he never saw the Bergers or the other kids again. My guess is they were already dead or about to be."

"Yeah, I'll bet you're right."

"Listen, there's one more thing," Jake said. "Tobie is not having any luck getting cooperation from the men who are on those thumb drive files. They're all calling their lawyers and circling their proverbial wagons."

"Are you kidding me? You can see their faces plain as day. Do they really think they can get away with it?"

"Deep down? Probably not. But calling a lawyer and trying to put some sort of bullshit spin on it is second nature for these guys. It's what they do. Some of them are swearing it's all photoshopped and bogus. They're threatening to sue us if we keep bothering them."

Reeve shook his head as he arrived at the diner's front

door. "Un-friggin-believable. What about Jessie's father? Has he made any contact?"

"None whatsoever. I suppose it's possible he's unaware of the media blitz that ran yesterday morning, but considering everything Miss Haynes told us about him, I doubt it. I know he's a recluse and all, but you would think he would at least have one of his minions reach out to us to find out what's going on."

"Jessie says that unless he can find a way to use it to his own advantage, her father won't do anything to help her. In fact, he may try to discredit her—and us—if he sees some sort of benefit in it for him."

"Wow. Some father, huh?"

"Yeah, some father. Okay, keep me posted."

"You got it."

"Thanks." Reeve disconnected and entered the diner, automatically scanning the few patrons for a threat. An elderly couple sat in a booth, drinking coffee and sharing a slice of pie, and a bald man sat at the end of the counter, reading a book and eating French fries. Other than that, Reeve had the place to himself. He sat at the counter, opened a menu, and scanned the possibilities. They offered several varieties of cheeseburger platters along with a few deep-fried chicken or fish sandwiches. Pretty much what he'd expected.

Jessie deserved better than crappy diner food and the current dump they were staying in. After they ate, he'd scan the internet and see if he could find better accommodations. Sticking to the use of cash would limit their options, but it couldn't hurt to look.

After placing an order with a teenage waiter, he moved to an empty booth by the window while he waited. He could see their room from this angle. Logic told him no one other than the OASIS team knew their current location, but he wouldn't be able to let his guard down for a moment until the Iceman sat in a high-security prison.

Or lay in a casket.

His stomach growled regardless of the oppressive aroma of grease permeating the place. He shuddered to think what kind of havoc all this fried food wreaked on his body. Once this case closed, he'd take Jessie someplace really nice to eat.

He jerked up in his seat. *Shit, not again.* But hell if the idea of taking Jessie out for dinner didn't sound like a good one. A small, tingly sense of hope chased away his momentary flash of panic. *Why not?* He leaned back in the booth and stared across to the motel room door, his mind filled with thoughts of the woman behind it.

He hardly knew her, never mind all the details of her past his team had uncovered. Yet on some level, he knew her very well. And that wasn't just the sex talking. There was more to it than the amazing hours they'd spent in each other's arms.

They'd met under extraordinary and hostile circumstances, with each of them toting some pretty heavy emotional baggage. Yet somehow they'd been good for each other. He'd kept her safe and helped her realize that leaning on someone during a crisis didn't make her weak. In return, she'd helped him realize that carrying a mega-ton of guilt was not only harmful and unproductive, it actually did a grave disservice to Tabitha Spencer and her parents.

He'd never know if Tabitha's death would have been prevented if he'd acted differently. That uncertainty would follow him to his grave, and he'd be kidding himself if he thought he'd ever reach a point where he'd never feel any guilt at all. But for the first time since the tragedy, Reeve's anger focused more on that douche Pugliesi and on the

Iceman. Tobie and the rest of the team had been telling him to do that all along, but he'd never listened. He'd convinced himself they were only saying that to assuage their own guilt. A childish and unfair notion, but he'd stubbornly clung to the idea all this time.

Hearing it from Jessie changed things. Her ability to see the event from an objective angle and point out simple truths blasted a big hole through the cement wall he'd erected around himself the day his sister died. Jessie absolved him, making it clear she trusted him with her life. Not even the ardent trust of his fellow SEALs when they were deployed in combat compared to her unconditional faith in him. Even with all the near misses so far, her confidence in his ability to keep her alive had only increased.

But would any of that matter on a personal level? Their current association was both precarious and unusual. What would happen when they no longer had to worry about the Iceman? Could he and Jessie have a normal relationship?

Reeve wasn't even sure he recognized *normal* anymore. The callous violence he'd witnessed as a SEAL, his sister's death, Tabitha Spencer's murder, the loathsome things he'd seen in those auction files. They'd all left a mark on him. What made him think he could handle a serious relationship with a woman?

Beyond going steady in high school a few times, he'd never been involved with a woman for more than a sexual relationship, especially since he'd returned home from his final tour of duty. A little shell-shocked and not inclined to talk about himself, he'd sought out women who weren't looking to settle down. Career women focused solely on their jobs and seeking only to scratch the same itch.

Jessie was different. Yes, she'd made it abundantly clear her independence was important to her, but not in the same way as the other women who briefly passed through his life. They didn't want a relationship because they didn't want to make a commitment to anything that might divert attention from their careers. Jessie didn't want a relationship because she didn't want to make the *wrong* commitment. She didn't want to wind up bound to someone who could make her life miserable. Her desire to be alone had been born out of fear rather than preference.

Reeve didn't want her to be afraid. Not of him, not of anything. He *did* want to pursue a relationship with her. The idea had been taking root and budding in tandem with his growing respect for her. Over the past couple of days, she'd wowed him with her dignity, compassion, and amazing strength. Qualities all the more remarkable in light of her family background. Not many could survive such an atrocious upbringing with their sense of self intact.

Jessie had not only survived it, she'd conquered it. She walked away, started from scratch, and built a good life for herself. Doing that with the support of a loving family was hard enough. Doing it on her own was monumental.

And if that weren't enough, despite her own current personal hell, she still cared about others, desperately wanting to help the girls in those files. She cared enough to reach out to him and try to ease his pain. The more he thought about her, the more he wanted to be with her, both in bed and out.

She'd resist. But he welcomed the challenge of convincing her to give their fledgling relationship a try. Once this ugly business with the Iceman was done, Reeve would make convincing her his sole mission.

And it would be done. Soon. It didn't matter how many lawyers those cretins on the thumb drive hired. They weren't going to be able to spin themselves out of this scandal. Before long, one or more of those assholes would wise up and cut a deal. Whatever information they could provide on the Iceman would soon be common knowledge, and his face would be plastered all over every media outlet available. With that level of publicity, he wouldn't be able to blackmail anybody anymore, leaving him with that much less cash to help him to maintain his low profile.

But until the details of the thumb drive went public, Reeve would have to wait on his newfound romantic goal. As long as the Iceman believed he still had the power to extort money from his wealthy clients, getting that thumb drive back would be his main focus. And as long as he believed Jessie still had it, she remained his primary target.

The waiter plopped a plastic bag in front of him. Reeve paid the bill and headed back toward the motel, scanning the area carefully as he walked. No new cars, no pedestrians walking nearby, no one peering out any of the motel windows. Good. They were still safe here.

And he would do whatever it took to keep them that way.

CHAPTER NINETEEN

JESSIE TURNED the lock and engaged the security chain. Stepping back from the door, she hugged herself, rubbing her hands up and down her arms. Why did the room feel colder now? For a long moment she stared at the door, and then barely stopped herself from going to look out the window to keep her eye on Reeve.

"Knock it off," she muttered to herself. "He just went across the street to get some food, for heaven's sake." She would not let the events of the last few days turn her into a clingy, needy thing, unable to be without her man. Her feelings for Reeve were strong, but that certainly didn't mean she was incapable of being by herself for fifteen minutes.

Taking a seat on the edge of the bed, she turned on the television and located a news channel. A wildfire burning out of control in California dominated the broadcast. She watched the news crawl rolling along the bottom of the screen. A couple of brief sentences mentioned the house in Sandy Hollow, indicating the explosion was "under investigation." Nothing at all about her or Reeve or the OASIS agency. *Good.*

Muting the volume, she idly channel surfed for something interesting to watch while she waited for Reeve. The different images flashed on the screen, but she didn't really see them. Mental pictures of Reeve and what they'd shared together filled her head. Less than a week ago, she would have laughed at the idea of having a man in her life outside of the bedroom. Tonight, it didn't seem so funny, but rather an intriguing contradiction of inconceivably terrifying and wildly exciting.

The motel's old black landline phone sitting on the nightstand rang, startling her out of her thoughts and onto her feet. She stared at it, afraid to pick it up. Who could be calling on that line? Only Reeve's team knew they were staying at this motel. *Duh, it must be someone from his office, then.* Shaking her head at her silly nervousness, she marched to the phone. "Hello?"

"Jessie?"

"Candy? How did you know—"

"Jessie, help me, please! He's crazy!"

Candy's anguished voice raised gooseflesh on Jessie's skin from head to toe. Shivering, she gripped the phone tightly. "Candy, what's wrong? Where are you?"

"She's with me." The oily, confident voice of the Iceman unraveled a sickening rope of nausea in Jessie's stomach.

"Please don't hurt her," she croaked out.

"Well that depends on you, Miss Haynes," he said calmly. "You have something of mine, and I want it back."

"I don't have anything." A feeble stall as her mind raced with terror.

"Yes, Miss Haynes, you do. I left something with you to look after for me. For your friend's sake, you better hope you still have it. Look in your bag."

"Hold on." Jessie put the phone down. Even though

Reeve had the thumb drive in his pocket, she picked up her tote bag and noisily ran her hand through its contents, using those scarce few seconds to try to think of something.

She would have to tell the Iceman she still had the drive, of course, but she had no idea what to do beyond that. Reluctantly, she picked up the phone again. "I found a thumb drive that isn't mine."

"Good. Then this should be easy. I would like to make an exchange, Miss Haynes. The thumb drive for the lovely Miss Bartlett. You do want to see your friend again, don't you?"

"Yes! Please don't hurt her." She swiped at the tears rolling down her face, unable to bear the thought of Candy being tortured.

"Do as I say and she'll be fine. Meet me at the beach tomorrow at six a.m." He gave her terse directions, which she scrawled on a notepad next to the phone. "Bring the thumb drive and come alone. I've got people watching you and Mr. Buchanan, as well as all his friends—some of whom are mutual, by the way. Did you know that?" He chuckled quietly. "I'll know if they set a trap."

"I understand," she said as she tore the sheet off the pad and stuffed it in her pocket. "How do I know you'll keep your word?"

"You don't. But I promise you that if you don't do as I say, you will never see your friend again. And I'll see to it that she curses your name before she dies." A sudden yelp followed by a weepy whimper from Candy preceded another of his infuriating chuckles. "Are we clear, Miss Haynes?" He hung up without waiting for a response.

Her hands shook as she dropped the receiver into the cradle, and she fought off the choking need to throw up.

Betrayed!

Someone from OASIS had betrayed them. She wanted,

more than anything, to believe the Iceman lied, but there had been so many close calls, the possibility of a mole in the organization could not easily be dismissed. So what the hell should she do?

Save Candy, no matter what.

While her soul shouted the only possible answer, her conscience cleared its throat, reminding her that less than twenty-four hours ago she'd promised Reeve she wouldn't keep secrets from him. But if Reeve prevented her from going—and she knew he would—the Iceman would torture and kill another innocent woman, this one her best friend in the world.

Tears filled her eyes. Much as she wanted to tell Reeve about the call, she just couldn't gamble with Candy's life. Guilt laced her decision, and having no other alternative offered no comfort.

Her helplessness accelerated her tears. What she wouldn't give for the opportunity to grab the little notepad from the nightstand so she could make a list. But she could never finish it before Reeve returned. Worse, she had a feeling that even with oodles of time to write it all out, she wouldn't come up with a plan that made her feel safe and in control.

Grabbing a tissue and blowing her nose, Jessie went into the bathroom and splashed cold water on her face. She had no time for tears. Reeve would be back any minute, and not only would she have to conceal her distress, she would have to conceal her decision to leave him behind. The thought of breaking her promise and making him so angry brought a fresh sting to her eyes, but she fought it back.

She soaked a washcloth in cold water before lying down on the bed and placing it over her eyes, hoping to forestall any telltale puffiness. Breathing deeply, she managed to stop shaking, but her mind still raced as images from the thumb drive flashed through her head. Candy was the sweetest, kindest person she knew, and the thought of the woman she loved like a sister enduring the same sort of merciless pain and degradation tore Jessie to pieces.

"Calm down," she whispered. For Candy's sake, she had to be strong and somehow find a way to get through the next few hours.

A quiet knock on the door started her heart racing again until she heard Reeve's voice. "It's me. I've got our chow."

"Coming," she called out as she rolled off the bed and tossed the washcloth in the bathroom sink. *Chow* was their agreed upon safe word. If he'd said *dinner* it meant she shouldn't open the door and should dial 911 immediately. Of course, she already knew the Iceman wasn't hanging around outside, waiting for an attempt to overpower Reeve. Not when he'd already deftly arranged for her to come to him.

She blew out a deep breath before opening the door. *Showtime.*

Reeve entered and placed the food on the small table as she shut and relocked the door. She'd barely turned around when he snared her into his arms for a searing kiss that left her breathless. She pulled away with a shaky laugh. "Down with your inner teenager. I'm starved."

"Yeah. Me too. Although I'm afraid it's more of the same old diner fare. Fried and greasy." He released her and started pulling food out of the bag.

"It'll have to do," Jessie said lightly. "But once I'm back home, it's going to be serious diet time."

"Yeah, me too," Reeve agreed as he sat down and bit into a burger. "I talked to Jake. It appears Tobie is running into some roadblocks getting any kind of cooperation from the men we've identified in those files. They're all consulting with their lawyers."

"But that's ridiculous! They have to know they aren't going to get away with it."

"I agree. But they're still refusing to cooperate."

Jessie bit into a French fry. How could those men believe they wouldn't pay for their crimes? Once those images hit the media, the public would be out for their blood. Unless... Oh hell, had they already made sure the images wouldn't ever go public?

The men in those files had access to an obscene amount of money. The lure of it would be a strong temptation to anyone. What if the Iceman had used that enticement and bought Tobie off? Perhaps she hadn't even contacted those men, and she was lying about it to keep Reeve from guessing the truth.

Jessie didn't want to believe it. Reeve seemed to trust Tobie and the rest of his team implicitly. But it sort of made sense. The Iceman must have at least speculated they might have discovered the thumb drive already, and that they would have copied the files, rendering the drive useless to him. Unless he knew those copies had been destroyed and that the drive would be returned to him, all thanks to his person—Tobie?—on the inside at OASIS.

Nor could she put aside the disturbing fact that the Iceman kept finding her so quickly. How? No one but Reeve and whoever he contacted at the agency knew their movements.

She knew Reeve wasn't involved. No amount of money could persuade him to let Tabitha's killer go free. But she couldn't definitively make that statement about the rest of the OASIS team. Maddie had seemed genuinely outraged by the images she'd seen on her cousin's laptop, but what if it

had been an act? After all, hadn't she been the one responsible for letting the drug dealer get away to warn the Iceman
in the first place? Had she somehow been in on it from the
start?

With all her heart, Jessie cursed the Iceman for threatening her friend and for tossing her into this wretched vat of
mistrust. With that one damned sentence, he'd planted this
extremely fertile seed of doubt, leaving her to water it with
profuse paranoia.

A week ago, being backed into a corner with no one to
turn to wouldn't have daunted her. Over the years, she'd
gotten herself past one or another of life's roadblocks all on
her own, just the way she'd always wanted it. But this was
different and far, far out of her depth. Much as she hated it,
for the first time in her life she desperately wanted to do
something she'd sworn she would never do and, thanks to
that one sentence, something she now *couldn't* do.

She wanted to ask for help.

ICEMAN POCKETED HIS PHONE. "Well done, Miss Bartlett," he
said to the sobbing woman. "Don't worry, it won't be much
longer." He replaced her gag and shoved her back into the
trunk, slamming the lid down just as his cell phone rang. He
dug his phone back out of his pocket, smirking when he saw
Rob's name. "Where are you?"

"I'm just getting off the highway. Where are *you?*" Rob
demanded.

Iceman flipped his middle finger at the phone but kept
his voice nice and neutral. "I'm on the other side of town.
I've found a house we can use." He relayed the address and
directions on how to find it. "If you get lost, call me back.

Don't ask anyone for directions. The fewer people who see you here, the better."

"Where's Judith? Are we going to be able to finish this thing tonight?"

"We'll have her in the morning. I'll explain everything when you arrive."

"You'd better. I'm about out of patience."

He was out of patience? Ha! The idiot had no idea he was living on borrowed time. After the unexpected Fox debacle, Iceman had no intention of leaving any other loose ends behind, and Rob became looser and looser with every word he uttered. "I will explain everything, I promise. Besides, I have a surprise for you. I've brought a guest along, and she will be at your disposal until tomorrow morning." A beat of silence followed, and Iceman could imagine the perverse little grin appearing on the other man's face. "Rob? Did you hear me?"

"I'll be there in twenty minutes."

Iceman chuckled after he disconnected. Manipulating Rob was child's play, taking only the mere mention of guaranteed sex to bring him to heel. By this time tomorrow, Iceman would be rid of the simpleton. Permanently.

Too bad he hadn't been able to employ the same solution for Fox. Already, thanks to that little prick, the blasted OASIS agency had found the Berger place.

Iceman mourned the loss of the old house. Several times over the years he'd taken comfort from visiting it. Visiting *them,* his firsts. Reliving the first time he'd held full and exquisite control over other people's lives, their pleas for mercy a beautiful symphony to his ears. Whenever he returned, it was a treasured interlude with that most beloved of memories.

He'd set the explosives, not so much to destroy the

evidence of his handiwork, but to protect it from the prying eyes of those who could never understand. Those who would sully and diminish his first masterpiece. No one would ever see it but him.

And now it was gone. Sad, but he'd survive it. The Haynes woman's proximity to the blast had been more unnerving. Had she been injured or killed, her tote bag with the thumb drive might have been destroyed right along with her. Or, worse, might have fallen into police hands. There would have been hell to pay. Those sniveling reptiles he did business with would throw their own young under the bus to save their asses. He'd never see a dime of blackmail money and would be hunted like an animal.

He shook off those morose thoughts. The woman *hadn't* died in the blast. She and the thumb drive were safe, and he would have them both in the morning. He could leave the country, and once things died down he could sneak back and take care of Fox, or get one of his blackmail victims to do it for him.

He took one last look through his binoculars, making sure Buchanan wasn't looking out the diner window. Returning the binoculars to his knapsack, he pulled out of shadowy thicket about a hundred yards down the road from the motel and headed back toward the temporary quarters he'd discovered earlier.

A large colonial-style home, it was located just outside of town and set back from the road. A tall boxwood hedge all along the front blocked most of the property from view of the passing traffic. When he'd first driven by it this afternoon, he'd spotted a couple of newspapers scattered on the driveway, and a quick reconnaissance of the large grounds showed the house appeared to be unoccupied.

After easily disabling a cheap alarm system, a search of

the interior confirmed the house was indeed empty. Even better, according to the copy of an itinerary he'd found stuck on a corkboard in the kitchen, the homeowners wouldn't be back for another three days. Perfect.

Returning now to the hideaway, he left the woman in the trunk and made another circuit of the house, inside and out. Satisfied they would be undiscovered here for the night, he helped himself to a bourbon from the well-stocked liquor cabinet in the dining room and went out to the porch to wait for Rob. Once the little shitbag arrived, he'd go over the plan for the morning before sending him off with the blonde. Iceman himself would wait to enjoy her charms at a later time.

He'd already decided to take both women with him to South America. There just wouldn't be enough time to enjoy them here. He'd long ago bought off some members of the Border Patrol, so he wouldn't have any issues smuggling the women into Canada. One of his clients kept a private airstrip not far from the border at which Iceman kept a small jet of his own. He sipped his bourbon with a warm sense of contentment. In less than forty-eight hours, he'd have both the blonde and the redhead in his small, private villa in Buenos Aires.

Where he would throw them a long and very special fiesta.

CHAPTER TWENTY

REEVE ROLLED over and reached out to pull Jessie close, but only cool sheets greeted his fingers. He slowly opened his eyes, his lids lead heavy. A glance at his watch showed he'd slept for a few hours. Good enough. Physically, he could sleep longer, but they didn't have that luxury. He flung the covers back and swung his feet to the floor, rubbing his hand across the back of his neck.

The silence of the room penetrated his consciousness. "Jessie?"

His sleepiness evaporated under an onslaught of apprehension as he checked the dark bathroom. Empty. He raced to the door of the room and yanked it open, already knowing she'd ditched him before seeing the vacant parking space where the Mustang had been. "Dammit!"

He slammed the door and scanned the room. She'd taken her tote bag, leaving him nothing to search for some clue to where she might have gone. He ran back to the bathroom, going through the futile motion of looking through the few cosmetics she'd left on the counter, desperate for any sort of hint. Nothing. "Son of a bitch!"

She must have decided to use herself as bait after all. Cold sweat seeped from his pores at the thought of her pulling such a reckless stunt, and he slapped his palm on the bathroom vanity. This was what he got for letting his guard down with her. He'd thought nothing of her edginess last night, assuming her nerves were stretched to the breaking point and never once thinking she was hiding something. She'd promised not to keep secrets, and he'd believed her, simple as that.

He'd *wanted* to believe her and let himself do it because he was falling for her. But he should have realized the very reasons he was falling for her—her strength, self-driven nature, and strong will—were the same reasons she would never sit idly by in the face of a threat. But none of that mattered now. He needed to find her before the Iceman got to her. *Think!* Where could she have gone? Back to her house, or had she thought of something else?

He paused in the bathroom doorway, slowly surveying the room for any possible clue. The faint scent of the lavender-scented shampoo she'd used the night before teased him. His gut tightened painfully at the thought of never again feeling her silky hair in his fingers.

His gaze passed the telephone on the nightstand and then whipped back. He stalked across the room, grabbed the receiver, and called Jake.

"Jessie's gone. Send someone to her house in case she shows up there. I need you to trace any calls that came in or out of here last night on this phone. It would be right around when you and I were talking. That was the only time she was alone."

"Hang tight, buddy, I'll check." Jake put him on hold, and Reeve cradled the phone between his ear and shoulder as he gathered his clothes from the foot of the bed and shuffled into his pants and shoes. He tucked his gun into the waistband and dragged his shirt on to cover it.

He pulled the pen and the little white memo pad with the motel logo on it closer, ready to take down whatever information Jake came up with.

Jake came back on the line. "A call did come in there. I tracked it back to a prepaid cell phone, so I don't know for sure who called. But I do know the call hit a cell tower less than five miles from your location."

"Shit, Jake, he's here." His temper flared to murderous levels. Like a schoolyard bully, the arrogant cocksucker taunted him with his nearness. And now the slime-bucket had lured Jessie away. Reeve had never before felt such intense hatred for another human being. "How the hell did he figure out where we are? Have our systems or phones been hacked?"

"With the firewalls I've put in place? I doubt it," Jake said. "I'll look into it, though. If he did, he's better than anyone I've ever seen."

"Then how could he have known?" No sooner had he asked the question when the answer hit him. "The car. The damn Mustang. I never checked it for a tracking device. Son of a bitch! Why didn't I check it?"

"Ah, hell, why *would* you? Who would think he was tracking his own man like that? But if there is a tracking device, maybe I can find her. It'll take time, though."

"Time we don't have." Reeve looked down at the pad again. There was a rough edge at the top of the pad from the last page torn from it. His heart rate accelerated as he fingered the indentations left from the note written on the previous page. Maybe Jessie had left him a clue after all. "I may have a lead, but I have to find a pencil before I'm sure."

"You're not making sense, buddy."

"I'll explain later. I'll call you back."

"Reeve, wait. I was just about to call you before you did. Tobie wants you to—"

"Tell Tobie I'll call back in a minute." Reeve dropped the phone in the cradle and ran out of the room. He raced down the parking lot to the front entrance. "I need a pencil!" he shouted as he burst into the lobby.

Purple Hair was no longer on duty, his replacement an overweight twenty-something young man with a serious acne condition. Obviously a graduate of the same school of pathetic customer service, he blinked stupidly at Reeve before pulling a pen from his shirt pocket. "Here."

"I said a *pencil*!" Reeve snarled.

"Geez, take it easy, mister," the clerk said. "What's the difference?" He opened a drawer and fumbled around, finally extracting a stubby little pencil. Reeve snatched it and began rubbing it lightly over the indentations.

Directions appeared on the page, and he showed the pad to the clerk. "Where does this lead?"

"That's the way to the town beach."

Reeve called Jake back. "I need backup here right away."

"Tobie and Fitz are already on their way in the company jet. That's what I was starting to tell you," Jake said. "Candy Bartlett was abducted from her home yesterday."

"Jessie's friend? The one she was traveling with?"

"Yes. Apparently her parents dropped by her place for a visit. They found her door unlocked and signs of a struggle inside. They reported her missing, and it's been on the news all morning."

More cold sweat trickled down his face. "That's not a coincidence. The Iceman must have taken her. That's why Jessie went off on her own. He's threatening her friend." Jessie's actions made sense now, and Reeve's level of anger with her dropped from blazing fury to simmering ire. She still should have told him.

"Tobie and Fitz should be landing inside of twenty minutes. They wanted to get to you as soon as possible once they saw the news report about the kidnapping. I've updated them about Miss Haynes going missing. Tobie wants you to meet them at the airport to plan the next move."

"No, tell them to meet me at the town beach. That's where Jessie is headed. Hell, she may be there already."

"Reeve, Tobie was crystal clear about you not going off on your own. Go to the airport."

"Can't do it. The Iceman is already here, and Jessie is heading right to him. How long do you think she's going to last on her own?"

"Don't go off half-cocked! That's what happened befo—"

"The town beach! Tell them to meet me there!" He disconnected, meeting the wide-eyed stare of the clerk. "You got a car I can borrow?"

The clerk looked at him as if he'd spoken Klingon. Reeve reached into his pocket and pulled out his cash. "I need a car right now. I'll rent it or buy it from you."

The sight of some easy money woke the clerk up in a hurry. "Two thousand." Reeve counted off the necessary bills, and the clerk gave him a set of keys. "It's the green hatchback near the entrance."

Reeve raced outside and found the car. He'd been royally ripped off. The battered little car wasn't worth two hundred, let alone two thousand. He prayed it ran better than it looked. The engine started on the second try, and he tore out of the parking lot.

Visions of Tabitha's body sprawled on top of the garbage filled his head, and he pressed the accelerator farther down.

He would not be late this time. *He would not!* Jessie would live.

He repeated that over and over to himself as he wove in and out of the early morning traffic. Still, ugly images seeped into his mind. Only this time, it was Jessie's body he saw in the dumpster.

"No, dammit!" he swore aloud. He'd get there in time to prevent the worst from happening. He had to, he just had to.

Another loss would kill him.

"TIME TO GO."

Rob gave no response, just stared off into space with that stupid grin plastered on his face. Iceman shook his head. Rob had been like that for the last hour. Once he'd laid eyes on the Bartlett woman, his expression morphed to a look of rabid lust one might expect to see on a prisoner just granted a conjugal visit with a centerfold. His anger instantly forgotten, he'd dragged the woman off to the nearest bedroom, thus staying out of Iceman's hair all night. Perfect.

But Rob's lack of focus this morning could screw things up. "Hey!"

Rob jumped in his seat. "What?"

"Pay attention. We have to go." Iceman reviewed the plan one more time as they walked out of the house.

"Yeah, yeah. I got it," Rob moaned before his eyes darted to the trunk of the car where they'd again stuffed the Bartlett woman. "And when it's done, I get to take this one with me, right?"

"Right." Iceman had told him that to keep him in line, but considering Rob's preoccupation with the blonde, maybe he should have come up with something else.

Too late now. He'd just have to keep a close eye on him. The moment when he could dispose of the fool couldn't come soon enough. Reminding himself that forbearance always paid off, he slid behind the wheel and flipped the ignition, heading for the local marina.

In less than an hour, Iceman would have everything he wanted—the thumb drive, the women, and Rob Cochran deader than disco.

JESSIE RUBBED her hands up and down her arms, though it did little to combat the chill of the early-morning ocean breeze. The arctic dread seizing her insides only made it worse. No matter how many times she told herself this was just a simple exchange, she couldn't set aside her absolute conviction the Iceman had other plans for this meeting's outcome. From the minute she'd found him in her living room, his intent to cause her physical harm had been clear. She'd be a fool to think he'd make the swap and allow her to take Candy and walk away.

So we'll have to escape him.

She studied her surroundings, but not having any idea which direction he'd come from put her at a disadvantage. And what if he didn't bring Candy with him? Tears welled in Jessie's eyes, and she fought them back. She refused to think about what Candy's absence might mean. Her friend was going to be all right. She had to be.

What would Reeve do if he were here? Shoot the bastard, most likely. *Dammit!* She should have taken Reeve's gun when she left the motel. Although it was probably just as well she hadn't. She'd never touched one before, let alone fired one. Between nervousness, inexperience, and her recent spate of bad luck, she'd probably fumble around with the thing and end up shooting herself in the knee or something before she managed to stop the Iceman. No, shootouts were best left to Reeve.

Reeve.

Thoughts of him battered her dejected heart. Unable to sleep a wink, she'd watched him all night, his handsome face so peaceful while he slumbered. He'd be furious when he found her gone, and she could only hope he would find a way to forgive her. Somewhere in the last few days, he'd become an important part of her life. Not just as a savior, but as a friend.

Yeah, right. A *friend.* Who was she kidding? She was falling in love with him. Since childhood, she'd been afraid to love someone, but now she wanted to be in love more than anything. The events of the past few days convinced her caring for someone—depending on them, even—didn't mean surrendering your life to them.

Falling for Reeve hadn't fundamentally changed her personality, hadn't turned her into a weak-willed little flower. She still knew how to take care of herself, how to think for herself. No one could take those things from her as long as she didn't let them. And believing every man on the planet would try meant denying herself a shot at one of life's greatest experiences.

She gave a dry chuckle, the irony more bitter than humorous. She'd gone from one prison to another, only the second had been of her own making, living half a life thanks to self-imposed restrictions. *Well, the hell with that.* For the first time since she'd left her father's house, she wanted—no, she *needed*—to let someone in. Reeve.

But will I get that chance?

Her fear of waking him hadn't allowed her to give him

one last kiss goodbye before she'd slipped the thumb drive from his pocket and left the motel. Funny how something she hadn't even known existed last week could be the one thing she wanted most in the world right now—to taste Reeve's lips on hers once more, to feel his comforting presence.

She'd been wrong not to tell him about this meeting. Because *of course* no one at OASIS had betrayed them. She'd been a fool to let the Iceman persuade her otherwise. Reeve trusted them, and that should have been good enough for her. The only one guilty of betrayal this time around was Jessie, breaking her promise to tell him everything.

True, he'd vetoed the idea of her setting herself up as bait, but if he'd known about Candy, he might have relented or at least come up with some kind of plan, backed up by his team. Too bad she hadn't given him the option. She wasn't used to collaborating with others when presented with an obstacle.

Another habit to break if she got out of this alive.

Hell, she'd start breaking it right now. Maybe it wasn't too late to tell Reeve where she was and what was going on. Clawing through her tote bag, she pulled out the phone. Her heart skipped a beat when she saw its shattered screen. *Dammit!* It must have broken in the explosion. With a cry of frustration, she flung it toward the water.

Swallowing the sudden lump in her throat, she again searched the beach for any sign of life. Nothing but seagulls scuttling along near the water's edge, a few of them floating on the waves. Dropping her tote bag to the sand, she sagged to her knees. She ran her fingers through the sand, putting a few fistfuls in her pockets. Maybe she'd have an opportunity to throw it in his eyes. Not much of a plan, but better than nothing.

A few moments later, she heard something above the crashing of the waves and the rusty cries of the gulls. A humming, purring noise. Instinctively, she scanned the ocean. The rising sun shone into her eyes so she almost didn't spot the boat, a decent-sized yacht, actually, approaching the shore from the brightening horizon. The engine cut off about a hundred yards from the beach, and the anchor splashed noisily as it dropped into the water.

Jessie forced herself back to her feet, having absolutely no wish to meet her fate on her knees.

A man lowered a small dingy from the yacht and climbed down into it. He started the tiny motor and headed toward the shore, the startled seagulls screeching loudly and taking off as a unit in a flurry of gray-black wings. Gleaming white hair left no doubt to the seaman's identity, and her stomach dropped to her toes.

Time had run out and evil had come for her.

CHAPTER TWENTY-ONE

REEVE CURSED the other cars on the road, hating the drivers, none of whom appeared to be in any particular hurry. He whipped the hatchback around a slow-moving minivan, ignoring the flipped bird he received in response.

Images of Jessie in the hands of the Iceman or one of his depraved clients flooded his mind as he hurtled down the exit ramp, almost sideswiping a gray delivery truck. Paying no attention to the blaring horns, he sped down the road, nearly standing the hatchback on two wheels as he swung into the beach entrance. He may have been too late to save Tabitha, but he was going to make damn sure he saved Jessie.

The memory of Tabitha's death hit him like a hard, stinging slap to his face. He lifted his foot from the accelerator and brought the car to a stop on the long road leading to the beach parking lot.

He was doing it again, repeating his exact same mistake. Last time, he'd gone racing off without a plan, his only thought to save a young girl from being kidnapped. Tabitha died because he'd been reckless. This time, Jessie would be the one to pay the price. Although every cell in his body screamed for him to get moving, his conscience whispered he'd cause more harm by not taking a few valuable moments to think.

He had three objectives. First and foremost, he needed to find Jessie and keep her safe. Second, if Candy Bartlett was here, he needed to get her out of harm's way as well. Third, catch that evil white-haired freak and turn him over to the authorities.

Okay, so how should he go about achieving those objectives?

First, he needed to know the status of his team. He dug his phone from his pocket and called Tobie. "Are you on the ground yet?" he asked as soon as she picked up.

"Yes. Jake filled us in about Miss Haynes. Have you reacquired her?" Censure underlined her professional tone. If she didn't fire him when this case wrapped up, no one would be more surprised than Reeve.

"No. I'm at the entrance road to the beach. How long before you get here?"

"About fifteen minutes."

"We may not have fifteen minutes!"

"Focus, Reeve. Proceed with caution and get the lay of the land. Stay calm, remember your training, and do your job."

Her words pierced his panic. He *was* trained for this. If he let his newfound emotions for Jessie get in the way, she'd be dead for sure, and he couldn't let that happen. Couldn't lose someone else who meant so much to him. *Focus.* "Right. Hold on."

Pushing his anxiety aside, he drove down the beach road and braked at the entrance to the parking area. The Mustang—empty—sat in the first of the painted parking spaces, but there were no other cars in the lot. Which meant one of two things: either the Iceman hadn't arrived, or he wasn't traveling by car. "He may be coming by boat. Call the Coast Guard."

"Already done. Jake took care of that as soon you told him you were going to the beach."

Reeve gave a silent prayer of thanks for the efficiency of his team. He'd never make the mistake of going rogue again.

"Anything else?" Tobie asked.

"No. Just hurry. Let's get the bastard this time. I'll call you back when I get down to the beach." He pulled into the parking area and hid the hatchback as best he could in a shaded spot on the far side of the lot, just in case the Iceman arrived by car.

After double-checking his gun and putting his phone on vibrate, he headed for the walkway lined with wooden pickets that led down to the beach. Breaks in the fencing marked the beginning of some coastal hiking trails, but Reeve didn't bother searching them for Jessie. His hunch about a boat resonated in his gut. The Iceman would have told her to meet him near the shore.

Large rocks and tall sea grass provided him with some cover as he crouched his way along the path, but it also prevented a clear view of the beach. The rising sound of a boat's engine reached him, and he picked up his pace.

The narrow path ended at stairs leading down to the sand. Reeve slowed his steps, careful to keep low. He crab-walked the last few feet to the top of the stairs and scanned the sand and sea. A yacht bobbed offshore while the Iceman motored a small dinghy toward the beach.

Jessie stood unharmed near the water's edge. The dispir-ited slump of her shoulders went a long way toward diffusing Reeve's angry urge to rush down there and shake her until she realized how foolish she'd been to come here alone. Instead, he wanted to hold her and tell her everything would be all right.

Because everything *would* be all right. He'd make sure of it.

First things first. He scanned the area again. The beach was deserted and, other than an ocean liner way out on the horizon, so was the water. Which left only the yacht, and he saw no sign of an accomplice on its top deck. All good.

Once he left the path, however, and started down the stairs, there would be no rocks or grass to provide any cover. He'd be an open target to both the Iceman and anyone hiding behind the darkened windows of the lower deck. Not so good.

He had to take his shot now, before the Iceman got any closer to shore. Closer to Jessie. As long as she was free, she could run.

Fighting the intense urge to just put a round in the bastard's head and be done with it, Reeve took careful aim at the dinghy's small motor, planning to put the little boat out of commission before the Iceman could make it to shore. He lined up his target and tightened his finger on the trigger.

Something cold and steely pressed against the back of his neck. "Drop the gun."

Frustrated fury tore through Reeve as he dropped his weapon. "Who are you?" he snarled. "Another one of the Iceman's errand boys? Like his pal Fox?"

"I'm no one's errand boy! The Iceman works for *me!* And you walked right into our trap." The man gave a shrill, high-pitched laugh, and Reeve would have given his left nut to put his fist through the bastard's face.

He took a deep breath and corralled his racing thoughts. Perhaps he could use this to his advantage. The Iceman had a heart of stone, but maybe this man could be reasoned with. "What do you want with Jessie?"

"I want her to disappear."

"Why? What did she ever do to you?"

"She's been a thorn in my side for years. At least now she can make herself useful for a change." The man's undisguised sneer of contempt made it clear he had a very strong, personal ax to grind.

"Listen," Reeve said, "I do a lot of work for a lot of rich people. If it's money you need, I'm sure I can find a way to help you. Just let her go."

"No! It's high time Miss Has-It-All gets what's coming to her."

Icy fear coated Reeve's spine. Whatever the grudge might be, it ran twisted and deep with this guy. Deeper than money could fix. The slimeball needed to be neutralized. Fast. "I'm going to turn around now."

"Don't try anything!"

"I won't. I'm just going to stand up and turn around." Reeve didn't wait for permission but slowly rose and faced his assailant, a man in his early twenties. He had a bony frame that stood about five foot nine. A pricey haircut just missed covering up the fact that premature baldness would inexorably have its way, while sleek designer clothes failed to hide the beginnings of a stomach paunch. He held an expensive Walther PPK in shaky hands, and his narrow blue eyes darted about as if he couldn't decide whether to keep a closer watch on Reeve or on whatever was happening with Jessie down by the water.

"Just take it easy," Reeve said. "It doesn't have to be like this."

"Yes, it does! It's my turn now. Since birth, she held the keys to the kingdom, but she didn't want the Cochran fortune. Well I do! And now she's going to help me get it. Once she's gone, Mitchell will have no other heir but me. He adopted me. I'm his son! I'll continue his legacy in his name."

Ah, the stepbrother. Rob Cochran. Now the man's raving made some sort of sense. Jealousy could do strange things to people, and from what Jessie had told him about how her father treated his own flesh and blood, Reeve could only imagine how cruel the man must have been to his stepson.

"Jessie walked away from that a long time ago," Reeve said, careful to keep his tone neutral and his hands in the air. "She doesn't want anything to do with her father. She's not in your way."

"Shut up! You don't know these people like I do. It's always about money with them. It's all about scheming. I'll bet Judith had a plan all along when she walked out. Of course she did. She's a Cochran through and through, and you better believe she had it all worked out to her advantage from the get-go.

"Well I'm the one with the plan now!" The tremors in Rob's hand increased along with his anger. "Once she's gone and Iceman pays me the finder's fee, I'll pay back the money and Mitchell will never need to know. Then I'll prove to him I'm a worthy heir. Nothing's going to stop me!" He looked scathingly at Reeve. "Not even Judith's big, bad bodyguard. Put your hands on your head, turn around, and get moving."

Hopes sinking, Reeve did as instructed. Rob was absolutely crazy. Dealing with the Iceman had been daunting enough, but with this demented fuck added to the mix, the predicament spiraled more and more out of control with every passing second. Reeve had never wanted the support of his team more.

The pair on the beach faced them as Rob marched him

along the sand and called out to the Iceman. Jessie's shoulders drooped even farther when she turned, her face a mask of defeat. Reeve stared hard at Jessie, trying to offer comfort without words. Difficult, since they were both now trapped in one hell of a mess. Tobie and Fitz were on their way, but until they arrived, Reeve and Jessie were on their own.

And he was just about out of ideas.

"WHERE'S CANDY?" Jessie demanded as the Iceman got out of the boat and approached her.

"There's no need for you to worry about Miss Bartlett." His calm, silky tone made Jessie's skin crawl. "We'll be joining her soon enough."

His pronouncement didn't surprise her, but hearing him say the words out loud destroyed the last tenacious shred of hope she'd clung to so desperately.

"No," she said with a bravado she didn't really feel. "You said we would make an exchange. The thumb drive for Candy. Now where is she?"

He closed the short distance between them and seized her arm, his black eyes boring into hers. Nausea roiled through her at his touch. "You are in no position to make demands, Miss Haynes. You will give me that thumb drive and you will get in this boat. *Now.*"

He pulled her toward the dinghy as a voice cried out from up the beach. They both turned, and Jessie's heart lurched with hope at the sight of Reeve coming toward her. But he had his hands on his head, and the man following him—definitely not one of his fellow OASIS operatives—held a gun to his back. Her hopes fell, and despair quickly mingled with confusion when she looked at the second man.

What the hell? "Rob?"

"Hello, Judith. Surprised to see me?" he smirked.

"Why are you here? What are you doing with that gun?"

"What, you don't think I'm man enough to handle a gun?"

Jessie bit back a scream as he waved the weapon at Reeve.

"I may not be as tall as your bodyguard, but I know how to use a gun just the same." He tilted the barrel up in the air and fired a blast into the sky.

"You idiot!" the Iceman hissed. "Do you *want* the police to show up?"

Rob's eyes widened, and he quickly glanced up and down the beach. "There's no one around," he groused as he returned his attention to Reeve. "Not such a big-deal body-guard after all, are you?"

Reeve didn't respond. Jessie searched his face for some clue, some hint of a plan he might have. His eyes locked on hers like lasers, but she had no idea what she should do.

"Let's go, Miss Haynes." The Iceman tugged her toward the dinghy.

"No!" she said, pulling against his grip. "Not until you let Candy go." She turned to her stepbrother. "I don't know what he's promised you, Rob, but it isn't worth it. Help us!"

"Ha! Help you? I'm the one who wanted to get rid of you in the first place." He laughed at her gasp of shock. "That's right, Judith. I'm willing to fight for my inheritance. I'm not going to just walk away from it."

"What are you talking about? I have nothing to do with your inheritance."

"Like hell you don't! It doesn't matter what you say now,

anyway. You'll be gone soon enough." He turned his focus back to Reeve. "Get on your knees."

Reeve complied, and Jessie's heart beat a staccato rhythm in her chest. Their odds worsened by the second.

"Why, Rob?" She racked her brain, unable to think of any injustice she might have caused him. In truth, she hardly knew her stepbrother. She'd left for college soon after Rob and his mother had moved into the house, so she'd only seen him on holidays. Since he was six years her junior, they had little in common. After she'd left her father's house for good, she'd had no contact with Rob at all, knowing only what news Kim shared during their brief calls. How could he be holding such a malicious grudge against her?

"Why?" she repeated. "I never did anything to you."

"You never did anything for me, either. Sure, you like to pretend you're better than your father, but the truth is you're as mean and nasty as he is. I remember what you were like when you came home to visit. You just walked around with your nose stuck up in the air. You never even tried to be my friend. You could have told Mitchell to leave me and my mother alone. He would have listened to you!"

A lump rose in her throat. She *did* know how awful it was to grow up in that house. But she'd been so intent on her own survival she hadn't had the strength to worry about anyone else. Nor could she recall Kim even hinting that Mitchell hurt Rob. "I'm sorry. I didn't know you needed my help."

"Of course not! You were too busy with all your stuck-up girlfriends to pay any attention to me."

"Then punish me, Rob, if you feel you must. But let Reeve go. Let Candy go."

His lips peeled back in an evil grin. "I don't give a crap

what happens to that bitch now. I taught her a special lesson last night. She's very sorry for looking down her nose at me. She'll think twice before considering herself too good for somebody ever again. In fact"—he laughed coldly—"she's probably been ruined for other men, now that she's had a real man like me."

The madness blazing out of his eyes chilled Jessie to the bone as a frigid horror congealed in her stomach. "What have you done to her?"

"What do you think? I fu—"

"Shut up, both of you! We have to get out of here." The Iceman glared at Rob before pointing a finger at Reeve. "Shoot him and let's go."

"No, don't!" Jessie swung her gaze back to Reeve's face. His stare retained the same intensity as before, yet she still had no idea what to do. If she couldn't think of something, Reeve would die. Unbearable pain raced through her, and tears filled her eyes.

Rob snickered. "Not so high and mighty now, are you? The Iceman is going to teach you the same lesson Candy learned. Hell, I might even give him a hand. It's not like we're really brother and sister, so it won't be weird." He chuckled at his tasteless wit. "By the time we're through with you, there won't be much left of the proud Miss Judith Cochran."

He laughed again, and an explosive rage overrode her fear. Ripping free of the Iceman's grasp, she launched herself at Rob. She hit him with the full force of her fury, determined to scratch that smug expression off his face. They stumbled a few feet as she swiped her hand across his face, going for his eyes.

"My name," she screeched, "is Jessie Haynes! I want nothing to do with the Cochran name and I want nothing to do with you!" She pummeled his head and face, but he managed to duck away and grab a fistful of her hair. Screaming in pain, she clawed frantically at his hand as he dragged her toward the water. He dropped his gun to seize her arm. She reached for it, but Rob savagely dragged her into the surf before she could grab it.

"I'll teach you!" he roared as he hauled her farther into the icy ocean. She spotted Reeve fighting with the Iceman just before Rob plunged her head into the briny water. He held her there for an agonizing moment before pulling her up. She coughed and gasped for breath, barely managing to close her mouth before he put her under again. His fingers were like iron claws in her hair, and she couldn't gain any traction as the waves pushed and pulled at her. Just when she thought her chest would burst, he yanked her up again.

"Oh, no," he whispered in her ear as she sucked precious air into her lungs. "You don't get to die so easy. I need you alive to get the money. But I hope he makes you scream just like I made Candy scream."

He plunged her head back in the water again, but almost immediately pulled her out. His screechy laugh rang in her ears as he continued to dunk her in and out of the water as if he were a child playing with a bath toy. Jessie coughed and sputtered and fought like mad, but her strength was waning rapidly.

Her tears mingled with the sea. Each time Rob pulled her head out of the water, blurry glimpses of Reeve wavered in and out of her vision, but she couldn't determine what he was doing. Was he still fighting with the Iceman, or was that his dead body bobbing up and down in the waves?

She continued her now feeble struggles to break free of Rob's grip, her molten rage refusing to allow her to admit defeat. As long as there remained the slightest hope of getting to Reeve, she would keep trying or die. Blackness almost fully crowded her vision when she heard a shot, and then another. Rob jerked her head back with a violent yank of her hair.

She shrieked in agony as she fell backward, then the water closed over her face and poured into her throat.

THE ICEMAN'S attention followed the battling pair as Jessie lashed out at Rob with astonishing ferocity. Reeve flung himself forward, clasping his hands together and swinging them, connecting a solid blow to the man's calves. The Iceman staggered but didn't go down. Reeve rolled after him and barely made it to his knees again as the Iceman recovered his footing and pointed his weapon toward Reeve's face.

Throwing his left arm up and blocking the Iceman's gun arm, Reeve aimed a punch with his right fist directly at the man's groin. The Iceman turned to avoid the blow, taking the brunt of it on his hip. He stumbled a few steps, giving Reeve the critical second he needed to gain his feet.

With a roar, he tackled the Iceman, seizing his wrist and squeezing as hard as he could. The gun flew from his opponent's hand as they hit the sand. A blow landed solidly on his jaw, and Reeve saw stars, but fear and fury overrode the pain. He bashed his fists anywhere he could land them as the two men rolled into the water.

The Iceman fought back hard, punching and kicking with an almost inhuman strength. Waves sucked at them as Reeve delivered a punch directly to the Iceman's face. Blood gushed from his nose as he howled in pain and spun away, belly flopping into the water. He got to his hands and knees, spitting blood and coughing as the waves splashed his face.

Reeve got to his feet, his desire to hammer this man to a bloody pulp nowhere near satisfied. "Get up! Before the Spencers get the pleasure of seeing you rot in jail for life, I'm going to enjoy beating the living shit out of you for what you did to Tabitha. Get up!"

The Iceman spat another phlegmy red mess into the ocean. "Tabitha was a drugged-out little slut who got what she deserved. Why do you care about her anyway? She was only sixteen. Wouldn't it be beneath some do-gooder like you to go after a tasty young thing like that?"

Reeve kicked him in the side, not even trying to deny the surge of pleasure as he watched the man go tumbling farther into the water. He wanted to pulverize the man's face until there was nothing left. Ready to do just that, he took a step forward. The Iceman stopped coughing and started laughing, an evil, remorseless chuckle. Reeve never wanted so badly to kill someone in his life.

"What's so funny?"

"You are. You're so worried about getting revenge for the death of one girl, you're about to lose another." He laughed again, his gaze directed to a point behind Reeve.

Reeve whipped his head around. Rob stood several yards away, dunking Jessie's head in and out of the water. Her feeble, choking gasps penetrated his crimson rage and he lunged toward Rob. A flash of light snapped his attention back to the Iceman. The rising sun glinted off the vicious switchblade his foe now wielded as he sprang at Reeve. Leaping back, Reeve cried out as the tip of the blade ripped his shirt and tore across his flesh.

He staggered back another few steps as the Iceman gave him an evil smile, waving the knife back and forth. "What a shame," he taunted. "You were so close. But you've failed. Again."

Reeve kept his eyes on the knife, ignoring the fiery sting of the salt water dripping into the gash on his chest. The wound wasn't life-threatening, but he couldn't afford to give the Iceman another chance to cut him. More difficult to ignore, however, were Jessie's desperate coughs and gasps. He had to get to her before that maniac of a stepbrother killed her.

"Don't worry about her," the Iceman said, as if reading his mind. "I won't let Rob end her. I've got too much time invested in her to lose her now." He took another step forward. "You can go to your death knowing she will outlive you by at least a week. Possibly two. She *is* exquisite. I might not get tired of her too quickly."

"You'll never lay a hand on her, you sick fuck," Reeve snarled. Jessie's gasps grew more strangled. She wasn't going to withstand Rob's feral assault much longer. Which meant he had to subdue the Iceman. Fast. "You're the one that's going to lose everything. I'm going to laugh my ass off knowing you're getting passed around and treated like those girls you auctioned off. Hope you enjoy being a jailhouse bitch."

The Iceman's eyes narrowed, and he lunged forward with a rasping growl. Reeve leapt back but as he pulled his arm back to deliver another punch, he lost his footing on the wet, crumbly sand and landed on his ass. The Iceman charged, and Reeve awkwardly scuttled backward onto the shore on his hands and feet. A large wave struck the Iceman at the back of his knees, knocking him off balance just as Reeve's fingers brushed something cold and metal in the sand. Desperate for any kind of weapon, he closed his fingers around it.

Dropping back onto his butt, he fumbled the object out of the sand, quickly registering it was Rob's Walther PPK. He turned it the right way and raised it up in front of him in both hands. The Iceman recovered his footing and loomed over him. Reeve took quick aim and pulled the trigger.

The shocked look on the Iceman's face as blood poured from his chest gave Reeve sweet satisfaction, but he had no time to savor it. As the lifeless bastard toppled forward, Reeve rolled away. He got only as far as his stomach before the Iceman landed on his legs, no longer a mortal threat, but literally a dead weight.

Reeve strove to free himself, but their wet denim jeans stubbornly clung to each other, impeding his efforts as another wave threatened to suck him back into the sea. He watched in wretched frustration as Rob kept thrusting Jessie's head under the water, barely allowing her to catch a single breath in between. The sick grin on the man's face bespoke his clear descent into madness.

Jessie's gasps grew weaker, and with a desperate, whispered prayer, Reeve propped his elbows in the sand and fired.

CHAPTER TWENTY-TWO

ROB HOWLED IN PAIN, yanking Jessie's head out of the water before flinging her backward into the sea. He clutched his shoulder, staring stupidly at the blood seeping through his fingers.

"You shot me!" he screeched. "I can't believe you shot me!" He took an awkward step forward in the waves. Reeve prepared to shoot him again, but a shout from up the beach surprised Rob back into motionlessness.

Fitz and Tobie, guns drawn, thundered down the beach, yelling warnings at Rob not to move. Tobie reached the shoreline first. Pointing her gun squarely at his chest, she ordered Rob from the water and down to his knees, unmoved by his indignation as he screamed about his injury.

Fitz reached Reeve and pulled the corpse from his legs. Reeve made a frenzied scramble to his feet. He plunged into the water, crying out from the fresh burst of pain exploding in his chest as the salty sea found his wound. Jessie drifted a little farther out, her body motionless except for the bob of the waves. Panic propelled his agonized strokes through the water, and he reached her in seconds.

"Jessie! I'm here, hang on!" She didn't respond and her eyes were closed. Reeve towed her back to shore, his heart seizing each time the waves crashed over her head. He laid her on the sand, tilting her head back as he began mouth-to-mouth resuscitation, the coldness of her lips chilling him with terror.

"Breathe, Jessie! C'mon, baby!" He pinched her nose shut and blew more air into her lungs.

Fitz knelt beside them, pressing his fingers to Jessie's neck. "I don't feel a pulse." He began CPR compressions as Reeve continued breathing for her. "I've called 911."

"I hope she dies!" Rob screamed. "She's a lousy, stuck-up bitch!"

"Shut up!" Tobie poked him none too gently in the back of the head with her gun.

They worked in silence, Reeve cursing himself with every passing second. This was his fault. Once again, a woman's life had been placed in his hands, and once again he had failed to protect her. Failed to save her. Not just any woman, but Jessie.

Salt stung his eyes as his tears blinded him. Fitz kept doing compressions, but Reeve knew they were wasting their time. Grief crushed what had been left of his heart.

He blew another breath into her mouth and then looked at her face, wobbling in time to Fitz's compressions. Her lips, slack and tinged blue, called to him. Jessie would never stop trying. She was in there fighting, just as she had her whole life. How the hell could he even think she would do otherwise?

All in, all the time. He'd lived that motto with the SEALs. Jessie lived it her whole life.

He pressed his lips to hers, giving her another breath of air, and then another. He lifted his head slightly, ready to give her a third breath when Jessie coughed. Water sprayed from her mouth and over his face. He and Fitz quickly rolled her to her side so she could clear her lungs. She retched and spat what seemed like a gallon of water, her racking coughs now music to his ears.

"How are you feeling?" he asked when her coughs subsided.

"Like crap." She rubbed a hand to her head. "My scalp is on fire, and it hurts to breathe."

"An ambulance will be here soon," Fitz said. "The police too."

Reeve could already hear the sirens wailing in the distance. He helped Jessie to sit up. She slid her arms around his waist and clung to him.

"Don't leave me," she said shakily.

"Never." Tears streamed unheeded down his face as he held her close.

He'd been given a second chance, and he grabbed it with both hands.

JESSIE HELD Candy's hand as she slept in her hospital bed. Fitz had used the dinghy to check the yacht and found Candy bound and gagged in one of the staterooms. Her face and body still bore the cuts and bruises she'd received when the Iceman had kidnapped her and from Rob's subsequent brutal assault. Those wounds would fade in time, but Candy had a long road to emotional recovery ahead of her. Jessie vowed to be with her every step of the way.

Candy moaned in her sleep, her grip tightening on Jessie's hand.

"Shhh, I'm right here," Jessie whispered. She reached up with her free hand and stroked Candy's brow. "Just rest. Try not to think about it." Candy's grip relaxed a little, and the troubled wrinkle on her forehead faded as she drifted into a deeper sleep.

The door whooshed open, and Reeve walked in. It had been nearly two days since those hellish moments on the beach, and during that time they hadn't seen each other. After being treated for her near drowning, Jessie had been released from the hospital and had countless interviews with the police as well as with the OASIS staff. Every other waking moment was spent at Candy's side, including accompanying her on the air ambulance flight the Bartletts secured to transfer their daughter to a private hospital in New York.

Tobie Armstrong had informed Jessie that it took sixteen stitches to close up Reeve's chest wound, but he had not sustained any nerve damage and would make a full recovery. He, too, had spent the better part of the last two days recounting the events at the beach, and then working with his team at their Manhattan headquarters. Jessie's only contact with him had been a brief phone conversation last night, making arrangements to meet here to go to a memorial service for Tabitha Spencer.

She'd missed him, plain and simple. The mere sight of his face warmed away the constant chill she'd felt the last two days, and she drank him in.

"How's Candy doing?" he asked.

"She's in pretty bad shape. But she's a fighter. She told me this morning she's determined to testify when the time comes. That's a good sign."

"How about you? Are you still prepared to stand up to your stepbrother in court?"

"Absolutely."

Rob, of course, was pleading not guilty to all charges. He claimed the Iceman had been blackmailing him because of his gambling debts and therefore coerced him into acting against his will at the beach. At least, that was the nonsense he spewed before a very expensive lawyer in a very expensive suit arrived at the police station—at her father's behest, she was certain—and firmly instructed Rob to keep his mouth shut. Mitchell Cochran would no doubt spend a fortune to sweep the entire episode under the rug.

Jessie supposed she should be glad to know she'd been right—her father hadn't been behind the Iceman's attempts to kidnap her. And perhaps she should be equally glad his image had not been found on any of the thumb drive files, but she couldn't quite get there. She had no question he was capable of such an act. Plus, he did have an indirect hand in the whole thing anyway. If he'd been a decent father figure to Rob, a decent man at all, none of this would have happened.

She sighed. It didn't matter to her how many fancy lawyers her father hired or how many people he bought off to keep things quiet. It didn't change who or what he was. He ruined too many lives on a regular basis, just because he could. She hoped one day he would be held accountable for his actions.

Candy's parents returned from the cafeteria, and five minutes later Jessie and Reeve were on their way to the Spencers' suburban estate. A tense silence grew between them as the miles rolled away. They hadn't talked about it yet, so maybe he was still angry with her for going off to face the Iceman alone.

She glanced at him, startled by the expression on his face. She'd expected an irritated twitching in his jaw, but instead the grim line of his lips coupled with the tight set of his shoulder suggested nervousness, not anger. "What's wrong?"

"Nothing."

Bullshit. The closer they got to the estate, the more his face betrayed his claim. Clearly, he didn't want to attend the memorial. "You're not still blaming yourself for Tabitha's death, are you?"

His skin flushed. "How can I face them? Today of all days. I don't know why the Spencers insisted I should come."

"Probably because they want to thank you. You did what you promised them you would do. You brought Tabitha's killer to justice."

"Vigilante justice, maybe. I'm not sure that's what they had in mind. I've denied them the pleasure of seeing the Iceman found guilty and sent away for his crimes for a long time."

"I don't think they're going to care about any of that."

"Well, we'll see, won't we?" They drove through a pair of stone pillars marking the Spencers' property. An older man in a somber dark suit pointed them to a long row of cars lined along the driveway. They parked, and Jessie reached for his hand as they walked up the drive. He took it quickly, his grip tight, as if he were clutching a lifeline.

A butler answered the door and led them through the lavish house and out to an elegant patio where clusters of guests were scattered about. Beyond the patio, several rows of folding chairs were set up. A large picture of Tabitha's laughing face stood on an easel in front of the chairs. Next to the picture, a large hole in the ground had been prepared for the willow tree the Spencers were planting as a remembrance of their daughter.

Tobie Armstrong and the rest of the OASIS team stood together on a far corner of the patio. As Jessie and Reeve joined them, Tobie greeted them with the latest information on the case. "The DA and Fox have come to an agreement."

Once informed of the Iceman's death, she told them, Fox looked as if a two-ton load had been lifted from his back. He became the model of cooperation with both OASIS and the police, answering any and all questions regarding the Iceman he could, although no one could find out the Iceman's true identity. The clever bastard had somehow managed to remove all evidence of himself from the foster care databases.

In return for cooperating, the DA offered Fox a generous plea bargain in the matter of his attempt to kidnap Jessie. He happily accepted it, even though it still meant jail time. As far as Fox was concerned, apparently, a little time in prison was a small price to pay to be rid of the Iceman forever.

"So I guess we'll never know the Iceman's real name?" Jessie asked.

"Doesn't look like it," Ian remarked. "And that sucks. But I can live with it, knowing he's never going to threaten anyone again."

Jake spoke up. With his thick, dark hair and horn-rimmed bespectacled eyes, he put Jessie in mind of an older, sexier Harry Potter. "We heard back from the Sandy Hollow Police Department regarding the explosion. Some of the remains at the scene were definitely the Bergers. Others are still unidentified. Probably the other foster kids. Fox gave us their names, but it's unlikely they have any DNA in the system to test against."

"But how could they not have been reported missing all

those years ago? Didn't they have caseworkers?" Jessie asked.

"Ha," Maddie scoffed. "Welcome to the wonderfully underfunded world of foster care. So many of those poor kids slip through the cracks."

Jessie shuddered. "How sad that the most defenseless members of society so often go unprotected. I wonder if that's where some of the victims on those files came from?"

"It's possible," Jake answered. "That's one avenue I'm looking into because so far, I've only been able to identify a few of them from reported missing children and women records." His eyes held a haunted look, and Jessie didn't envy him his task. Looking at those files over and over was bound to mess with his head.

"What about the men on the files? Have any of them been arrested?"

"No," Fitz grumbled, his shaggy blond hair dipping down over one eye. "We've turned the thumb drive over to the police. But given that most of those men are wealthy or politicians, or both, their slick lawyers are keeping the arrests at bay for now. But it's only a matter of time."

"That's right," Maddie added. "The media doesn't have a copy of the files yet, but they already smell a story, and they're circling like sharks in the water. Once those files hit the mainstream, those asswipes are done." Jessie got the sense Maddie just barely restrained herself from cackling with glee at the thought.

"It won't end there," Fitz went on. "There were a lot of unidentified customers at those auctions. We're going to keep trying until we track them all down."

The entire OASIS team nodded in agreement, the resolute look on their faces assuring Jessie the matter wouldn't be buried by political pandering. Their determination impressed her.

"We hope," Tobie added, "we can bring some comfort to the families of those girls, at least those we can identify."

"Thank you, all of you," Jessie said. "For helping me, for rescuing Candy, and for not letting this drop. I'd like to do whatever I can to help those girls too. I'll contribute whatever I can to your fee."

As a unit, the team shook their head no. "Not necessary, Miss Haynes, but thank you," Tobie said. "Money is not an issue. We're still going to take the jobs that pay the bills when we need to, but we're all agreed those girls are our number one clients now. We won't let them down."

"Absolutely," Reeve said. "This isn't over."

Mr. and Mrs. Spencer appeared from the house, walking from group to group, greeting their guests. Their sadness was evident, but from the snatches of conversation she overheard, Jessie suspected the recent developments were going a long way in helping them deal with their tremendous loss. Their strength solidified her own determination. She would do whatever she could to help any other families that may have been destroyed by the Iceman and his clients.

The couple approached their group, and Reeve's grip on Jessie's hand grew tighter. She squeezed back, hoping to ease his dread of the next few moments.

"We want to thank you all for coming," Mr. Spencer said, "and for everything you did. My wife and I are profoundly grateful."

The team nodded their acknowledgment, each offering their condolences in turn.

"Thank you," Mrs. Spencer said, a light sheen of tears in her eyes. "The ceremony will start in a few moments so the rest of you can take your seats. Mr. Buchanan, we'd like to speak with you privately, please." She took Reeve's other hand, and Jessie gave him a discreet elbow to his side when his grip on her own hand tightened to the point of pain. He released his clutch and allowed Mrs. Spencer to lead him and her husband to the area in front of the chairs.

Tears stung the back of Jessie's eyes as she watched the trio share a deep conversation. She'd fallen for Reeve, harder than she ever thought she would fall for someone in her life. But if he couldn't forgive himself for what happened to Tabitha, it would slowly devour his self-respect, threatening any chance they had at a future together. He'd already taken some baby steps toward self absolution, but she had a feeling this conversation with the Spencers would be the final push he really needed.

Which meant that maybe, just maybe, they could plan for the future.

WITH LEADEN FEET, Reeve allowed himself to be tugged along by Mrs. Spencer. They reached the first row of chairs, the lovely photograph of Tabitha claiming their attention. Reeve stared at it, a lump rising in his throat as the images of her death crowded his brain.

"This is how I'm going to remember our little girl," Mrs. Spencer said. "I've seen the photos of what that man did to her, and I thought they would torture me forever. I don't know that I'll ever fully be free of them, but it helps me to know he didn't get away with it. So whenever those pictures haunt me, I'm going to think of this photograph. I'm going to make myself think of the good times." She dabbed at her eyes with a handkerchief before turning to face him. "And I have you to thank for that."

"Mrs. Spencer, it was my fault—"

She placed a finger on his lips. "No. Before the drugs got the best of her, our Tabitha was a wonderful, compassionate young woman. We saw that same darling girl returning to us as she made her recovery. She would never want you to feel bad about this. She would know, as we do, where the true blame lies in all of this." She dropped her finger and her tears flowed freely now, but they did not diminish the hope and compassion in her eyes.

Her kindness and strength touched him, and Reeve knew he had no business feeling sorry for himself. Doing so would be an insult to these amazing people. "I'm so sorry for what happened to your daughter, and I want you to know that the OASIS team is going to do everything it can to see that all of those men are held accountable. We all want to do it. For Tabitha."

Mrs. Spencer pulled him in for a hug. "Thank you," she whispered. "You are a good man."

Reeve stepped back, and Mr. Spencer shook his hand. "We, too, will be doing what we can to see that those animals get what they deserve. I'm speaking with my attorneys about initiating lawsuits against some of them. I don't care if I don't win a dime. If it puts those men in the spotlight and reveals them for what they are, it will be worth it."

The minister officiating the memorial service nodded at them as he stepped up to the podium next to Tabitha's photograph. They took their seats, the Spencers insisting he sit with them. Reeve cried as Tabitha's friends and relatives stood up and shared their stories about her. Surprisingly, he found he could actually laugh at some of the humorous ones told by her high school buddies.

The minister said his final blessings as two of Tabitha's cousins lowered the willow tree into the ground. Mr. and

Mrs. Spencer each picked up a garden spade and tossed the first shovelfuls of dirt over the roots. Mrs. Spencer then turned and extended the shovel to Reeve.

As he added soil to the hole, a weight lifted from his shoulders. He would always wish the outcome had been different, but he knew now he'd done the best he could for Tabitha and her parents. And his best had been helpful. Coming to the service today had been the right thing to do. Maybe it wasn't a great day, but it was a worthy day.

He passed the shovel to the next person, and his eyes searched through the guests until he found Jessie, seated with Tobie and the rest of the team. Her warm smile loosened the last knot in his chest, and he made his way to her side. After a brief stay at the post-ceremony reception, they said their goodbyes and headed for Jessie's house.

They didn't speak in the car, each lost in their own thoughts. Once inside, Reeve didn't waste time with words, pulling her close and kissing her deeply. He'd missed her unbearably the last two days, and her passionate response left no doubt she felt the same. Between kisses, they tore at each other's clothes as they worked their way up the stairs. They fell to the bed amid laughter and heat. This time, their lovemaking didn't feel like an escape, but rather a homecoming.

For the first time since Ann Marie died, Reeve knew he'd found his family.

JESSIE SIGHED CONTENTEDLY as Reeve rolled to his back and pulled her close. She tried to remember the last time she'd been this utterly and completely relaxed. Her massage on the beach at Key West, maybe, although not quite in the same way. Then, she'd been relaxed and content. Right now, in this moment, she felt relaxed, content, and... *complete*. There really was no other word for it.

Would she ever have realized the disservice she'd been doing to herself if not for the events of the past several days? In an ironic sense, maybe Rob and the Iceman had done her a life-saving favor.

Thoughts of the Iceman were enough to cast a cloud over her good mood, and it sucked that the bastard still had the power to ruin a cherished moment. Understandable though, she supposed. Even though she knew the Iceman was dead, had seen for herself those repulsive black eyes staring lifelessly at the sky, his actions were going to haunt her for a long time.

"Welcome to the wonderful world of PTSD," Reeve said.

She lifted her head, giving him a wistful smile. "How did you know?"

"After everything that's happened, I'd be surprised if you *weren't* suffering from it, to some small degree at least. I can recommend a good therapist if you like. Helped me a lot when I got back to civilian life."

"Maybe down the road if I need it. But I think, for me, taking action is the best medicine. I meant what I said earlier about assisting OASIS. I know I'm not a trained investigator, but I can still help. Whether they're dead or alive, identifying those girls won't be the end of it. They and their families will need help. Candy is going to need help, so I want to set up a support group for the victims."

"That's a great idea."

"And I want you to teach me how to use a gun, as well as any other sort of self-defense techniques you think I can use."

"I'll be happy to show you anything you want to learn.

Tobie has insisted I take some time off rather than firing me, thank goodness, so we can start anytime. Lesson number one is not putting yourself in unnecessary danger." His chest rose as he inhaled deeply, and Jessie could almost predict his next words. "We still need to talk about what happened that day. You should have told me when the Iceman called. It was foolish of you to face him alone."

"I wanted to tell you. I really did. But I couldn't risk Candy's life."

"So you were willing to endanger your own?" His sharp tone stung, but she knew it came from fear more than anger.

"I hoped it wouldn't come to that. And in my defense, I did decide to call you from the beach and would have if the phone had worked. But it doesn't matter now, and in the end it all worked out."

Reeve snorted. "Just barely. Listen, I think you and I could have something really special, but I have to know you won't keep things from me."

"I think we could have something special too, but I can't change who I am. I *won't* change who I am." She propped her chin on his chest, careful to avoid the bandage covering his knife wound. "You have to understand, I can never allow anyone but myself to be in charge of my decisions. Not even you."

"It's not about being in charge of your decisions. I have no desire to control you. But I don't want you to hide things from me. Especially things that could be potentially dangerous. I can't live like that, always wondering if you're keeping secrets. I lost my little sister that way."

She reached up and stroked his strong jaw, rubbing her thumb over the tantalizing little scar she'd come to adore. "I understand that, I really do. Secrets have no place in a relationship. I promise not to keep things from you, but you have to promise you'll respect my decisions, even if they differ from yours."

He blew out an angsty breath. "I don't know if I can do that. Not if it's something threatening. All I can promise is that I'll try."

"Not good enough. There's a reason I want to learn weaponry and self-defense. I don't want you to feel you have to protect me all the time. I want you to feel comfortable in knowing I can take care of myself."

He stroked her hair as a ghost of a smile appeared on his lips. "I'm falling in love with you. I want to have a family with you. I guess that means we're going to have our ups and downs. But I promise to respect your decisions."

"Good, because I love you too. And having a family sounds like heaven. Since my mother died, I haven't had a real family. I thought I could go through life on my own, not needing anyone, but I can't. I need you. I'll need you always, but not as a protector. As a partner."

His smile broadened, melting her heart. "I wouldn't have it any other way."

EPILOGUE

GOD DAMNED JUDITH!

Mitchell Cochran flung the report to his desk, each irritating detail of it committed to memory. His daughter's name mocked him from every page. She'd always been more trouble than she was worth.

Marriage to Tony Wallace would have set things up pretty good for her, the least Mitchell could do for his only daughter. All the little twit had to do was sleep with the old man whenever the pathetic bastard managed to get it up. Not too much to ask considering all the luxuries she'd receive in return. But she'd refused. Refused! The most advantageous deal for Cochran Enterprises in decades had been at stake, and his ungrateful daughter refused to do her duty.

As if she were free to make that choice and go about her business without repercussions. *Fool.*

So, she didn't want to be the wife of one of the wealthiest industrialists in the world, mistress of the vast Wallace estate, with myriad servants at her beck and call? Fine. When he'd met the Iceman, Mitchell found the perfect form of revenge. He made arrangements for Judith to become the servant. A very specific kind of servant. One at the beck and call of some very vulgar yet exacting men. A fitting degradation for her uppity attitude.

His fingers tapped a rapid beat on the desk. He never would have thought the Iceman capable of screwing up the perfect plan and losing control of the situation like that. If he weren't already dead, Mitchell would have shot the asshole himself.

But there were still others to be dealt with, those whose interference had brought a great deal of unwanted attention to the Cochran name. Not to mention they'd gotten hold of the thumb drive. He'd had specific uses planned for several of the men on those videos, the politicians in particular. Now those men were worthless to him.

Mangling a paperclip, Mitchell entertained visions of several satisfyingly painful demises for each and every member of that cocksucking OASIS team. The mere thought of their interference sent his blood pressure skyrocketing.

Damn them! He seized his laptop, pitching it across the room. With a snarl, he grabbed his chair and hurled it through the window. Alarms blared, and his head of security called through the intercom system.

Mitchell pressed the respond button. "Turn off that fucking noise. Get someone in here to clean up this mess and set up a new laptop right away."

"Yes, sir."

The alarm quieted, and Mitchell stormed from his home office toward his private quarters. His wife looked at him with wary eyes as she stepped from her sitting room. Stupid bitch. "Come to my room in ten minutes," he barked as he passed her. "Wear nothing."

"Of course, my love," she whispered.

He went straight to the bar in his library and poured himself a scotch. Downing it in one swallow, he poured a second as he moved to his bedroom, placing the decanter on the nightstand. He walked over to the floor-to-ceiling windows opposite his bed. The glory of his vast estate spread out like a triumph. *His* triumph, the crowning symbol of his power, and his favorite view in the whole house.

Yes, he must remember he had power. Loads of it. He had several heads of state on speed dial, all ready to do exactly as he ordered. He could squash that insignificant little detective agency like a bug if he so desired, and he did. But not so fast. They deserved to suffer for their insolence. And suffer they would. One by one, he would ruin their lives, cause them pain.

Including his daughter. He would save her for last. At first, his instinct had been to forget about seeing her in bondage and just send someone to kill her *and* her bodyguard boyfriend. Haste rarely benefited him, though, and waiting for the report from his own investigators had been worth it. Apparently, his daughter was in love with Buchanan. It would be interesting to see how far the relationship progressed.

The more he thought about it, the more he liked that idea. Let her think she had nothing to worry about now. Who knew? In time, she might give him a grandchild.

Maybe a granddaughter, a lovely young girl to take and mold and shape precisely the way he wanted. No one would interfere with her rearing this time. He'd been a fool to let his first wife have any say in Judith's upbringing. He should have gotten rid of Elizabeth a lot sooner. At least he'd learned from the mistakes of his first marriage.

Or maybe Judith would have a boy. One Mitchell would personally train to carry on his legacy, assuming the kid didn't turn out to be some weak-willed little pansy. And if he did? Well, there was a market for them too.

Mitchell smiled. Maybe he would even keep Judith alive to look after the baby. His revenge would be all the more potent with her knowing her lover died an agonizing death and Mitchell was raising their child as he wished while she could do nothing but watch. He could do whatever he wanted to whomever he wanted.

Because he had the power.

And patience, unlike his imbecile of a stepson. When Mitchell married Kim, he had planned to groom Rob to take over the legacy. But it rapidly became clear Rob would never have what it took to run such a vast empire. The only admirable quality the idiot possessed was an apparent lack of conscience.

But it wasn't enough. Mitchell would pull whatever strings necessary to have the charges against his moron of a stepson dropped. A trial was out of the question. The publicity would reach circus-like proportions, destroying his ferociously guarded wall of privacy. Once the charges were dropped, Mitchell would see to it his stepson met with an accident pretty damn quick.

Neither Rob nor the Iceman had any inkling Mitchell had engineered their introduction to one another just when Rob needed to get his hands on some fast money. Nor did Rob have any idea Mitchell had arranged for one of the men on the tapes—a gangster thug named Tommy Pruitt—to make sure Rob knew the Iceman paid money for girls. And Mitchell didn't want his stepson around long enough to put it together. While he was at it, he would also dispose of

Rob's college buddy, the one who'd gotten all the publicity rolling. Nothing would be left to chance.

The bedroom door opened, the reflection in the window revealing his naked wife. She closed the door and stood in front of it, head down, hands clasped before her, waiting for his instructions. She'd wait there all night if he chose, not moving, not saying a word without his permission.

He drained his glass and then thrust out his arm. "Pour me another."

She hurried forward and took the glass. While she filled it, he kicked off his shoes and sat on the foot of the bed where he could still look out over his land. She brought him his drink. The amber liquid swirled a little in the glass as her hand shook. She was frightened of him, of his mood. *Good. She should be frightened. She has no power.*

"On your knees," he commanded. She quickly obeyed, and he smiled. It had taken him a while to break her to complete compliance, but it had been worth every gratifying moment. She would do anything he told her without question.

"Please me," he whispered. "Don't use your hands."

She clasped her hands behind her head, where they would remain as firmly as if they were bound unless he instructed her otherwise. She tugged at his belt with her teeth.

He sipped his drink and stared out at his moonlit domain. The scotch, the view, and his wife's industrious efforts to satisfy him took the edge off his anger. A few hours of putting Kim through her paces—and reminding her his belt was not just for holding up his pants—would take care of the rest. He hadn't forgotten her disloyal remark to Rob the other day, or that she had been speaking to Judith recently. She wouldn't know why, but tonight she would receive her punishment for those offenses.

Kim had no idea he had every room and phone in the house bugged. Often, after one of their sessions, he would send her back to her own sparse quarters and then listen to her sob for hours. Witnessing her wallow in her abject helplessness was one of his most treasured marital pastimes, second only to making her beg for mercy he would never bestow.

Tomorrow, with a calm, clear mind restored, he would begin arranging the downfall of OASIS. According to his own investigators, Tobie Armstrong and her team were excellent at what they did. Good. They would be worthy opponents. But it wouldn't matter in the long term. Over the years, he'd mastered the art of obliterating his enemies, planning their destruction so carefully and methodically they never saw it coming. This time would be no different, and he planned to savor every minute of it.

Kim leaned back on her heels, pulling his belt free and placing it in his outstretched palm. She began working his zipper down with her teeth, quivering as he draped the belt down her back, idly sliding it back and forth over her bare skin. Warmth spread through him. *Ah, power.*

Delicious power.

THANK you for reading Trusting The Bodyguard. I hope you enjoyed Reeve and Jessie's story. Would you like to read about the day Jessie's father disowned her? Sign up to join The Troy Inner Circle for this special bonus scene. Join The Troy Inner Circle Today

If you enjoyed Reeve and Jessie's story, you would make

this author very happy by leaving a review on your **favorite storefront** and/or **Goodreads**. Reviews are crucial to authors, and a brief line or two goes a long way to helping other readers find my books. Thank you.

THE ADVENTURES **of the OASIS Team continue with Fitz's story in TAMING THE BODYGUARD Book 2 in the OASIS Series. Here's a sneak peek:**

IT WAS JUST SEX, for pity's sake.

Ignoring the nervousness flickering in her eyes, Erienne Stuart flipped up the vanity mirror, and exited her champagne-colored Mercedes Benz SL, thankful the warmth of autumn's second summer meant she didn't need a jacket. The raucous tune of an old George Thorogood song drifted through the open door of the Steel Horse Tavern, the resident biker bar of Candlewood, CT. With the flock of hummingbirds flitting about in her stomach, she doubted even George's recommendation of a bourbon, a scotch and a beer would be enough to quell her nerves.

She could turn around right now and forget the whole thing, but in all her thirty years Erienne had never been one to back down from an unpleasant task and wasn't about to start now. Besides, there was every possibility this undertaking could turn out to be an enjoyable experience. She'd never know unless she tried.

Decision made, she took a deep breath before remembering she shouldn't do that, not if she wanted to keep her body-hugging, coral-colored silk sheath from splitting its seams. Maybe buying it two sizes too small hadn't been such a good idea after all. Releasing her breath, she walked inside.

A few couples gyrated on the large dance floor but most of the patrons were either at the bar, which took up most of the wall to her right, or clustered around the high, square tables scattered about the perimeter of the dance floor. Beer was the prevailing scent of the room, although from the large array of bottles perched on the shelf behind the bar, she figured just about any preferred drink could be accommodated.

Several young men at one table looked her over, and she willed herself not to blush. The nearest one got up and approached her. The sway in his step indicated he and his companions had been here a while. His belly flopped a little over the top of his worn jeans, further cementing the idea that drinking large quantities of beer was a frequent pastime. She wasn't exactly sure who she was looking for, but she was fairly certain drunkenness on her partner's behalf wouldn't help her.

She turned and strode toward the bar, ignoring the howls and good-natured jeers the drunk's buddies tossed at him. A glance in the large mirror behind the bar showed him scowling at her before turning back to his laughing friends with a shrug.

The seats at the bar were all taken, but there was space to stand between some of them. Several men were looking at her, either directly or through the reflection of the mirror. Fingers of doubt poked her resolve. Her plan had seemed simple enough, but now she wondered...

After a quick scan up and down the bar, she chose to slip in next to the one guy who wasn't paying any attention to her. His dark blond head tilted down a little as he tapped the screen of his phone, and a nearly empty beer glass stood before him. A short-sleeved, black tee shirt accentuated firmly toned arms, the right bicep sporting some sort of a military emblem with the phrase "The Only Easy Day Was Yesterday" written under it, the sleek muscle flexing a little as he worked the phone. Bringing her gaze up, she noted the shirt did wonders for his broad chest, too.

She stood quietly next to him, uncertain what to do next and thankful the seats on her other side were occupied by a young couple who had eyes only for each other. The bartender, a thirtyish-looking woman with short, spiky black hair and an armful of brightly colored tattoos worked her way down the bar. Erienne eyed the bottles on the shelves. What should she order? A beer maybe. Tonight was about breaking taboos, and she'd never tried a beer before. Somehow, her usual white wine spritzer just didn't seem right.

Damn! The man next to her lowered his phone and drained his beer, his eyes looking over the rim of his glass and landing on her reflection in the mirror. His attention caught, and his arm froze for a second before he lowered the glass back to the bar, openly staring at her. Oh well, she was going to have to talk to someone here sooner or later, so she might as well get started. Ignoring the second flock of hummingbirds joining the first in her stomach, she faced him as he turned in his seat. Her smile faltered as his honey-colored eyes practically pinned her in place.

"What brings you in here, sweetheart?" he asked. "Slumming?"

The birds started doing double-time but she made herself speak. "Would it bother you if I was?"

He slowly raked his gaze up and down, and she strove to maintain a somewhat bored expression on her face. It wasn't easy. As he looked her over so deliberately, she now knew what it felt like to be undressed by someone's eyes. A man's eyes. *This* man's eyes. Heat pooled between her thighs as he continued his calculating assessment. The warmth of a blush swept across her cheeks and she could only hope the dim lighting of the bar concealed it.

Because, if truth be told, she *was* slumming. The men she'd known throughout her life would never dream of looking at her like this, not in public, not with a crowd of people surrounding them. But this man didn't seem to care. The bar was busy enough, but not super crowded, and plenty of people could see what he was doing, see that he was sizing her up with what she could only describe as naked lust.

A sexy smile emerged from between his short, slightly scruffy beard and mustache. "Nuh-uh, sugar," he said, returning his gaze to hers, his eyes crackling with amber fire. "I wouldn't have a problem with that at all. Slum away."

Her mouth went dry. He was dead serious. She had no idea it could happen so fast, so easily. She'd come here tonight to lose her virginity, but now that the moment was quite possibly at hand, she wasn't so sure she could go through with it.

"Buy you a drink?" Fitz saw the fear in the blonde's eyes. She hid it well otherwise, but the truth was crystal clear in those sweet baby blues of hers. Others might not have noticed, but in his line of work if he hadn't honed the ability to tell whether people were lying or putting on an act, he might have been dead a long time ago. She wasn't dangerous, though. No doubt about that. She came from money, her carriage and demeanor a dead giveaway, no matter how hard she tried to hide it.

He wondered what brought her here. The Steel Horse had a reputation as a biker bar, and thus held a certain appeal to the students from the Ivy League college one town over, so she wasn't the first rich girl to wander into the place. Every now and then a group of them would show up wearing tight leather skirts and even tighter cut-off shirts. After ordering a pitcher of something silly and fruity, they usually just sat at a table, looking around with wide eyes and keeping to themselves as they whispered and sniggered their way through their drinks. They went to the bathroom in packs and rarely strayed far from one another.

Occasionally, one or two of the more brazen of them would play a flirty game of pool with one of the tattooed regulars, but they always left with their friends. Fortunately for them, the Steel Horse was frequented mostly by blue-collar laborers who were also biker enthusiasts rather than real hard-core bikers, the kind that lived by their own set of rules as far as women were concerned. The guys here – himself included – were all on the make, sure, but there were more than enough willing women in the bar. Fitz never had trouble finding one to spend his energies on.

But the long-legged, stacked, stunning — albeit timid — blonde package of sex standing next to him was a few years past college age, which made her that much more appealing. Unlike the college girls, this one was old enough to know what she was doing, and he certainly wasn't above giving her a nudge in the direction she was dressed to go. The skin tight, orangey-pink dress she wore left nothing to the imagination, and it had been a long time since he'd been with a woman. His last job had been long and difficult, leaving no time for any kind of a social life. Now that it had wrapped up, he was more than ready for a little R & R of the horizontal kind.

He slipped his phone into his back pocket, careful to keep the gun tucked into the back of his pants out of sight. "Terri!" he called to the bartender, "I'm running dry, darlin'."

"Sounds like a personal problem," Terri laughed as she walked over.

"I'll take a boilermaker." He turned back to his new companion. "What would you like?"

The question appeared to catch her off guard. She scanned the bottles behind the bar for a second, her brow wrinkled in confusion. Terri folded her arms and looked at Fitz with a smirk. The blonde turned back to him with a dainty shrug. "The same," she said

Inwardly, he smiled. He hadn't pegged her for a "let's do a shot" kind of gal, but he was glad to see she had some spunk. That could bode well for what he had in mind for later on. She'd come alone, too, so she wasn't entirely afraid to take some chances. His night was looking better and better already.

Terri delivered their drinks, and Fitz picked up his shot glass, catching the eye of several other male patrons in the mirror behind the bar. It occurred to him that the blonde was damned lucky she met him before anyone else. He knew she didn't have the street smarts she'd need to effectively dismiss some of the pushier guys here, the kind that often needed something more blunt than a simple "no thanks, not interested" before they got the message. Fitz could recall two occasions where he'd had to step in and tell an obtuse yet persistent guy to back off a woman when her own objections weren't being understood.

One by one, he faced down each man's stare long enough to let them know he'd staked full claim to the golden goddess beside him. A tall guy with dark hair and a large tattoo of a hornet on his neck stared back a little longer than most before he, too, dropped his gaze. Good. Fitz had no qualms about fighting somebody for her, but he had a feeling she'd be long gone before any scuffle got settled.

"Cheers." Her soft voice reclaimed his attention. Biting back a grin at her delicate toast, he clinked his glass with hers. He tossed the Jack Daniels back, watching her as she studied his movements and then quickly followed suit. Her eyes flew wide open and she fought down a sputter as she groped for her beer. Her cheeks turned rosy but she hung on to her composure, watery eyes the only evidence of her discomfort when she set the mug back down on the bar.

Oh yeah. He'd lucked out when she came to stand by him. She'd need a little wooing. A game or two of pool, a couple of slow dances when the band started, but she would be worth every effort. He had no doubt about that. "What's your name, princess?"

"Erienne."

"Erienne what?"

"I'd rather not say if you don't mind." She smiled at him, but nervousness crept back into her eyes.

An ugly thought struck him. "You're not married are you?" He hoped to hell she wasn't because no way was he getting in the middle of anyone's marriage, no matter how much he wanted her. That was trouble he didn't need right now. Ever.

She lifted her left hand, and waggled her bare fingers at him. "Nope."

"Rings come off easily enough."

Her smile disappeared. "I'm not married, and I don't appreciate being called a liar." She yanked open the sparkly silver purse dangling from her shoulder. "I'll buy my own drink."

"Whoa, slow down, I didn't mean to hurt your feelings. Just want to be sure I'm not poaching another man's territory." He'd have to remember she was pretty skittish, whatever her reason for being there might be. If he wanted to see her naked later, he'd have to handle her carefully now. "I'm sorry."

Her eyes softened and she gave him a slight nod.

The band took to the stage. It was retro-night at the Steel Horse, and they opened with a raucous version of Twist and Shout. Fast dancing wasn't Fitz's favorite thing, but he'd do it if it would put her at ease. "Wanna dance?"

She looked at the couples cavorting around the dance floor and shook her head. "I've never played pool. Can you show me how?"

"Sure. Let's go." He picked up their beers and stood. "Lead the way, princess."

She gave him another one of those nervous smiles before heading around the perimeter of the dance floor to the pool tables. Two of them were already in use, but the third one was available. She walked toward it, ignoring the drunken frat boys near the door who were openly staring at her. Not that Fitz could blame them. The silky material of her dress skimmed over her hips and ass in a sinful invitation no man's eyes could decline. He could just picture his hands sliding the dress down over her curves and revealing her creamy skin, inch by delectable inch.

"I saw her first," one of the frat boys muttered as Fitz passed.

Tightening his face into a well-practiced scowl, he stopped and faced the little dweeb. "And? What's your point?"

The wanna-be Romeo's eyes narrowed as he and two of his buddies got to their feet. Fitz would have laughed if it weren't so important to make sure the lamebrains knew the foolishness of trying to interfere now. He would have no trouble laying them all flat. Hell, drunk as they appeared to be, it wouldn't even take him two minutes to do it. But he just wasn't in the mood, and it was two minutes he would rather spend with the mystery blonde. The sooner he could put Erienne at ease, the sooner he could entice her to a more intimate locale.

Fitz stared hard at the kid who spoke first. He supposed it might be more expedient to flash his gun at him, but that could potentially lead to police attention, and Fitz's boss wouldn't appreciate that. Fortunately, the frat boys weren't drunk enough to be stupidly brave, and the one who'd complained turned back to the table and sat. A quick glance at his *compadres* showed none of them were willing to pick up the gauntlet, and Fitz moved on.

Unaware of the silent duel that had taken place over her, Erienne carefully studied the rack of pool cues hanging on the wall, as if there would be some sort of marker on them to indicate which one would be best for a beginner. Fitz placed their beers on the small shelf surrounding a square post between the tables and joined her. He picked up a cue and hefted it for weight. After years of abuse by drunken players, they all pretty much sucked, not that she would know the difference. Still, he hated to do things half-assed so he'd make the best of the materials at hand. "Since you're a beginner, you'll probably do better with a heavier cue. It will give you a little more control."

"And control is important?"

He met her gaze dead on. "Always."

A faint blush tinged her skin but she gamely picked up

two cues and tested them for weight. "I think this one's heavier," she said, putting the other one back.

"Maybe, but it's not long enough for you. You'll do better with a bigger shaft."

She blushed deeply this time. Damn, she was easy to tease. But he'd better knock it off before he spooked her away completely. He helped her find a better cue and then set up the balls on the table.

"I'll go first this time," he said. "After you've played a little and get used to the feel of the stick, then you can break the balls." Oops. He really had meant for that to be instructional, not raunchy.

She arched a golden eyebrow at him. "If you're going to talk to me like that, don't you think you should at least tell me your name?"

He chuckled, relieved to learn she had a sense of humor. "Mordecai Fitzjames."

"Mordecai?"

"It's an old family name. Most people call me Fitz."

"Is that what you prefer I call you?"

He gave her another quick glance up and down before he could help himself. "Sweetheart, you can call me any damn thing you want."

Blushing furiously, she straightened up a bit. "Well, how about I call you 'coach' and you get on with teaching me how to play?"

"Fair enough." He leaned over and gave the cue ball a solid whack. The balls scattered across the table and two of them went in the pockets, just as the band wrapped up their song.

"You got two balls!" Erienne cheered in the ensuing quiet. "Is that good?" Several people snickered but she paid no attention as she looked up at him.

"Um, yeah, that's good." Fitz bit back his own laugh. "Normally, that would mean I keep shooting, but I want to make sure you get a turn."

"No, I want to learn how to do it right."

"You will. I'm a good teacher, but I'm also a good player. You won't learn anything if I clear the table and you don't get a chance to shoot. We'll play for real after you get the hang of it." Although if he had his way, they'd be out of here long before she became any kind of a pool hall wizard.

He showed her how to chalk her cue and then how to hold it. "Now, get down low over the table and look at how the cue ball lines up with the blue ball." He bit the inside of his cheek for a second before continuing. "See how it's lined up with the corner pocket?"

"Yes."

"Okay, now pull the stick back, then give the cue ball a fast hit and pull the stick back to the original position quickly."

She closed one eye and concentrated a moment more. Fitz took the opportunity to let his eyes wander over her lush figure, from her silky hair drifting over her shoulder, down her graceful back, to her rounded butt as she bent over the edge of the table. She took her shot, giving her ass a little wiggle. His mouth actually watered.

"Fudge!" Erienne straightened up and whirled around. "I missed."

Fitz swallowed. "That's okay. You can try again. I'll help you." He looked at the table and found another easy shot. "Try the red one."

"Okay." She bent over the table again. "Like this?"

"Exactly." He stepped to her side and bent over her, placing his hands on hers and bringing his head next to hers. A scent, soft and sweet, cut through the smell of spilled beer and stuffy air, her perfume far more intoxicating than the shot he'd had earlier.

"Now what?" she asked.

"Now we hit it. Dead center of the cue ball." He guided her hand back, his fingers brushing the outside of her thigh as he did. He snapped the cue and the red ball dropped into the pocket they'd been aiming for.

Erienne pushed up in excitement and Fitz reluctantly dropped his arms as he stood back. She'd fit so nicely underneath him it seemed a shame to let go.

"It went in the hole!" Her eyes sparkled like pale blue ice.

"Yeah," he laughed, "it did." One more innuendo and they would officially be behaving like junior high students. But she didn't seem to be aware of them, and he found that refreshing.

"I'm going to try again." She scanned the table. "The purple one." It was another easy shot and she let out a small shriek of satisfaction when she sank it on her own.

The next shot was harder and she missed. Fitz took a turn, dropping two of the more difficult shots, leaving her a few more easy ones to try. She missed her second attempt and asked him to help her with a third. It was a tricky angle and she was lying flat across the table with one foot on the floor. He leaned over her, stretching his arms around her to help her line up the shot. As her perfume invaded his nose again, a hazy vision of tangled sheets and golden hair spread on a pillow flooded his mind. She jerked the cue and the shot went wide. No surprise there. He'd been too busy fantasizing to actually line it up.

"I thought you were an expert at this," she said impishly from beneath him. She turned her head and their lips were millimeters apart. The laughter in her eyes drifted away, replaced by desire tinged with a little nervousness.

The band launched into an old rock ballad. "Let's dance," he whispered, feeling a strong need to make that nervousness go away.

She nodded slightly, and they straightened up. He took her hand, leading her to the dance floor. She looked around at the other couples, and then looped her arms around his neck as the other women were doing with their partners. He slid his arms around her waist and pulled her a little closer, but not too close. This was all about making her comfortable, so he'd let her set the tone.

She tilted her head back a little and smiled at him. Encouraged, he slid his hands a little further around her waist. Heat shimmered through him as she slowly slid one of her hands up the back of his neck and slipped her fingers into his hair, just barely touching his scalp with captivating circular motions. Her eyelids drifted shut and she leaned her head against his chest. With a barely contained growl of pleasure, he wrapped his arms around her and dispensed with the notion of keeping any space between them. Her firm breasts were heaven against his chest, and he smiled in anticipation of seeing them in all their glory in another hour or so.

Maybe less.

CHAPTER TWO

Fitz turned her around in that slow, shuffley way that couldn't really be considered anything other than foreplay done upright and set to music, silently praising whoever it was that invented the barroom rock ballad slow dance. Just as he closed his eyes, he noticed a man staring at them. That shouldn't have been surprising. Most of the men in the place had taken a good look at Erienne at one point or another this evening. The frat boys and those men at the bar hadn't been the only ones he'd warned off with a glare.

But this guy was different.

First, he was doing a piss-poor job of pretending *not* to stare. Second, just before the guy had jerked his gaze away, Fitz was certain the man had been staring at *him*, not Erienne. As they danced their slow lazy circle, he periodically opened his eyes and scanned the crowd, spotting the guy a few more times, once in deep conversation with another guy at the bar, and twice more staring at him. Maybe the guy was gay and had wandered into the wrong bar. Whatever. It had to be pretty obvious to the man by now that Fitz's sexual preference placed him squarely on the boy-girl team.

The song ended and the band switched back to an upbeat tempo. Fitz reluctantly loosened his hold, and Erienne stepped back a millimeter and looked up at him, her eyes darkened to a smoky blue. "Can we...can we go somewhere else?" Her voice was a raspy whisper.

Although his libido was doing a rather lewd happy dance, Fitz managed to suppress the mile-wide grin threatening to surface. "Whatever you want, princess."

"I'll need the ladies' room first."

He guided her back toward the bar and pointed to a little hallway at the end of it. "In there. I'll wait for you here." She nodded and headed off. His eyes feasted on her butt as she walked away until she disappeared into the ladies room. He called to Terri, and quickly settled his bar tab.

"Have fun, Casanova," Terri smirked as she retuned his credit card and sauntered away.

As Fitz put the card back in his wallet and double-checked he had a few condoms tucked in there, his phone rang. He dug it out of his pocket, his heart sinking when he saw Tobie Armstrong's name on the screen. His boss calling him now could only mean bad news. With the morose feeling he was about to kiss good bye any quality time with Erienne, he moved into the hallway for the bathrooms where it was quieter. "Hi, Tobie."

She got right to the point. "I just got word that Tommy Pruitt was shanked in lock-up last night. He's dead."

"Dammit!" Fitz's last undercover operation for October Armstrong Security and Investigation Services - aka OASIS - had helped get the nasty little bastard arrested. But it was Tommy's brother, Dave Pruitt, the authorities really wanted to get their hands on. "I don't suppose you're calling me to say that before he died, Tommy told everything he knew about his brother's operations, and even as we speak Dave is being processed and fingerprinted by New York's Finest."

"Fat chance. Getting Tommy to flip was always a long shot. He adored Dave."

And, Fitz knew, Dave adored Tommy. It was common knowledge among New York's underworld that messing with Tommy was risking the legendary wrath of Dave. "I wouldn't have believed there was anyone stupid enough to shank Tommy. Not unless they had a death wish."

"Word is that Dave has already put out contracts on those responsible for Tommy's murder," Tobie said.

"Contracts? More than one? How many guys shanked him?"

"I don't know, but all this went down during a small inmate riot. It's all still being sorted out. The Department of Corrections isn't sharing a lot of information about the attack. But Dave is blaming a whole host of people for putting Tommy inside in the first place. The arresting officers, the assistant district attorney, and the judge who denied Tommy's bail have all been placed in protective custody."

"Sounds like everything's under control." If all the principals were already being protected, maybe his evening wasn't ruined after all. Tobie's company was exclusive. She charged exorbitant fees from wealthy clients, and delivered exemplary results. The City of New York couldn't afford her rates, so it wasn't likely she was calling him to come in for a bodyguard detail. "Well, thanks for letting me know. I'll call you tomorrow. Right now I've got a hot—"

"Forget it. There's a contract out on you, too."

"What?"

"My sources tell me that Dave doesn't believe you escaped the arrest scene on your own. He's saying you set Tommy up. Which means there may have been a leak somewhere."

Fitz's pulse began to throb in his temple. "Who the hell would have told him?"

"I don't know yet. I'm not even sure there was a leak. Pruitt could just be flying off the handle. But we cooperated with a lot of official departments on this one – the police, the FBI, ATF. If there *was* a leak, that's where it came from. Not from us."

"I know that." Fitz trusted his fellow OASIS agents with his life. He knew some of them from as far back as boot camp, and had served with all of them at one time or another during his tours with the Navy SEALs.

"Maybe someone in the D.A.s office was bought off," Tobie went on. "And let's not forget we've pissed off some very important people when we had them arrested for participating in Iceman's auctions."

Fitz's blood boiled as he thought of the now deceased

Iceman and those men to which he'd auctioned his victims. Men, many in public office, who had bought and sadistically tortured young women. The only good thing the Iceman ever did was record those men in action. "Those scumbags deserve everything they get."

"And then some. But until they are tried and sentenced, any one of them can still be dangerous. Many of them still have the power to compromise police investigations and leak sensitive information. We're already looking into it. If there was a leak, we'll find it. But right now, we know that Dave's threat is real and we need to keep you safe. Ian and Jake are going to look after you. Where are you?"

"I don't need babysitters. Give Jake and Ian something more useful to do. I'll come to the office as soon as I can get there."

Two women passed him on their way to the ladies room, reminding him Erienne would be along soon, not that it was going to do him any good now. Damn Pruitt and his stupid contract anyway. But Fitz knew better than to ignore the threat. Pruitt was a lethal bastard, and had more than enough money to hire a top notch hit man.

Or hit*men*. What if some of Pruitt's goons had found him already?

Fitz moved to the hallway entry and quickly scanned the room. There was no sign of that guy who'd been looking at him, or the guy he'd been talking to at the bar. Just where the hell had they gone? They hadn't passed him to go to the men's room.

"Fitz? Are you still there? Where the hell are you?"

"Sorry. Yeah, I'm here. I'm at a bar called the Steel Horse. It's just outside Candlewood. But tell the guys to meet me at my place. I've got a date, and I need to get her out of here safely. There's a couple of guys here that might be a problem."

"A Pruitt problem or a poaching on your woman problem?"

"I'm not sure. Either way, I can't leave her. If it is a Pruitt problem, they've seen her with me. She's not safe." Not to mention Erienne had caught the attention of way too many guys here. Even without the threat of Pruitt, she was in over her head in a place like this.

Tobie swore. "Stay there. Wait for backup."

"No. If these guys are Pruitt's men, they won't have any qualms about opening fire in a public place like this. It will be easier for me to give them the slip if they think I don't suspect anything."

"All right. I'll have Jake and Ian meet you at your place. But until you get there I want you to call or text me every five minutes. And do not turn your phone off for any reason."

"Okay. I'm on my way."

Fitz disconnected and scanned the bar again, annoyed with himself for having let his guard down. No matter how gorgeous and pliant Erienne was, he'd been careless not to pay more attention to his surroundings. That's what he got for thinking with the wrong head.

Mentally urging Erienne to hurry up, he kept a constant vigil of the bar area, dance floor, and pool tables. The guy with the hornet tattoo still sat at the bar, but his attention was riveted to a dark-haired young woman as she read his palm. Still no sign of the other two guys. He wanted to believe they hadn't been from Pruitt, but the hairs standing up on the back of his neck told him he probably wasn't that lucky. Fate was screwing with him. He could feel it. Why else would a blonde and horny goddess fall into his arms, only for him to discover he had to take a pass?

Yeah, fate was a cruel bastard.

ERIENNE WASHED her hands and then looked through her purse, making sure she had everything she would need. Condoms? Check. Personal lubricant? Check. Her research indicated her nerves might prevent her from getting sufficiently aroused. But thinking of Fitz waiting for her outside, remembering the way her body responded when he'd stretched himself on top of her on the pool table had her believing the lubricant would remain unopened. Her panties were still damp.

After touching up her lipstick and combing her hair, she reached into her purse and pulled out her perfume atomizer only to discover it wasn't her perfume. With a chuckle she tucked the small canister of mace back into her bag. She certainly wouldn't keep Fitz in the mood if she sprayed *that* on her neck.

Not that she was worried about keeping his attention. Although inexperienced, she wasn't stupid. Fitz definitely wanted to be with her.

Her hands shook a little as she rooted around for the perfume, but she wasn't anywhere near as nervous as she thought she would be. Initially, she owed her lessening nerves to the shot and the beer, but that wasn't entirely it.

Her attraction to Fitz was real. At least on a physical level. His whiskey brown eyes were warm and full of good humor. The silky texture of his blond hair had been paradise to her fingers. *And that body!* Six feet of tight muscle and broad shoulders. Every time he'd touched her it was as if he enhanced her own femininity. She couldn't remember the last time she'd felt that way.

All too often, Erienne's devotion to her career left her little time to relax and have fun. She didn't regret her decision to continue her late mother's biofuel research, but sometimes she missed having the time to do the things other women her age did.

Like date and have sex.

Well, she wasn't expecting – or looking for – any kind of dating relationship with Fitz, but she thought he was an excellent prospect to help her with the sex part. Something primal inside her told her he would be a good lover. Her plan was working out much better than she'd hoped. She was still a bit nervous about the whole thing, but that was only natural. The good news was since she'd met Fitz her excitement level had risen, and she no longer worried she wouldn't have the courage to go through with it.

She returned her perfume to her purse, and her fingers brushed against the mace. In her gut she knew she wouldn't need it, not with Fitz, but what was the point of carrying it if she couldn't find it? With a shrug, she moved it to an easily accessible pocket of her purse.

The door to the ladies' room opened and two giggling girls came in. "Did you see that guy on the phone?" said one. "Damn, he was hot!"

"Hell yes!" said the other. "Makes me wish I wasn't here with Frankie."

Erienne caught sight of Fitz talking on his phone before the door swung shut and smiled, feeling a little smug that she had the attention of the hottest guy in the room. Knowing he'd be occupied for another few minutes, she pulled out her own phone and dialed her cousin, Kylie. The call went straight to voicemail. Good. Kylie had been very clear on what she thought of Erienne's scheme.

The two girls were still laughing and talking with each other, paying absolutely no attention to Erienne, but she kept her voice low anyway. "Hi, it's me. Don't be mad. I decided to go through with that plan I told you about yesterday. I'm at the Steel Horse, but I'm leaving in a minute with a guy named Mordecai Fitzjames. He seems alright. I'm not sure where we're going yet but I'll call and leave you another message when we get there. Please try not to worry. I've got a really good feeling about this. I think it's going to be a very good experience for me. Talk to you soon." She tossed her phone back in her purse. With a last quick glance in the mirror, she smoothed a wayward strand of hair into place and exited the ladies room.

Fitz was no longer on the phone and she approached him with a smile. He barely looked at her as he took her hand. "Stay close to me."

Fine by her. Close to him was exactly what she wanted.

He led her to the exit and stopped just outside the door, turning his head left and right as if he were looking for someone. "Is something wrong?"

"No, but I'm afraid something's come up so we're going to have to take a rain check. Where's your car? I'll walk you to it."

What? He was sending her home? Ten minutes ago he'd been all over her. "Did you get some bad news?"

He whipped his gaze back to her. "What do you mean?"

"I saw you on the phone. Was it bad news?"

"Something like that."

He scanned the parking lot again, definitely looking for someone, and not appearing too pleased about it, either. Her mind tripped back to when they'd first spoken at the bar. He'd asked if she was married. Maybe that was the problem. Maybe *he* was married and his wife had called. Maybe she was on her way here to collect her gorgeous, wayward husband.

Erienne pulled her hand from his. "Don't worry about me. If you have to leave, you go right ahead."

A determined glint entered his eyes. "Where's your car?"

"Is your wife on her way? Is that why you're trying to get rid of me?" Her petulant tone grated her own ears but she couldn't help it. She wasn't sure if she were more angry or disappointed.

"My wife? What are you talking about? I'm not married."

"You couldn't wait to leave with me until that phone call. Now you can't ditch me fast enough. No wonder you were quick to think I was concealing a marriage earlier. I bet you're the one with a spouse to hide."

He took her hand again, and pressed her palm to his lips. "I swear I'm not married," he whispered, his beard tickling her hand as he kissed it again. "Believe me, there is nothing I would rather do than take you to bed this minute." Heat tingled up her arm from where his lips and fingers touched her. "But I can't right now. If you give me your number, I promise I'll call you in a few days."

A few days! Absolutely not. She was ready to do this now. As ready as she was ever going to be anyway. She'd come too far to have her hopes dashed like this.

He kissed her palm again, the warm light in his eyes a sensual promise. "That's not a line. I will definitely call you. Give me your phone number."

She believed him. He would call her and they could go out and then, hopefully, pick up where they left off. Only that sounded too much like a date, and after the pain of her last boyfriend's betrayal, that's not what she wanted. Her goal was to lose her virginity with no strings attached. Besides, despite his devilish appeal, Fitz was not the kind of man she dated. It was his killer body she wanted, and she wanted it now.

Eager to regain the warm, sticky, dreamy feeling she'd had as they danced, she rubbed her thumb over his full lips. Encouraged by the flare of heat in his eyes, she moved in closer and slipped her hand up his neck, tangling her fingers in his sumptuous hair. A growl purred in his throat as he closed the distance. She parted her lips and he accepted her invitation, his tongue caressing every part of her mouth. The warmth at the pit of her belly turned to lava as he wrapped his arms around her and pulled her flush up against his granite chest.

Oh yes, he's the one. Her world dissolved to a sensual haze as she held on tight. Perhaps it had been a sheer stroke of luck, but Erienne knew he would be an expert lover, and after having this heady taste of what was in store she didn't want to settle for anything less. She doubted she'd be so lucky a second time if she had to go back inside and start all over.

He broke away from her lips and trailed succulent little kisses along her jaw and down her neck. "Erienne... princess," he muttered, "I really can't right now. I have to—"

"Yes, you can. I know you want me," she whispered.

"You bet your sweet ass I do."

"It's all right, I want you, too."

"That's not the problem. I really have to go."

Determination fueled her brain, reminding her of the stack of old romance novels she and Kylie had found as children playing hide and seek in the attic of their grandmother's house. Once discovered, those novels proved to be an irresistible temptation. She and Kylie had always snuck up there to read them whenever they visited their grand-mother. The men in those books seemed to crave virgins. She knew the mores of the times were different now, but not so much that a man wouldn't appreciate being a woman's first lover. That's the sort of stuff they bragged about to their friends, wasn't it? Visions of Kevin's angry face tried to creep across her mind, but she slammed the lid on that line of thinking. She'd been wrong about him on so many levels.

"Shhh." Erienne kissed Fitz's neck like he was kissing hers. "You don't want to pass this up. Trust me."

He chuckled against her skin. "I'm sure it will be fabulous, darlin', but—"

"No, you don't understand." She smiled inwardly as she played her ace in the hole. "I'm a virgin."

He jumped back from her so fast she could have believed he'd been poked with a cattle prod. "You're what?" he croaked.

"A virgin. Well, sort of. But I don't want to be one anymore." She reached for him, missing the warmth of his body, but he grabbed her wrists and halted her progress.

"So, what, you were planning to jump into bed with the first guy you met at a bar?"

"Well, technically, you weren't the first guy I met." She smiled up at him, hoping her stab at levity would remove the scorn that twisted his mouth into a scowl.

No such luck. "Are you crazy? Do you have any idea how dangerous that is?"

"Oh, come on, Fitz. Strangers hook up at bars all the time. You're not dangerous, are you?" Doing her best to be flirty, she tilted her head to one side. "You said you were a good teacher. I know I'm a good student, and I'm guessing someone like you has lots of experience."

"Not with virgins."

"Well then, now's your chance to get some." She straightened up and gave her hips a little wiggle. "Some real hands on experience, if you know what I mean."

He shook his head and rolled his eyes. "C'mon," he said. Dropping one of her wrists and stepping into the parking lot. "Where's your car? You have to go home."

Disappointment warred with disbelief within her. He meant it. He really wasn't going to spend the night with her. She should have known it was all going too smoothly.

"That's your car, isn't it? The Mercedes?" He towed her along toward it without waiting for an answer. "Get your keys out."

Erienne stopped, almost toppling out of her shoes as he kept striding along. She grabbed the door handle of the nearest car and yanked her other arm free. He whirled and reached for her but she backed up. "Thanks for the escort, but I'm not leaving yet."

"Erienne, please, you've got to go. It's not safe here."

"What do you mean?"

"I don't have time to explain. Please trust me."

"Why should I trust you? You're nothing but a tease!"

She spun and took one step before he managed to grab her arm. "Erienne, I can't let you do this. It'll be a big mistake."

"Well, it's my mistake to make."

"I can't let you stay here."

"What are you? The morality police? If you're not interested then I'm going to go find someone who is. It really isn't any of your business." She jerked away and headed back toward the bar, wrath fueling her steps. How dare he? He didn't want to sleep with her? Fine, that was certainly his prerogative. But trying to dictate her actions as if she were a child? No way.

"Erienne, wait." He caught up with her and stepped in front of her.

"Leave me alone!" She tried to get around him.

"Erienne—"

"Hey! I believe the lady said she ishn't interested."

GREAT, *just what he needed.*

Fitz faced the frat boys as they approached, obviously drunk yet seeking to come to a lady's aid. He moved in front of Erienne, blocking their path. "Stay out of this, guys. It's not your concern."

One of them, the same one he'd warned off inside the bar, stepped forward. "We're not gonna just shtand here and let you force her," he slurred. "That'sh rape, buddy."

His friends muttered their agreement. The five of them squared off their shoulders and stood up a little straighter, scowling at Fitz all the while. The effect might have been intimidating if they weren't also weaving a bit like a pack of alcohol-infused bobble-head dolls. Physically dealing with them wouldn't pose much of a problem in and of itself, except he would have to let Erienne walk away to do it. And if he let her go, she'd march right back into the bar to implement her ridiculous plan.

A plan that, as she'd correctly pointed out, wasn't any of his business. He shouldn't really care, and heaven knew a foolish virgin was a distraction he didn't need right now. Those other guys he saw earlier were gone, and probably had nothing to do with his last case anyway. He should let her go on about her merry way while he met with his teammates and figured out a plan to deal with Pruitt.

That's what he *should* do, but he still couldn't help being concerned about her well-being anyway. He eyed the frat boys. While their intentions were honorable and heroic enough at the moment, they *were* pretty drunk. Alcohol could do strange things to people, and they outnumbered her. Despite their high intoxication level, she wouldn't be any match for them if things happened to turn ugly.

He faced her again. "Erienne, please let me walk you to your car. I can't stay here much longer, and it's not a good idea for you to stay here alone."

"Why not?" Anger crackled in her eyes, and something told him the word "docile" wasn't in her vocabulary. She arched a golden eyebrow at him. "Well? Surely you're not suggesting that a man can stay here by himself but a woman can't?"

"That's right, man," one of the frat boys chimed in. "Haven't you heard of women's lib? Bucking the patriarchy?" He and his buddies laughed uproariously.

Fitz threw them a glare. "Excuse us." He pulled Erienne a few feet away. The boys stopped laughing and watched them with the intensity of a hungry dog waiting for his master to drop a scrap of food. They were one step away from hanging their tongues out of their mouths.

"Look, Fitz, I've only known you for a little while. I thought we could have some fun but you obviously don't want to. That's your business. But how I spend the rest of my evening is *my* business. Got it?" She moved to step past him and he blocked her way.

"Erienne!" he hissed, losing patience with the whole situation. "It's not gonna happen. You are not staying here."

She practically snarled at him as she planted her hands on his chest and shoved. Her effort barely moved him but it galvanized her drunken knights into action.

"Leave her alone, you bastard!"

Fitz turned to face them as they fell on him en masse. Erienne broke away, a flurrying flash of pink as she skirted the lot of them and headed back toward the bar.

His attackers brought him to the ground, but fortunately one of the drunken fools hit the pavement first, thus softening the impact. Fitz managed to deliver a sharp elbow jab to the guy's temple. Judging from the yowl that elicited, he had only four of them left to deal with. With a mighty heave he rolled over and managed to pin two of his combatants underneath him, one on top of the other as he straddled them with his knees.

The remaining two got unsteadily to their feet. One grabbed Fitz's right arm, so he belted the kid with his left fist, connecting with the kid's nose which began gushing immediately. The fight fizzled out of him as he dropped Fitz's arm and brought his hands to his face. "Shit! I think you broke my node!" he said, his words somewhat strangled.

"I'll get him, Bob!" The second topside assailant swung at Fitz's head, but he easily deflected the blow with his forearm. He was pitched to the side as the ones beneath him bucked and struggled to stand up.

Fitz rolled away and regained his feet. One of the boys launched himself off the ground directly toward Fitz and was greeted with a solid fist to the stomach. The boy doubled over with an *oof* before he staggered away a few steps, vomiting up a fair portion of all the beer he recently consumed. Fitz whirled to face the rest of them.

The boy who'd first went down was still down, eyes shut. Fitz panicked for a second that the kid was really hurt until he heard him give a loud snore. Bob of the broken nose was leaning against a car with his head tilted back and moaning. One of his friends was trying to pull him away as he kept a nervous watch on Fitz.

That left only one knight-errant ready to do battle. The one who earlier muttered something about seeing Erienne first. Arms spread wide, he charged with a wordless roar. Fitz jumped out of the way and kicked the would-be champion right in the ass as he staggered by. The kid went sprawling, and Fitz dropped down and put his knee in the kid's back. He grabbed an arm and twisted it up high between the kid's shoulder blades.

"Listen, jerk off," Fitz said, ignoring the kid's yelps of pain, "you're damn lucky I don't have the time to really kick your ass. Now mind your own busin—"

"Hey!" one of the other guys yelled. "Hey, they're taking her!"

Fitz looked up as a feminine scream pealed across the lot. The two goons he'd seen earlier had Erienne by the arms and were dragging her away from the bar entrance. A large black van screeched into the parking lot, and the side door slid open. Erienne struggled and screamed as her captors pulled her toward it.

Dropping the kid's arm, Fitz lunged to his feet and raced across the lot. "No! Let her go!"

GET TAMING **The Bodyguard** today and see what happens next!

JOIN MY FACEBOOK READERS GROUP, Maura's Mavens. We'll talk about the OASIS team and their adventures in a non-spoilery way. There may be the odd giveaway now and then. And most likely lots of man-candy.

. . .

Books by Maura Troy
   The OASIS Series
   Book 1: Safe with a SEAL: Trusting the Bodyguard

Book 2: Safe with a SEAL: Taming the Bodyguard

Click here to join Maura's Facebook Group: https://www.facebook.com/groups/204642791675234

Click here to follow Maura on Twitter: https://twitter.com/MauraTroy

Click here to follow Maura on Instagram: https://www.instagram.com/mauratroy1/

Click here to follow Maura on Goodreads: https://www.goodreads.com/author/show/21985241.Maura_Troy

ACKNOWLEDGMENTS

A book is never written in a vacuum. I have so many people who helped and guided me along the way:

The fabulous members of CoLoNY/RWSC past and present have all contributed to my growth as a writer.

The LaLaLas, whose various journeys on their own paths to publishing were nothing short of amazing, and always inspired me to keep going. A special shout out to Valerie Bowman for starting that group.

My Wednesday Night Girls - Tina Gallagher and Amanda Sumner. Even though we talk more than we write on Wednesday nights, we always seem to learn something. And some extra thanks to Amanda for her fantastic editing. I will master commas yet!

My beta readers - Kylie Gilmore, Wendy LaCapra, Barbara Bettis, LM Pampuro, Melissa Crispin, Gwen Hernandez, Linda Avellar, Denise Alicea, Sailaja Ledalla, Mary Evans, Patricia Byrne, Carol Waite, Maureen Raftery, Caryn Brittain, and Beth Falk. Your comments and honesty were so helpful and very much appreciated. Thank you.

A million thanks to my friends and family who always cheered me on, even though I'm sure they were wondering just how long this endeavor was going to take me. Trust me, guys, I was wondering that, too.....

Made in the USA
Coppell, TX
19 August 2023

20537007R00184